DESERVE TO DIE

A PSYCHOLOGICAL THRILLER WITH A HEART-STOPPING ENDING

MIRANDA RIJKS

INKUBATOR
BOOKS

1

TAMARA

I glance around the small living room. Wide cracks zigzag down the walls from the corners and paint curls off the ceiling. At the edge of the wooden curtain pole, a cobweb heavy with dead flies and moths hangs like a net. The avocado-green curtains are pulled shut, but there are dark, greasy smudges, fingerprints on the fabric, where they have been tugged open and closed.

A large black, artificial leather sofa, sagging in the middle and no longer shiny, sits up against the back wall. At least it looks vaguely clean, unlike the small wooden coffee table with its cup rings and crumbs.

He leans down and picks up a mug of coffee, but not before I see the mould lining the inside. I shudder.

'A lovely place you've got here!' I say, turning towards him and fluttering my eyelids, trying to ignore the stale, musty smell that suggests he never opens his windows.

'Thanks,' he grins. 'I was lucky to pick up this flat, so close to the centre of Horsham.' He has good teeth, neat and bright white, contrasting against his thick black beard. Thank goodness his personal hygiene appears to be of a higher standard than his domestic cleanliness.

'What would you like? Red, white or beer?' He speaks in a low voice and strides forwards so he is in my personal space, extending his hands as if to embrace me. I take a step backwards.

'White would be great.' I smile and turn to inspect his bookshelf. 'You've got quite a collection!' I look at the shelves, heaving with large hardback books. Mostly they are design books: interiors, architecture and graphic design.

He grins. 'Wine coming up!' He hurries towards the small kitchen. I have no desire to inspect it. If it's as filthy as the living room, it doesn't bear thinking about. I just hope that he washes his wine glasses in a dishwasher.

I perch on the edge of the sofa, my bare legs sticking to the fake leather. The largest television I have ever seen outside of John Lewis spans almost the full width of the wall opposite me. There are no female touches about this place, and I wonder if he's ever had a live-in girlfriend.

'Here you go,' he says, handing me a glass filled to the brim. He places his glass on the coffee table. I am glad he is also drinking wine. It will make things easier later on. He sits down next to me, so close I can feel his body heat.

'You're beautiful.' Fixing his gaze on mine, he removes his round, wire-framed spectacles and places them on the arm of the sofa. He looks marginally better without the glasses, his eyes not quite so currant-like, his bulbous nose not so prominent. As he leans in to kiss me, I place the glass of wine on the table. It's now or never. I let him pull me towards him and as his lips clamp over mine, I allow my mind wander. But it's difficult with those sharp bristles scraping my upper lip and my chin. He kisses surprisingly well, and within a few seconds I can feel myself relaxing. I don't need to think about what I'm doing. My body responds to his.

But then I remember, and I lean back.

'Wow!' he says breathlessly, stroking my hair and the side of my face. 'Wow!'

'You're not so bad yourself,' I say coyishly, gently biting my lower lip as I lean forwards to reach for my wine glass. I stroke my own neck and let my fingers slip down to the rise of my breasts, unsubtly undoing the top couple of buttons of my blouse. 'Tell me more about your job. I've never seen so many books on design.' I gaze at the bookshelf.

'That's boring,' he says, his hand clasping my right knee.

'No, really it's not. We've spent all evening talking about me. Tell me about you!'

It's true. Dylan Headley is a good conversationalist. He doesn't talk much about himself and instead asks lots of questions. I've spent most of the evening telling him about me and it's been tiring, ensuring I don't let slip or contradict myself. It has surprised me. I thought someone like him would be me, me, me; expounding about ex-girlfriends, what he's looking for in a relationship, how he's been hurt in the past. But so far I've got relatively little information out of Dylan. And now I need him to open up.

'I'm thirty-one, single, and have worked in the same job as an Account Director for a design agency for the past eight years, although obviously I wasn't a director when I joined. There's not much to say, other than I can't believe my luck that such a gorgeous woman as you is sitting here in my flat next to me.'

I laugh. 'Flattery will get you everywhere.'

He leans in for another kiss, but I quickly raise my glass to my lips. After taking a sip, I say, 'Tell me more about your job.'

He shifts along the sofa a couple of inches, so that his jeans-clad thigh touches the length of my upper leg. His fingers begin stroking me, inching up underneath my short suede skirt.

'I help the design agency bring in more business and I liaise between the clients and the design team. Really, it's boring.' He kisses the side of my neck. 'You smell so gorgeous.'

I put the wine glass down and let him kiss me again, but this time his fingers start undoing a couple more buttons of my blouse and soon his hand is caressing my bare skin.

I pull away. 'Slowly,' I murmur, my breath tickling his neck.

He leans his head back and sighs. 'I don't know if I can go slowly.' He licks his lips and then eases open his eyes, glancing down at his crotch with a smirk on his face. The bulge in his jeans says it all. I smile coyly, letting my fingers gently sweep across it. Then I lean forwards and pick up my glass again, ensuring he has an excellent view of my cleavage and lacy bra.

I hand him his glass and take a couple of large gulps to finish my wine. 'What's the agency called where you work?'

'SAID. It's an acronym of the owner's names and their children.'

Stacey, Arthur, Ivy and Dominic, I think to myself.

'It's mainly business to business. We help companies with their advertising campaigns, corporate identity and communication and stuff.'

'So you're a full design agency?' I ask.

'Yes. Branding, web and digital, video, print, advertising, social media content – the whole works.'

I tilt my head to one side and bring my brows together. 'Is your managing director Dominic something or other?'

'Dominic Nicholson. How do you know about him?'

'I read some article or other recently that mentioned him. The agency has a memorable name.'

'Yes, I suppose it's unusual.'

'So what's he like, this Dominic?'

'Everyone calls him Dom. He's a good bloke and a fair boss. I like working for him. Why?'

I try to ignore Dylan's fingers that are squeezing my right

nipple and kneading my breast as if it is a cow's udder. 'It sounds like a good place to work.'

'Yes, it's all right. But I don't want to talk about that. We've got more important things to do!' He pulls me towards him so that the remaining closed buttons on my blouse snap open. Damn. I hope none of them have ripped off. But I let him kiss me.

After what I hope is long enough not to appear rude, I pull away again. 'The company I work for is looking for a new design agency,' I say, trying to inject my words with a sense of insouciance.

'Really?'

'Yup. It's a big budget too. Over a million pounds annually.'

'Bloody hell!' he says, pulling himself up slightly.

'Why don't you show me your company's website and I'll pass on your details to my boss.'

'What, now?' he groans.

'Yes now. And then we can concentrate on the more important business!' I run my fingers over his bulging crotch and give it a slight squeeze.

He leans across to the small grey plastic side table at the far end of the sofa and picks up his phone. I am right next to him, ready and waiting. He punches in the code to unlock his phone. 170461. His mother's birthday. How unoriginal, but at least it will make it easy for me to remember. He brings up SAID's website and hands me the phone.

I pretend to look through it, making noises of appreciation. 'This is great. It's exactly what we're looking for. I'll definitely get Martin to call you in the morning.'

I place the phone on the coffee table.

'Shall I get us some more wine?' I suggest. Both our glasses are empty.

'I'll get it,' he says, stretching.

I jump up. 'I'm up already. Just point me in the right direction.' I lean forwards, my breasts almost in his face, and stroke the length of his lips with my index finger. He moans.

'Good things come to those who wait!' I say.

His eyes flutter open. "There's a bottle of wine in the fridge. Don't be too long!' He shuts his eyes again.

I consider slipping my feet back into my stiletto shoes, as I'm not keen on walking bare footed on the dirty floor, but I don't want the clip clop of my heels to alert him to my movements. I pad gingerly towards the kitchen, holding the empty glasses in my left hand. I glance at Dylan, but his eyes are still closed, so I dip my right hand into the open handbag that I placed on the chair near the door to the hall. The little plastic medicine spoon is wrapped in a tissue on top of my wallet. I grasp it and carry on walking towards the kitchen.

I open the fridge door and try not to grimace. The shelves are filthy, and it smells like the inside of a rubbish bin. There's not much; just an opened pint of milk, some mangy-looking butter smeared with marmalade on a dish, a couple of ready-made curries from M&S, several cans of beer and a cheap bottle of wine lying on its side.

I take the bottle out and unscrew the top. I need to be quick. My glass has lipstick marks on the rim. I pour the wine into it and place it on the countertop next to the toaster. With my back to the door, positioned so that if he should come in, he won't see what I'm doing, I take the spoon out of the tissue, unwrap the little bit of cling film over the top and place the spoon along with the ground-up contents in the bottom of Dylan's glass. I then pour in the wine and stir the spoon vigorously, ensuring that I don't make any noise by clinking the spoon against the glass. I hold the glass up to the light to check it's not cloudy. Then I palm the spoon, the left-over cling film and tissue in my right hand, and pick up his glass with my left hand. I walk out of the kitchen, and when I'm adjacent to my handbag, I drop the contents of my right hand in it. Holding the stem of the glass with both hands, I walk back over to Dylan.

He is watching me, his eyes glazed with lust. 'Where's your glass?'

'I only wanted to carry one at a time in case I spilled any. I'm a crap waitress!'

I turn around and go back to the kitchen to collect my glass.

When I return, I straddle Dylan, shifting my short, tight skirt higher up with my left hand and holding my glass with my right. He moves as if to put his wine glass down. I run my tongue along his lips and then pull my face away.

'Drink!' I say.

I take a small swig from my glass. He takes a large swig from his.

'Oh my God, I want you so much!' He leans forwards, but I'm in the way. I wriggle my tits in his face.

'Finish the wine and then let's get down to business.' My voice is as husky as I can make it.

He tips the wine down his throat, and then I take his empty glass, putting it and my full glass on the floor next to us. The carpet is so disgusting, it won't matter if it spills.

He kisses me long and hard, and his fingers fumble to undo the strap of my bra. Eventually he releases the hooks and brings his hands forwards to cup my breasts. I want to stop him, but I remind myself: it's worth prostituting myself just a little bit.

After a while, when his hips start grinding into mine, I pull back. I can't leave this for too long.

His eyes flicker open and his head turns towards me.

'Have you got a bath?' I ask, running my tongue along my lips.

I know the answer to this already. Zoopla is a wonderful website. I know exactly how much he paid for this flat and its precise layout – if he hasn't done any refurbishments which, by the state of the place, I assume he hasn't.

'Yeah.'

'Why don't you run a bath and we can both get in it. It would be fun.'

I don't need to convince him any more. He is up from the sofa and stripping off his shirt.

'Oh my God. You are so sexy!' he murmurs, striding towards me.

'The bath!' I say, lifting up my wine glass and pretending to take a big swig.

'Must I?' he sighs.

'Yes.' I wink at him.

He turns away from me and walks out of the room. His back is hairy, and the sight of it sends a shiver through me.

THE WATER PIPES reverberate through the small flat as the bath fills up. After almost five minutes, the clanking becomes increasingly sporadic and then, with a final shudder, it stops altogether. I glance at my watch. If my research is correct, the effects will take place soon.

I walk down the small corridor and stand outside the bathroom door. It's open just a few inches.

'Are you in the bath yet?'

'Yes. Come and join me!' His voice is languid. I poke my head around the door. I don't want to look at his hairy naked body in the bath water, so I keep my eyes fixed on his face.

'Have you got another loo I can use?' I know he has.

'Yes. The room next to the front door.'

I turn and walk away.

'Don't be too long!' he says, but his vowels are beginning to sound extended, his voice more of a drawl.

Everything is working perfectly.

Back in the living room, I do my blouse up and pull my skirt down. I'll wait another ten minutes to be certain. I take down one of the more interesting-looking books and flick through it. The interiors may be cutting edge in their design, but they do nothing for me. Evidently they have had no impact on Dylan's decor.

'Dylan!' I shout out. There is no answer. I walk back to the bathroom.

His head is leaning back against the bath, his mouth wide open and his eyes shut. He gives a snort in his sleep, which makes me jump. Laughing to myself, I stride back to the living room. The rubber gloves are stored in the pocket of my hand-bag, along with the packet of razor blades and a disposable plastic apron. I extract them carefully, tug the gloves on and tie the apron around my midriff. Returning to the bathroom, I extract a single blade, placing the rest on the side of the sink. And then I wonder if, with his mass of facial hair, perhaps Dylan doesn't shave. 'Shit,' I mutter to myself. I fling open the doors of the cupboard underneath the bathroom sink and to my relief see a razor and a packet of blades. They're a different brand to the ones I bought, so I swap them over, putting his packet in my skirt pocket.

And now for the dirty business. I haven't done this before, but I have carefully researched the procedure. I pause for a moment. It's one thing doing the planning, quite another carrying it through. I'm not a bad person. No, definitely not. I'm a good person who has to do one or two bad things for the greater good. I remind myself that Dylan is expendable. It's debatable whether he's deserving of this, but it's irrefutable that he's dispensable. He hasn't got any kids or close family. He's a slob, and his flat is a disgrace. He doesn't appreciate the job he's got. Besides, it's not as if he's going to feel anything or suffer.

I take a deep breath. The time has come.

I position the bathmat so I am kneeling on it, the plastic apron protecting my knees and body.

Dylan appears comatose as I lean over his naked torso, and for a moment I wonder if he is still breathing. Not that it matters. I pinch his arm just to be sure. He doesn't move. I place his right hand across his groin, his arm covering his now-flaccid penis, then lift his left hand out of the hot bath water. I am careful not to get drips on me or the side of the bath. His arm is heavy but, by shifting him a bit, I manage to get it to lie on the edge of the bath. It gives me leverage to slice the blade into his wrist. Vertically, of course. I know what I'm doing. And as he is right-handed, the incision needs to be on his left wrist. I push down hard. As soon as the blood starts flowing, I let his arm flop back into the bath. The blood comes so fast, swirling through the bath water like a gushing red river. For a long moment I am mesmerised, but then I remember.

I have work to do.

I drop the razor blade into the bath. Then I swap the dirty, wet pair of gloves for some clean ones, placing the used gloves inside a Ziplock bag that I brought along especially for the purpose. I wipe down the packet of Lorazepam to make sure there are no prints on it and place it on the side of the sink. It's surprising how easy it is to buy illegal prescription medication. And a man like computer-savvy Dylan, of course he will have bought illegal drugs and wiped the evidence off his mobile phone. He's got about five times the recommended dosage in his body right now, but it won't have been so fast-acting to have stopped him from cutting his wrists. There are two pills left in the seven-pill strip pack.

I walk out of the bathroom and shut the door behind me. I don't need to be there for when life completely drains out of his body. Back in the living room, I chuck out the remaining wine from my glass and clean it thoroughly before placing it back in his kitchen cupboard, to the rear of the eclectic collection of wine and beer glasses. Then I empty the wine bottle and wipe both empty bottles down, just in case I've left any prints on them. I look for a recycling bin, but he doesn't appear to have one. Typical for a selfish man like Dylan.

I take off the gloves and place them inside the Ziplock bag and tug on another clean pair. One can never be too careful.

I sit back down on the sofa and pick up his mobile phone, typing in 170461 to open it up. He uses a Gmail account for his personal email. I scroll through the messages. Most of them are to Jamie Headley – who he calls *Bro*. He met up with him for a drink last night. He also sends Jamie photos of his dates, and their Tinder photos. And there are a lot. Dylan likes to play the field, the little shit. Jamie in return scores the pictures out of ten. He lifted my photo and sent it to Jamie last week. 'She's hot,' Dylan wrote. 'Out of your league,' Jamie replied. *Too right, Jamie*, I think. And then I notice Jamie, the bastard, only scored me a seven.

I type out an email, addressing it to Jamie. It's full of sentimental nonsense. '*Sorry to do this to you, bro, but I can't be in this world anymore. I'm bailing out. The pressure at work is too much. That bastard Dom never lets up. I've kept it from you, bro, because you care too much and you'd tell me to leave, and go and beat the bastard up. But that wouldn't achieve anything. I'm in too deep. I'm sorry but*'

I leave it there. I don't want to overdo it and besides, it'll look a bit odd that our chirpy Dylan hasn't let on to his brother how crap his life is. I'm pleased with the sentence, *I'm in too deep*. I wonder what they'll think Dylan has done. I don't fill in the To: field. Instead, I save the message in his Drafts folder and leave the email open, so it will be the first thing someone will find when they switch it on. Then I carefully wipe down the phone.

I stand up and look around. It's time to leave.

I don't need to wipe my prints down from anywhere else, because I have been inside this flat perfectly legitimately. I pick up my bag and take my coat off the hook by the front door. I take out my phone and scroll to my password protected to-do list App. I type in my password and pull up the extensive list and Gantt chart I have painstakingly created, the list that details every minute step I need to take to achieve my goal. I click on the button next to step one. Bingo.

'Bye, Dylan,' I say as I drop my phone back in my bag. I open the front door, walk through it, and let it close gently behind me.

On my way home, I pass a homeless man huddled inside a filthy sleeping bag. I extract £100 from my wallet and gingerly shove it into the opening under his chin. It's £100 that I can't spare, as it only leaves me £10, but I like to atone for what I do.

2

STACEY

'Did you have a good day at school?'

Ivy and Arthur are strapped into their car seats and I'm driving the short distance home. As normal, five-year-old Arthur doesn't stop talking, while his more introverted older sister remains silent.

'And what about you?' I ask Ivy. It worries me that she bottles things up inside. I would much rather she dump her worries on me than try to figure out life's conundrums all alone. Aged seven-and-a-half, she's too young for that. She shrugs her skinny shoulders and says, 'Normal. It's fine.'

'I've got good news! Mina is bringing Ben and Rosie over for tea.'

'Yippee!' Arthur wriggles around in his car seat, doing as much of a happy dance as the seat belts allow. Ivy simply smiles.

'Are you and Rosie still good friends?' I ask.

'Yes, sort of,' Ivy replies.

Mina and I met at antenatal classes, and when Ivy and Rosie were born within two months of each other, we became the best of friends, sharing our baby-care woes and supporting each other through life's up and downs. Our flowers, as we call them, (although Ivy is strictly a leaf and not a flower) have grown up together. When I got pregnant with Arthur, Mina was just five months behind me, and now Ben and Arthur are also in the same class at a little private prep school in a leafy part of Horsham.

We are lucky. The school fees are only a little bit of a stretch for Dom and me, but for Mina, who is a dance instructor – pole dancing, to be precise – and her husband Paul, who is a fire-man, money is permanently tight. I invite Mina and the kids over a lot, not just because our house is much bigger than theirs, but also because it means they don't need to buy food for every meal of the week. I hope Mina never thinks she's my charity case because she absolutely isn't. She's my best friend and she's hilarious.

And this afternoon I am absolutely bursting to share my news.

As we pull into the drive, I press the fob to open the up-and-over doors and slide my Volvo XC90 into the garage. It wouldn't have been my first choice of car, but Dom bought it for me a couple of years ago. He said it looks cool and will keep us safe. I'm not sure about the first part of that statement, but then I'm far from the only mum at school driving this model.

'Homework first,' I instruct Ivy as they rush into the house.

I think it's ridiculous that seven-year-olds get so much homework. Isn't good teaching what we are paying for? I don't remember having homework before the age of eleven, but then again, I didn't go to a private school.

AT FOUR O'CLOCK on the dot, the doorbell rings. Unlike me, Mina is always punctual. Arthur races to the door and is just tall enough to let them in.

Ben and Arthur rush outside to the garden, while Rosie disappears upstairs to Ivy's room.

'Sit down! I've got so much to tell you!' I beam at Mina, placing a mug of fresh mint tea in front of her. Our kitchen is sleek and white and totally impractical for a family with young kids. I wouldn't have chosen it myself, but it came with the house, and as it was sparkling new with all the latest kitchen gadgets, there has been no reason to change it. The white Corian sink stains horribly, and the floating white shelves adjacent to the stove – which looked so good holding up strategically placed *objets d'art* when we viewed the house – are now cluttered with the detritus of family living: clay pots made by the kids, my Happy Mother's Day mug, bills that need paying, notices from school, and a large spotted bowl into which I shove all the things that don't have an obvious home. Badges, rubber bands, pens and the like.

'You look like the cat that got the cream!' Mina says, folding her legs up underneath herself, gazelle-like, on one of my kitchen chairs. She is tiny, with shoulder-length frizzy black hair that she ties back with elastic hair bands. The corkscrew curls always come loose and bounce around her small, pretty, coffee-coloured face. She lives in leggings and an array of bright sweatshirts, normally chosen to match her considerable collection of multi-coloured trainers. She cradles her hands around the mug. I call Mina my Teflon-coated friend. She is one of those people who can drink scalding hot beverages and touch burning hot things without flinching.

'I've got exciting news and we have cake to celebrate!' I grin as I place a small coffee and walnut cake on the table; home-made-looking but shop bought, of course. I don't have to pretend to Mina. She knows I'm a lousy cook.

'Spit it out, then!'

'I have signed a contract for *Pinkapop's Adventures* with Howden Brook Publishing.

You know who they are, right?'

'Just the biggest publishing house in the whole world. That's amazing, Stacey! Congratulations.' She claps her hands.

'And what's even more exciting, rights have been sold in every country in the world, and it's being optioned to be made into an animated film. They're hoping that the major networks might pick it up!'

'Oh my God, you're going to be the next J. K. Rowling!' Mina leaps off her chair, runs around the table and flings her arms around me. 'You won't forget me when you're super rich and famous, will you?'

'Haha, of course not. But it's not a done deal, it's only being optioned.'

Mina returns to her chair while I cut the cake. She always asks for a small slice but ends up coming back for seconds. She is one of those lucky people who can eat whatever she wants without putting on weight, but then again, her active job keeps her fit.

'What does "being optioned" mean exactly?' She digs her fork into the cake.

'It means that we're giving the film rights to a production company for a set period of time so that they can turn the book into an animated film. But they don't have to do it, so it may still not happen.'

'That is totally awesome! You'll have Hollywood stars battling to do the voiceovers. And then you'll be invited to Leicester Square for the red-carpet opening, followed by Cannes and Los Angeles. Think of the dresses you'll get to wear!'

I'm laughing at Mina's over-enthusiasm. I can't imagine that happening to ordinary me, but I suppose it's not beyond the realms of possibility. Of course, the fabulous deal does come with its downsides.

'I've got to finish the book before Christmas,' I say, grimacing.

'What, the writing and the illustrations?'

I nod.

'How much more is there to do?'

'At least a third. I'm panicking just thinking about it.'

'I'm happy to have the kids more over the next few weeks. It's no bother, really.'

'Thanks, Mina. You're a great friend.'

'It's in return for getting me red-carpet tickets, obviously!'

The thought of the amount of work still left to do makes my sternum clench. I try to avoid deadlines because they bring out the worst in me. Panic stifles my creativity. I could probably just about manage the writing, but the intricate illustrations take ages.

'I'm signing Rosie and Ben up for swimming lessons at the local pool. Would you like me to take your two as well?'

I shiver. Mina knows all about my water phobia. It's been so long since I have been in a pool, I'm not even sure I still know how to swim. It's also a bone of contention between Dom and me. He wants the kids to learn how to swim, which isn't unreasonable. But he wants me to take them. I'm the one working from home with the spare time. I take them to all their other after-school activities, and although he does the occasional school drop off, it's always me who does the collections. There is no way I am getting in a swimming pool, and the thought of watching my two babies struggling in water gives me palpitations. But if Mina could take them, then perhaps that would be all right.

She can sense my hesitation. 'I'll call you just before they get into the pool and as soon as they're out of it. I can even Facetime you from the poolside, if you'd like.'

I shake my head and shiver.

'You know the kids all wear floats, don't you? It's impossible for them to drown. Besides, if any of them got into trouble, I'd jump straight in, and I'm a good swimmer. I did a life-saving course in my early twenties.'

'Ok,' I say, without much conviction. 'If you could take them, that would be good. Dom will be happy.'

The oven beeps to let me know the pizza is ready. I jump up and take it out. The pizza is large, oozing with gooey cheese and dotted with a variety of meats and vegetables. I don't even need to ask Mina to get the kids. She's outside, chivvying the boys into the kitchen, getting them to wash their hands in the utility room sink. Rosie and Ivy trundle down the stairs, Ivy trailing behind. I sense a *froideur* between them.

'I'm starving,' Rosie says. She has her father's build, and I reckon she'll be taller than her mother by the time she's ten.

'Here we go,' I say, placing their plates in front of them. Mina and I always make the kids eat fresh salad alongside fast food. That's the deal, and mostly they do as they're told.

'Look at this!' Arthur says, pulling a piece of cheese into a long string with his fingers. 'It looks like a bogey!"

The boys collapse with laughter. Rosie rolls her eyes, whereas Ivy struggles to contain a grin.

'No it's not!' I say.

'It's snot!' Mina retorts, and we all collapse around the table roaring with laughter, howling so much I don't hear the front door open and close.

When I see Dom standing in the doorway to the kitchen, two hours earlier than he is normally home, looking white-faced and drawn, I jump up off my chair.

'How come you're home so early? What's happened?' I ask, walking over to him to give him a quick welcome home kiss.

He turns so his back is to the children, still absorbed in their merriment. He speaks quietly.

'Dylan killed himself.'

3

TAMARA

I check myself in the mirror. The dark hair still takes me by surprise, even though it's been dyed this hue for a couple of weeks now. I look good. Groomed, with neatly arched eyebrows that highlight my blue eyes – which are enhanced with coloured contact lenses and extra-long false lashes - and a perfectly made-up face, framed by gently curling hair that flows down my back, thanks to the new hair extensions. I'm wearing a cream silk shirt, and a navy wrap-around skirt that looks quite staid and boring, but can allow a glimpse of thigh should I so choose. I'm topping it off with a boxy little Chanel-style jacket, my lucky gold necklace and kitten-heeled shoes. It's probably a bit formal for the job, but I'd rather look too smart than too casual.

I pat my lips together, spray a little squirt of Jo Malone's Lime, Basil and Mandarin perfume onto my wrists – which is fresh and fragrant rather than the florals, which I find sickly sweet – and I'm ready to go. I like to be early for everything. It allows me time to prepare myself. Planning is everything.

SAID's offices are on the second floor of a shared office block in a business park just beyond the perimeter of Gatwick airport. It's a dull location for an edgy company. I use the shared ladies' toilets on the ground floor, then head up in the elevator to the second floor. The entrance to SAID is on the left. I ring the buzzer.

'It's Tamara Collins to meet Dominic Nicholson.'

'Come in.'

They don't have a reception, but a young woman, who looks barely old enough to be of working age, jumps up from her desk near the entrance and greets me. It's an open plan office, bigger and brighter than I anticipated. There must be twenty or so people sitting there, staring at large Apple Mac computer screens. A few faces glance up. I feel self-conscious. Their dress code is seriously dress down, with jeans and T-shirts being the norm. I should have done my research better.

'Dom will be along in a moment. Have a seat in the meeting room. I'm Ellie, by the way.' She bounces along in front of me, her high-wedged trainers, skinny jeans and dyed red hair making her look like a giraffe. I stare straight ahead, and am happy to disappear into the seclusion of the meeting room. A large black, glossy table and transparent acrylic chairs dominate the room. A glass-fronted fridge housing all sorts of different fizzy drinks and juices hums adjacent to the door, and there are three large jars on the table, filled to the brim with jellybeans, pretzels and Liquorice Allsorts. Cute.

'Have a seat. Would you like a tea or a coffee?' Ellie asks.

'Neither, thanks. Water will be fine.' I point at the bottle of mineral water on the table.

'Okay. I'll let Dom know you're here.' She bounces away and lets the door swing closed behind her.

There are no windows in this space, and the air conditioning is blowing cold rather than hot. I shiver and draw my jacket further around me. I stare at the pictures on the walls – examples of advertising campaigns SAID have completed for various blue-chip clients. I recognise several.

'Tamara, it's great to meet you!' Dom strides into the room, hand outstretched. He has a firm handshake, not so strong that it squeezes your hand, but not too flaccid either. It suggests confidence. 'Please, sit down.'

He is better looking than his photos suggest. The thick-rimmed tortoise shell glasses look trendy and sit well against his tightly-cropped curly mid-brown hair. He has the slight shadow of a man who hasn't shaved for a couple of days, and a warm demeanour. He is wearing a tight-fitting bright white buttoned-down shirt with a collar that's bigger than normal. The top couple of buttons are undone, showing a hint of chest hair. Tall and slender, he has the physique of a runner and the confidence of a successful boss.

'Would you like a drink?'

'Thank you, your colleague has already offered.' I pour myself a glass of fizzy mineral water. 'Would you like one?'

'Yes, thanks.' He sits down opposite me, placing a leather binder and a black Mont Blanc ink pen on the table.

'It's good to meet you, Tamara.' He opens the binder, and I can see my CV and a notepad with scribbled writing. It's small, so I can't read it upside down. 'You have an excellent CV. So, why don't you tell me about your previous experience and what you're looking for?'

I am disappointed. I had high hopes that Dom Nicholson would be a good interviewer. I have prepared and learned by heart the answers to the hardest and most probing questions. I wonder if it was a waste of time, but then chastise myself. One can never be over-prepared.

I tell him all about my work history, the roles, the responsibilities and my greatest achievements. He scribbles the occasional note.

'Very impressive,' he says at last, leaning back in his chair. 'It sounds like you have exactly the type of experience we're looking for. What questions do you have for us?'

'I'm curious as to why you have a vacancy for Account Director?' I tilt my head to one side and fix my gaze on Dom's hazel eyes. They are interesting, shaded with flecks depending upon how the light falls on them.

He looks away, a flicker of discomfort on his face. 'Sadly, our Account Director has died.'

'Oh goodness,' I say, bringing my hand to my mouth. 'I wasn't expecting that. I thought you'd say he or she got another job.'

'Yes, it was a shock for everyone when Dylan passed away. He was only thirty-one.'

'I assume it was sudden, then?'

Dom flinches. 'Yes.'

'I lost a close friend recently in a car accident,' I say, letting my gaze fall to the floor.

'Unfortunately it wasn't an accident.'

'Oh!' I say. 'Was is it—?' And then I cover my mouth with my hand. 'I'm so sorry. It's absolutely none of my business.'

'You should probably know. He took his own life.' Dom looks ashamed. What a curious reaction.

'I'm very sorry for your loss.'

'Dylan's shoes will be hard to fill. You mentioned that you have some good contacts in the pharmaceutical and leisure industries. Generally, I oversee the bringing in of new business, but it would be helpful to share the load. What are your thoughts on that?'

'Actually, I love sales. I've done a lot of pitching and been quite successful over the years. I brought in contracts of over a million pounds a year in my previous job.'

'That's very impressive.' Dom's eyes widen. 'How soon could you start if we offered you the job?'

'Actually, I could start straight away. I took voluntary redundancy last month when the agency was taken over by a massive American firm. The new owners weren't interested in the employees or the relationships we had with our clients. They wanted to get rid of as many of us as possible. Voluntary redundancy suited me because I'm not keen on working for large companies. I much prefer working in small businesses, preferably family-owned and run. I like to know that I'm making a real difference.'

Dom nods, and I am heartened to see a smile edge along his lips.

'What salary are you looking for?'

'I would accept anything within the range you are advertising. Obviously, the more the better!' I throw him a cheeky grin. 'And I like incentive-based bonuses. Having said that, doing a good job motivates me much more than money.'

'That's decided, then! Subject to your references, I would like to offer you the job, Tamara.' He leans over the table and extends his hand. I shake it, holding on to his warm, dry hand for a beat too long.

'How wonderful! I can't wait to start.'

'Let me show you around and introduce you to the rest of the team.' Dom stands up, walks to the door and holds it open for me. I let a little leg show as I slip out of my chair.

'I notice from your CV that you live in Horsham,' he says.

'Yes. I moved there last year when the writing was on the wall with the new takeover. It was a pain having to take the train into central London every day. Working here will be much more convenient. I assume I can drive or take the train?'

'Indeed. We may even be able to share the journey from time to time.'

'Oh, you live in Horsham too?' I look surprised. 'Have you been there long?'

'Yes. Nearly ten years. It's a great town.' He waves his hand at a camp-looking man who is on the phone, pacing at the back of the office near the windows. 'That's Jeff. He's our Creative Director.'

'I thought you were the brains behind the creatives?'

'We share the role. We work for a couple of clients in the same industry sectors, so it's better if we split the creatives to avoid any conflicts of interest. Anyway, Jeff is far more of a natural than me. Creativity oozes from every bone in his body.'

'But your reputation in the industry is that you're the best?'

Dom looks away, a hint of embarrassment on his face. I haven't got a clue what Dom's reputation is, but I know that flattery is a wonderful weapon. Jeff puts the phone down and minces over towards us.

'Jeff, this is Tamara Collins. I am hoping that she will be our new Account Director.'

He nods at me and says, 'Welcome on board.' But his eyes don't light up with enthusiasm; the opposite even. I sense he's feeling pain. Dylan's passing perhaps. I pre-empt it.

'I'm so sorry for your loss. It must be very hard to contemplate someone else stepping into Dylan's role. I promise to be as sensitive about it as I can.'

He nods at me and mutters, 'Thanks.'

Jeff and Dom start talking about a problem with a client. I zone out.

Tick. That was so much easier than I'd anticipated. I'm good at this.

4

STACEY

Dom has been sleeping so badly the past three weeks, he's taken to going downstairs in the middle of the night, switching on the television and eventually dozing off on the sofa. Unsurprisingly, he has dark rings under his bloodshot eyes, and he looks as if he's aged by several years.

When he arrives home from work, the children are already in bed. I greet him in the hallway. With its tall window, located directly opposite the front door, that floods the generous space with light and offers tantalising views of our mature garden, this is one of the spaces that sold the house to me. Sometimes I sit at the bottom of the stairs and luxuriate in living in a house with a proper hallway. It's a far cry from the small council house I grew up in.

'Another bad day?' I ask Dom, throwing my arms around him.

'The post-mortem results have come through.' His voice is muffled as he buries his face in my thick, dark brown hair.

'And?'

'Confirmed suicide.' He pulls away from me and shrugs off

his coat, letting it drop onto the bench in the hall. 'The coroner's inquest won't happen for another three months or so.'

'What does that mean?'

'The family can organise his funeral now, but the official cause of death won't be confirmed until then. I expect the coroner will want to interview me.'

'Jeez. Haven't the police already put you through enough?'

Dom sighs. 'Yes, but they're only doing their job.'

'Harassing you and implicating the agency.'

Dom walks through to the kitchen, opens the fridge door as if to take out a beer, then he changes his mind. 'I need something stronger.'

'Whiskey?' I suggest.

'Yes.'

'I'll get it. Supper won't be long. Do you want to say goodnight to the kids? Arthur is probably asleep, but I expect Ivy's still awake.'

'Ok.' He gives me a peck on the lips and disappears off upstairs.

I am worried about Dom. He has taken Dylan's suicide very badly. We all have, I suppose. It was such a shock. It's just the note Dylan left, puts all the blame on SAID and Dom. Apparently he was struggling in his job, said it was an awful place to work, implied bullying. It's weird. I know I haven't worked there for seven years, but Dom has always tried so hard to create a happy workforce. Staff turnover is exceptionally low. Of course it is pressurised, but I thought the likes of Dylan thrived in that kind of environment.

I think back to the last time I saw him. It must have been three months ago, when I went into the office to print off the manuscript of *Fairy Sparkle's Magic Mysteries*. I was sending the final draft to my publishers and wanted to make sure the book was laid out properly. Dylan stood next to the printer and teased me, saying how I was the last person he imagined making a living off children's story books. I wish I had asked him what he meant, but he got pulled away, joking with a couple of the girls on the design team. He seemed the same old, happy-go-lucky Dylan I first recruited eight years ago.

And now he's gone.

I pour Dom a glass of whiskey and drop in a couple of ice cubes. I dollop out a portion of chicken casserole for both of us, along with some boiled potatoes and French beans. Dom's footsteps are heavy as he walks downstairs.

'They're both fast asleep,' he says, taking a plate of food from me. We sit down opposite each other at the kitchen table. He tips back his whiskey in two rapid gulps. Then he stands up again. 'I need another one.'

I know better than to voice my concerns that he's drinking too much. I need the stress to ease off Dom's shoulders. He is normally there to calm me down. I can't remember a time when our roles have been reversed. And it's not as if I'm feeling tranquil right now. The deadline for *Pinkapop's Adventures* is keeping me awake at night and since Dylan's death I've been finding it increasingly hard to concentrate during the daytime. My productivity is abysmal.

'How's morale in the office?' I ask.

'Bloody awful.' Dom speaks with his mouth full. 'Everyone is feeling shit. Of course we are. We all failed to miss the fact that one of our key colleagues was suffering from depression. And what's worse, they've printed details of Dylan's death in two of the industry magazines. So now everyone knows what a crap company SAID is. Cash flow is tight, and we desperately need some new business.'

'How's the new woman doing?'

'Tamara. She's good. Very good, in fact. Super-efficient, and pretty confident she can bring in some new business. But she's only been with us for two weeks, so it's still early days.'

We finish off our chicken in companionable silence. Dom

and I never feel the need to speak for the sake of speaking. I look at my husband and, as I do several times every single day, think how lucky I am to be married to this gentle but determined man.

'Ice-cream?' I ask, lifting both our plates and carrying them over to the dishwasher.

Dom nods. Ice-cream is my comfort food. SAID created the advertising campaign for a particularly delicious new brand of dairy- and sugar-free ice-cream. The freezer is stacked full of the stuff, sent to Dom as a thank you for the successful launch of the product. It's just as well we both love it.

I have just placed large scoops in both our bowls when the phone rings. I place the bowls on the table and walk over to pick up the phone.

'Stacey, it's Corinne. Just wanted to say congratulations! It's amazing news and I'm so excited.'

'Sorry, Corinne. I'm not sure what you're talking about.' Corinne is a mum from school. I don't know her that well, but we're members of the same book group, so I see her socially at least once a month. I've never particularly warmed to her. She comes across as rather superior. With her horsey face and mane of ash blonde hair that she flicks from side to side whenever she wants to make a point, Corinne takes herself quite seriously. She never joins in when Mina and I collapse in fits of giggles over particularly bad sex scenes, but she's quite happy to supply us with a stream of gossip on other mums – those that aren't lucky enough to be a member of our book club cabal. I've often wondered what she says about Mina and me.

'Mina told me. About *Pinkapop's Adventures*.'

'Oh thanks. Yes, I signed the contract three weeks ago.'

'And she said that it's going to be made into a movie.'

'Possibly. It's been optioned. But there's a long way to go.'

'What documents do I need to sign?'

'Sorry?'

'I'm assuming I need to sign some stuff.'

I am totally confused. What on earth is she talking about? I am silent for a moment. Dom looks at me and raises an eyebrow, his ice-cream spoon sticking out of his mouth.

'Because I gave you the idea, I'm assuming I need to sign a contract. I've done a bit of research, and the going rate for concept creation is about ten to twenty per cent.'

I can feel heat flooding my cheeks.

'Concept creation?' I ask.

'Well, I gave you the idea, didn't I? *Pinkapop's Adventures* is about a little character that takes children on dream adventures when they're asleep at night?'

'Yes,' I say hesitantly.

'It was at the book club meeting a few months back, at your house, and we were talking about ideas for your children's books. I came up with the concept. Don't pretend you've forgotten?'

'I'm sorry, Corinne, but I don't have any recollection of this at all. And even if you did come up with the idea, you can't claim anything. I don't want to fall out with you over this, but it's ridiculous.' I am pacing up and down the kitchen now, and Dom is looking at me with a frown on his already drawn face.

'I don't want to fall out over it either, but I need you to put your thinking cap on. I'm sure one of the other girls will remember the conversation. I'll ask around. You really need to give credit where credit is due. Let's have a chat about it tomorrow or the next day.'

'No, I haven't got time for this!' I say. But she has already hung up. I stare at the phone in dismay.

5

TAMARA

'You don't have to come.' Dom has his back to me and is adjusting his tie by looking at himself in the reflective glass of a framed poster in his office. He looks dapper in a dark navy suit and thin black tie.

'Of course I will come,' I say. 'I may have never met Dylan, but I have his job. I want to pay my respects.'

'Fair enough.' Dom turns around to face me. It's the first time he has properly looked at me today, and I relish the way his hazel eyes move slowly over my body, appreciating the figure-hugging black dress that I bought especially for the occasion.

'Your taxis are here, Dom,' Ellie says.

The mood is sombre as all nineteen of us troop into the lifts and go downstairs to the fleet of cars waiting for us. The staff have scrubbed up well, but no one is as smart as me in my beautifully cut designer dress that I bought on DesignerDress-Savings.com for a fraction of its original price. I ensure my necklace is hidden under the circular neckline of my dress, shrug on my Reiss black woollen coat and hang back with Dom. Jeff, Dom and I get in the last taxi.

The men don't talk during the journey to the crematorium and I follow suit, looking out of the car window and occasionally staring at the back of Dom's head, as he sits in front of me in the passenger seat. I wonder what his hair feels like. It looks like it might be thick and wiry, but I suspect it will be smooth and smell divine.

When we arrive, the rest of the staff are milling outside in a huddle.

'You'd better go in,' Dom says.

I let Jeff lead them inside but hang back to stay with Dom.

'Go and join them, Tamara. I need to wait for my wife.'

I pause. I would rather wait with him but I need to bide my time, so I nod and, with a straight back, stride in after the SAID employees. Because I am the last to join them, I am seated on the end of the row, near the centre aisle, with a perfect view of the pulpit and the coffin covered in wreaths of white lilies.

I like crematoriums. That may sound strange and perhaps it is a little macabre. But crematoriums bring people together; they provide a sanctuary of remembrance and pave the way for new beginnings. At one point, I considered becoming a pastor, but as I don't believe in God or the afterlife, it would have been living one big lie. But it would have brought me closer to people; I could have been the ultimate puppet master of people's emotions. My unfortunate reality is, I need money, so I'm destined to work in commerce. I have a good brain – an excellent brain perhaps. I see patterns. It's like life is a big game of chess and I'm several steps ahead of everyone else. I am grateful for that every day of my life.

Some suitably mournful music is playing. After five minutes or so, during which I read the funeral programme from front to back and wonder about the unattractive black-and-white photos of Dylan, the hum of voices in the room quietens. An older couple stagger to the front row of the pews, supported by a better-looking version of Dylan. Dom and his wife, Stacey, tiptoe in after them. Stacey has more lines around her eyes than the photo of her on Dom's desk portrays, but she is equally attractive in the flesh: thick, dark, wavy hair that cascades down her back, and violet blue eyes. They take seats in the second row from the front, perfectly positioned so I get a good view of Stacey whenever she looks to the left. She has let her figure go a bit, especially around the waistline. And she's wearing a stupid little black pill box hat, more suited to a wedding than a funeral. Even Dylan's mother isn't wearing a hat. But I try not to stare too much.

The service is just like any other funeral service, with eulogising by a vicar who most probably never even met Dylan and standard Church of England hymns and prayers. And then the Dylan lookalike stands up and walks up to the pulpit, his back straight and his eyes glazed.

'My older brother, Dylan, had everything to live for, and his death makes no sense to anyone who knew and loved him. He was always good at art, and that skill turned into a passion for design. After studying graphic design at college, he got an intern job at the advertising agency, Jeanneau's, and within six months was offered a full-time position. Dylan was the kind of bloke who excelled in everything he did, but exceptionally, he was a thoroughly nice chap.'

Jamie swallows hard and his hands shake as he shuffles the little cards he has written his speech on.

'He got his job at SAID just two years later and rapidly rose up through the ranks, eventually becoming Account Director. In the early days, Dylan loved his job. More latterly, he just stopped talking about it. I, and I guess most of you, assumed that his role was so familiar to him that he had other more interesting things to say. But it seems that Dylan was hiding a dark secret. He was deeply unhappy at work, and this translated into a misery that ate into his soul, eventually compelling him to take his own life.

'Dylan was one of life's achievers, but he was also kind and funny. Very funny. He had lots of friends, evidenced by the full house we have here today. He didn't have a girlfriend at the time of his untimely death, but he was dating and was full of excitement about a new woman he had recently met. It makes no sense to us, his loving family, that he took his own life. I will never forgive myself for missing the signs of his deep unhappiness. I just hope that something good can come out of his death; that we can learn how to spot the signs before another family has its heart torn apart.

'Please join my parents and I at the Rose and Crown after this service to celebrate the life of my extraordinary brother. Dylan, we will never forget you.' His voice cracks. Then he wipes the back of his hand across his eyes and stumbles down the steps to his seat. His shoulders convulse with sobs that he tries, but fails, to stifle.

The vicar carries on with his service, but I lose track of what he's saying. Instead I focus on Dom and Stacey. Her shoulders are also shaking, and then Dom puts his arm around her and pulls her towards him. He places a kiss on her cheek. Sweet.

I wonder if I should feel bad about Dylan's demise but, despite seeing the heaving shoulders and hearing the gentle sobs all around me, I don't. Dylan had an easy life. He didn't contribute to society or make a difference. He just was. It was only his death that released him from banality, a bit like the first tile that sets off the chain of toppling dominoes. Perhaps if he knew what a glorious chain-reaction he has set in motion, he would be proud.

After the service, everyone moves to the foyer of the crematorium and then there is a queue for shaking hands with Dylan's parents and his brother, Jamie. I make a beeline for Dom and Stacey so I am just one person behind them in the queue. Dom still has his arm around Stacey's shoulders. As they start talking to Dylan's parents, Jamie stands rigid, his hands clenched together. Dom steps sideways so he is directly in front of Jamie. He extends his hand, but Jamie ignores it and narrows his eyes.

'I have nothing to say to you,' he hisses.

Dylan's dad looks at Jamie, a beseeching expression on his haggard face.

Dom handles it well. He retracts his hand and nods at Jamie. 'I am so sorry.'

Stacey gets a better reaction from Jamie. There are tears in both of her eyes, and when she leans forwards and stands on tiptoes to give him a kiss on the side of his cheek, Jamie accepts it and then squeezes his eyes shut.

There is one person in front of me in the queue, and then it is my time.

'I am very sorry for your loss,' I say to Dylan's parents and brother. 'I didn't know your son, your brother, but I work at SAID and his loss is felt there very deeply.'

Close up, Jamie is much better looking than Dylan; clean shaven, his nose is aquiline and his cheekbones more chiselled. I hold my breath as he looks up at me, his eyes watery and red. But I don't need to worry. He just harrumphs, nods, and focuses his gaze on the man behind me in the queue.

THE RECEPTION IS HELD in a depressing side room of a local pub, away from the main bar, with a dark-beamed ceiling and a hideous maroon floral carpet. There is the faint smell of stale beer and cat pee. A white linen cloth covers a long trestle table. Placed on it are rows of empty wine glasses and teacups, along with a couple of cheap flower arrangements at either end. A young girl with goth-style hair and makeup pours out warm white wine. I wonder if she is chosen especially for wakes.

Another girl places teacups under the spout of a large industrial tea urn.

After collecting their drinks, the SAID crew huddle together. Many of them are wearing dark glasses, despite the dull November weather. I hover on the fringe of the group. I don't know any of them well enough to engage in small talk, and as I didn't know Dylan – or at least, not in the way they did – it's safer for me to say nothing.

'Tamara, can I introduce you to my wife, Stacey?'

I swivel around to face her, a warm smile on my face.

'I'm sorry to meet you for the first time in these circumstances,' I say.

Her handshake is feeble and as I anticipated, but her voice is deep, rather husky and quite sexy. It surprises me. I had expected her to sound all saccharine and high-pitched, commensurate with my mental image of someone who writes cutesy kids' story books.

She looks over my shoulder and I have to force myself from turning around to see who is more important than me. She grasps Dom's hand.

'I want a word with Jamie,' she says quietly.

'I don't think that's a good idea,' Dom replies.

But she ignores her husband and, muttering 'Excuse me' to me, weaves her way through the mourners towards Jamie.

'Just going to the ladies,' I say to no one in particular. I then follow Stacey across the room. I take out my mobile phone, which is set to silent, and pretend to be studying it as I stand as close to Stacey and Jamie as I can without drawing attention to myself.

'I'm truly sorry, Jamie,' Stacey gushes. 'I know you blame Dom, but really, it's come as much of a shock to him and the rest of the team as it has to everyone else.'

'Thanks, Stacey. It just doesn't make any sense,' Jamie says, sniffing. 'I saw Dylan only the evening before it happened. He was going on about the holiday he was planning to Ibiza and wondering whether it would be too soon to invite the woman he had just started seeing. Surely that isn't the language of a man about to slash his wrists?'

'What do the police say?' Stacey asks.

Jamie shakes his head. 'That it's suicide. He took an overdose and slit his wrists. They found a suicide note on his laptop.'

'Oh.' She pauses for a moment, her fingers clasping Jamie's hand. 'And how are your parents?'

'Broken,' he says. 'And scared. They relied on Dylan's salary. Ever since Dad broke his back at work ten years ago, they've been living off benefits. He even paid the rent of their flat. He did good, did our Dylan.'

'Did he have any life insurance?'

'Of course not. Who aged thirty-one has life insurance? We're shafted, and what's worse is, I was only made redundant last month, so I'm out of a job and can barely afford to pay my own rent, let alone help out Mum and Dad.'

'I really am sorry,' Stacey says. And then she looks up at him, her eyes wide, her lips parted and the tip of her tongue extending beyond her front teeth. Bloody hell. Is she flirting with him? She tips her head to one side. 'I'm going to ask Dom if SAID can help you out financially. I'm sure he will.'

'Really?' Jamie's face lights up. 'That would be amazing, Stacey. Thank you so much.'

6

STACEY

Briony is my literary agent and the person to whom I owe most of my recent success. I was trained as an illustrator, but it wasn't until Ivy was about two years old that I discovered I also had a talent with words. I used to make up little bedtime stories and poems to soothe Ivy to sleep.

One evening, Dom brought Briony home. They had run into each other at the train station.

'We were the best of mates at school, but lost touch years ago,' Dom explained. For the first thirty minutes whilst Dom and Briony consumed a bottle of red wine and reminisced about their glorious childhoods, I felt jealousy and a little fear weasel its way through my gut. It was stupid, because I have never had reason to think Dom was being unfaithful to me. Despite the pressures of having a young child, we were still in love. But it wasn't until Briony started referring to her partner, Sarah, that I truly relaxed.

To be truthful, I still find Briony a bit scary. She is one of those uber-confident women, brimming with enthusiasm and efficiency, already a partner in a leading literary agent by the time she was thirty. She wears edgy clothes that normally clash, red and purples are her favourite combinations, although latterly she's taken to yellows and neons. Her hair is very short and almost fully grey, despite her young age. And everything she wears is a little too tight for her girth. Matching her attire, her energy is vibrant, and one can't help but be swept up in her enthusiasm.

About six years ago, she was coming out of the bathroom when she overheard me making up a little story about the Gurgles who lived in our radiators. When Ivy was asleep and I made my way downstairs to join her and Dom, they had already plotted out my future. She took me under her wing, and within a couple of months I had a publishing contract with a boutique children's publishing house. Writing and illustrating books has given me a purpose beyond motherhood. It's been a gentle pursuit without too much pressure. It doesn't pay the bills and, up until now, has barely earned me enough to pay for a handful of new outfits, but I feel a sense of pride in describing myself as a children's author and illustrator. I knew I didn't want to go back to work at SAID after the kids were born, but I did want to do something beyond being a stay-at-home mum.

But with the imminent success of *Pinkapop's Adventures*, things have changed.

Now, just the day after Dylan's funeral, Briony is on the phone to me explaining how the next few months will be panning out.

'There'll be a publicity tour around the States. You'll start in New York, then go to Boston, onto Chicago and across to Los Angeles. It's still to be confirmed but you'll probably head to Dallas, then back across to Philadelphia, possibly Miami before returning home.' Briony speaks quickly.

'How long will I be away for?'

'About three weeks. The exact itinerary is yet to be finalised, and obviously it depends if the film option is taken up. If it is, then you might need to stay in LA for a week or two.'

'But I can't be away from the children for that long!' I exclaim.

There is a heavy silence. 'Stacey, this is a once in a lifetime opportunity. I'm sure Dom will look after the kids.'

I don't know what to say. But I feel a rising panic.

'Anyway, are you on track to meet the deadline?'

I want to scream "No," that I'm going to let everyone down. But I don't. 'It's coming along fine,' I lie, crossing the fingers of my left hand.

'Great! I'll be in touch when I have more info.' She hangs up on me.

I SHOULD HAVE BEEN honest with her about how far behind I am with the illustrations. But most of all, I should have told her about Corinne. Things have gone from ridiculous to disturbing. I am trying to push it to the back of my mind, but by the time Dom is home from work, I am in a complete pickle.

The children must have picked up on my mood because bedtime descended into a farce. Arthur had a tantrum in the bath; bubbles and water soaked both the bathroom floor and me. I was so drenched, I had to change my clothes. Ivy refused to talk to me, burying her nose deep inside a book and then sobbing that Rosie had been horrible to her. After lots of tears, I eventually managed to calm them down with their nightly hot chocolate, but the whole bedtime rigmarole took me about forty-five minutes longer than normal. Just before Dom inserted his keys in the front door, I burned our supper. So now he is walking into the kitchen where I am cursing and trying to bat away both the smog and the revolting smell of burned plaice.

'What's up, darling?' Dom asks as he tilts my chin up to place a warm kiss on my lips.

'I'm feeling the stress. Briony wants me to go on some mega publicity tour of the States, and Corinne is threatening to send Briony a solicitor's letter saying I've stolen her idea.'

Dom peels off his black polo neck jumper and sits down heavily. 'We can't let that happen. It's your intellectual property. You do realise that if either the publishers or the film production company gets a whiff of issues with the IP, the contracts will be cancelled?'

'I know, Dom. You don't need to spell it out!' I snap. 'It's a load of bullshit!'

I have taken a couple of salmon slices out of the freezer and am defrosting them in the microwave.

'I'm going to have it out with Corinne. She's a jealous cow.'

The microwave pings, I open the door, remove the Pyrex plate...but somehow it slips from my fingers and the fish slides onto the floor. The plate smashes into a thousand little pieces.

I scream. I can't help it! It's just one of those evenings when everything is too much.

Dom jumps up. 'Stacey, calm down!'

There is nothing worse than someone telling you to calm down when you feel like you're going to explode.

'I'm fine,' I say through gritted teeth, bending down on my knees and furiously sweeping up the fragments of glass.

Dom crouches next to me and takes the dustpan and brush from my hands. 'No, you are not fine. Go and pour yourself a glass of wine and sit down at the kitchen table.'

I do as I'm told and look over at my husband who, after a long day at work, is now clearing up my mess.

'I'm sorry darling,' I say.

He tips the fragments into the kitchen bin.

'If the deals around *Pinkapop's Adventures* are all too much for you, you don't need to do it. We could always find you a co-writer or illustrator and you could license it out.'

'But I want to do it!' I exclaim. 'It's my big break.'

'I know, but stress isn't good for you. We don't want a repeat—'

'For God's sake, Dom. I am not having a breakdown.' I think back to what happened fifteen years ago, before I met Dom. The memory makes me shiver.

Dom puts a warm, reassuring hand on my shoulder and bends over to give me a kiss.

'Let's order a takeaway.'

Tears well up in my eyes with gratitude for my supportive husband.

AFTER WE PLACE our order with the local Chinese restaurant, I pour Dom a beer and we move to the living room. I put my legs over his lap as we sit together on the pale grey sofa and adjust the salmon pink and dusty blue cushions. I want to steer the conversation away from myself.

'Have you had the chance to investigate how you can pay or donate money to Dylan's parents?'

Dom sighs. 'No. It's been a hectic day. I'm not even sure it's a good idea. I need to think about it a bit more.'

I disagree with Dom. I think it's imperative that SAID make some kind of gesture in Dylan's memory, but now isn't the time for picking an argument. Instead I ask, 'How is everyone at work, now the funeral is over?'

'It'll be a long time before we're all back on track. The only good thing is Tamara. I feel bad saying that she's better at the job than Dylan was, but she really is. Look at this.' Dom shifts to take his phone out of his trouser pocket. He pulls up an app, or perhaps it's a software programme I've never seen before. 'This is how organised she is. She's got us all working on a new CRM software programme so we can keep track of everything that needs doing for each account. Everyone gets a list of the tasks they need to do for the day.'

'Even you?' I laugh.

'Especially me. She's got me ticking off lists left, right and centre. I've never met anyone as organised as her. And even better, she's secured us a meeting with Stanwyck.'

I frown. The name means nothing to me.

'They're only the world's largest luxury yacht builders! If I had a boat, it would definitely be a Stanwyck.'

I try to stifle my shiver. My phobia of water and Dom's love of sailing have been a significant bone of contention between us since the day we met.

'The contract could be huge and global. We're going to Liverpool to pitch to them next Tuesday. I'm afraid we'll have to stay the night, as the presentation is at 5 p.m.'

I lean over and kiss his cheek. 'That's great. I hope you win the contract.' It's true, I hope SAID wins the contract. I just wish it wasn't for a damned boat builder.

'What did you think of Tamara?' Dom asks.

'I literally just said hello to her at the funeral. I can't really comment. Why don't you invite her here for dinner next week so I can get to know your new superstar?'

'Thanks, Stace. I will.'

7

TAMARA

W e are on the train to Liverpool. First class, because we need the table to work through the presentation and enjoy the peace and quiet of an almost empty train.

Dom raised his eyes when I led the way onto the first class carriage. I know he never travels first class because I checked through the expenses file. But Dom is going to do things differently now he has me.

'It was ten pounds more than standard class each way,' I say as a throwaway comment as I place my little suitcase in the luggage rack and take my place by the aisle. 'If you book in advance and buy off-peak singles, you can get great deals.'

That used to be true, although I'm not sure it is anymore. But I can't see Dom checking the price of train tickets. Besides, if we win this contract, we'll be able to fly up to Liverpool and back on a private jet in future.

We start off the journey sitting opposite each other, but it's tricky working off the same laptop.

'Shall I come and sit next to you?' I suggest.

'Might be easier,' Dom says.

I choose my moment and almost slide on top of him as the train lurches around a long bend.

'Gosh, I'm so sorry,' I say.

Dom laughs, but flushes slightly, so I'm pretty sure he got a good view down my cleavage.

We finish off the presentation and run through who is going to say what. I only let my hand touch his once, when I pass him a cup of coffee. I wonder if he feels the jolt of electricity that sears my skin. What a surprise.

WE CHECK into the Premier Inn at Liverpool's Royal Albert Docks. I would have preferred somewhere a bit classier, but the location is perfect, right on the docks, walking distance from the Tate Liverpool and just a stone's throw away from Stanwyck's offices. Besides, it's not your typical Premier Inn, as the building is a former tobacco warehouse with exposed brick and vaulted ceilings. Our rooms are on different floors, but that suits me at this early stage.

I change into a tight navy pencil skirt and a cashmere pale pink V-neck sweater that suits my new hair colour, and slip my feet into stilettos. It's a classic and classy outfit, suitable for posh boat builders. I'll be almost the same height as Dom, but I doubt he's the sort of man who is intimidated by a tall woman. I finger my lucky gold necklace, do a twirl in the mirror, then put my coat over my arm, pick up my newly acquired soft leather briefcase and stride to the lifts. I give myself a quick once over in the mirror in the lift, and when the doors open on the ground floor, I stride out confidently, smiling widely at Dom.

I KNEW the presentation would go well, but I didn't know it would go that well. They were almost gushing at the end, begging for us to work for them. I'm good at presentations, and it never ceases to amaze me how bad most people are. It requires two things: research and listening. I have studied every piece of information in the public domain about Stanwyck, and I've researched and analysed every communications strategy they've ever implemented. Dom is good at presentations too. Articulate, to the point and modest. And it helps that he is obsessively passionate about boats. The more time I spend with him, the more I'm liking him. It's an unexpected bonus.

'I think we might get the business!' I say, doing a little twirl as we exit the building into the freezing cold, dark dampness of this Liverpool evening.

'I think so too!' Dom grins. 'You did really well in there.'

'Thank you.' I tilt my head coyly.

'And although it's a bit too soon to count our chickens, I think we deserve a good dinner out. What do you reckon?' he suggests.

'That would be lovely.'

After checking that I'm a meat-eater, Dom selects a grill-type restaurant, all industrial decor with exposed brick walls and black metal girders. I suppose it suits his trendy designer image, although personally I think the style has had its day. We are seated at a table on the back wall under some gaudy black and white posters of old ships.

'Do you prefer red or white wine?' he asks.

'I don't mind. Your choice.'

'In which case it will be red. I don't drink white. Weirdly, it gives me indigestion.'

The waiter brings the wine quickly.

'To you!' He raises his glass up. 'I'm so delighted you joined SAID.'

I glance at the ground. 'Thank you,' I say, 'I'm loving the job.'

After taking a small sip, I lean forwards towards him. 'You seem to know a great deal about yachts. Are you a sailor?'

He laughs. 'I wish. I've always loved sailing and used to do a lot of it when I was younger. Sadly, it's not possible these days.'

'Why's that?' I frown.

'Stacey, my wife; she's water phobic.'

'Oh, that's awful. I can't imagine anyone hating the sea. I love it. That vast expanse of nothingness, just you and the elements. There isn't a better feeling in the world.' I gaze off into the distance.

'So you sail too?'

I nod. 'But not nearly as much as I would like to. Work and life tend to get in the way.' I pause and then, placing my forearms on the table, I lean forwards. 'I haven't had the chance to ask, but what's your background and why did you set up SAID?'

'It's not a very interesting story!'

'I'm sure you're being typically modest. Please tell me!' I urge.

Dom takes a sip of red wine. 'After studying graphic design at college, my first job was with a division of Publicis. I thought I was the bee's knees, when in fact I was the most junior of the junior dogsbodies. I moved to another agency, and after a few years realised I enjoyed the business side of things as much as the design itself.'

I nod enthusiastically. 'And SAID?' I prompt.

'When Stacey and I got together, we decided to take the leap and set up our own agency. We started out with one client: a small chain of women's wear shops. And then we got lucky. The chain of shops was taken over by a big stock exchange-listed company.

'We were asked to pitch for the whole public company's

communications work and, against all the odds, we won. Talk about running before you can walk!'

'That's amazing!' I exclaim. 'I didn't realise your wife was in the business too.'

'I couldn't have done it without Stacey. She's a great designer.'

'But she doesn't work for SAID any longer?'

He shakes his head. 'She decided to quit after our first child was born.'

The food arrives. A thick steak for Dom and poussin for me. I don't normally eat big meals in the evenings, but I don't want to be one of those ridiculous women who obsess over what they eat and frustrate the men around them.

'So Stacey doesn't work now?' I raise my eyebrows.

'Actually she does. She's an author and illustrator of children's books. She's just won a fantastic contract. Various TV networks are interested, and they might be creating an animation of her new book, *Pinkapop's Adventures*.'

'Wow, that's amazing! And such a cute name. I'm in awe of people who do that. Please pass on my congratulations. How does she come up with her ideas? It must be so hard in this day and age, when everything has been done before?'

It is luck that I have appear to hit on a raw nerve. Dom goes on to tell me all about some woman called Corinne who claims that she came up with the idea for *Pinkapop's Adventures*. I purr sympathetically as he explains the consequences of Intellectual Property violations.

'That reminds me.' Dom swallows a mouthful. 'Stacey wanted to know if you'd like to come over for dinner at the end of this week or the beginning of next.'

I bite the inside of my cheek to stop myself from beaming too widely. 'I'd love to. Thank you. Friday evening would be perfect.'

'That's a date. I'll let Stacey know.'

'How did you and Stacey meet?'

'Through mutual friends. She had been through a bit of a tough time personally and, having just moved to London, didn't know many people. For me, it was love at first sight.'

'Not for her?'

He laughs, although I don't understand why. 'She says it took eight dates before she realised I was the one for her. Anyway, tell me about yourself. Are you married?'

'Um, no. I was, but my husband died.' I eat a morsel of chicken, and it feels as if it's going to get stuck in my throat. I take a large swig of wine to dislodge it.

'I'm sorry to hear that. How terrible.'

'Yes, it was a bad time.' I swirl the wine left in my glass and keep my eyes looking down. 'But it was a while ago, and life moves on. I've started dating again.'

'I'm delighted to hear that. Anyone special in your life at the moment?' And then he looks embarrassed. 'I'm sorry, I keep on forgetting that it's inappropriate to ask employees about their personal lives!'

I toss my hair back and throw him a wide beam. 'I don't mind in the slightest. There's nothing to hide. No, my lover these days is work. But perhaps that will change soon.'

Dom shifts slightly in his chair. We are both silent for a moment as we finish off our meals. When I have cleaned my plate, I put my knife and fork neatly together and say, 'Please could you excuse me for a moment. I just need to pop to the Ladies'.' I stand and pick up my bag.

'Of course,' he says. 'Would you like a dessert?'

'No, just a coffee please.'

'Decaffeinated?'

'No. I like the hard-core stuff!' I laugh and walk away from the table, wriggling my hips just a little as I walk.

When I'm in the ladies, I stand in front of the row of metal sinks to examine myself in the mirror. My breasts are full and, thanks to my enhancement surgery, they are pert and not sagging. I pull my jumper so that it's tighter around my breasts. Other than the fact that my nipples are fully erect and pointing through the fabric, I am decent. I look good and I feel good. I finger my lucky gold necklace, then step back into the restaurant. I get a couple of admiring glances from other diners – men and women alike – as I stride past.

Dom is on the phone when I arrive back at the table, but when he sees me, his eyes widen just a smidgeon. 'I've got to go now. Yes, you too,' he says to whoever he is talking to. Stacey, I assume.

He hangs up. I hug my arms around myself to enhance my cleavage. I can tell that he is having to try extra hard to keep his eyes on my face and not let them slip down to my bust.

I steer the conversation back to him and his hopes for the future of SAID, and then the waitress arrives and Dom asks for the bill.

When we're back outside, shivering in the dank air, I step close to him and place my hand on his arm.

'Thank you for such a lovely evening.' I leave my hand there for a little too long. Dom steps away from me.

The reception area in the hotel is busy, and another couple step into our lift, forcing me to stand as close to Dom as I dare. They get out on the second floor, but I don't move. The doors ping at the third floor, where Dom's room is. I gaze up at him, my eyes on his, my lips parted. He hesitates for a moment but then, just as the doors are about to close again, he puts a hand out to stop them.

'Goodnight, Tamara. I hope you sleep well.'

And then he is gone.

~

WHEN I'M BACK in my hotel room, I open the secret password-protected app on my phone. I achieved a lot today: showing how invaluable I am to SAID; learning about Dom's background; gleaning some juicy nuggets about Stacey. And I know for sure that Dom fancies me. I tick off several points and allow myself an indulgent gloat at how well everything is coming together.

And yes, thank you, Dom. I do sleep well.

8

STACEY

I t is a miracle, but we are on time for school. Ivy and Arthur rush off to join their respective classmates queuing up in the playground, ready to follow their teachers into their classrooms. I walk over to the cluster of mums I know the best, including a couple from our book club. I'm relieved that Corinne isn't among them.

'Hi Fiona, hi Julie,' I say, breaking into their huddle.

They stop talking immediately.

I tense. There are five of them, and not one of the women is looking at me.

'Have I disturbed something?' I ask, sounding braver than I feel.

'No,' a couple of them mutter, but then Fiona says, 'Yes.'

'Oh,' I reply, not sure how else to answer. That feeling of being the only one not invited to a party or the last chosen for a sports team, makes me nauseous. I wish I had eaten breakfast before leaving the house.

'It's really off what you've done to Corinne,' Fiona says, her pretty face distorting into a sneer. 'You know that she's hard up ever since her divorce and she needs the money. Forgetting, of course, the moral obligation.' Fiona puts her hands on her jeans-clad hips. The others shuffle uncomfortably. It's one thing indulging in gossip, but quite another facing it head on. I almost admire Fiona for her bravado.

'This is none of your business,' I say. 'Besides, I don't know what Corinne has been telling you, but she categorically did not come up with the idea for *Pinkapop's Adventures*.'

I don't know what else to say, so I turn on my heel to leave the playground. I can feel my head trembling as if my neck isn't strong enough to support it. It's only when I'm nearly at the gate that I realise the children have gone inside to their classes. I always wave at them, and they're still at the age where they give me a vigorous wave back. But today I totally forgot.

And then I walk straight into Corinne.

'We need to talk,' I say, planting myself directly in front of her.

'Run along to your class otherwise you'll get a black mark,' she tells her daughter. The child must be ten or eleven. She's big, almost as tall as her mother. She runs off, her satchel bouncing up and down on her back.

I take a deep breath. I must be resolute. 'This nonsense has got to stop. And can you please stop spreading rumours about me.' I glare at Corinne, hoping that I look and sound much braver than I feel.

'It is not nonsense, Stacey Nicholson. I can't believe you've conveniently forgotten our discussion. The only original thing you came up with was the name, and I suppose the drawings, because I can't draw. It's you who are being totally unreasonable and selfish. I've got no wish to talk about it anymore. I'm considering putting the matter in the hands of my solicitor.' She turns on her heel and starts jogging away. It's only then that I notice she's dressed for the gym, in expensive trainers and designer jogging bottoms. One thing is for sure; the clothes she is wearing give no indication that she's hard up.

'Corinne!' I shout after her, but she ignores me and disappears around the street corner.

'Shit,' I mutter to myself as I hurry to the car. Dom told me to ignore her, to only confront her if she actually does send me a solicitor's letter. Too late for that now, but I wonder if I should discuss the matter with Briony, my literary agent.

I am still debating this in my head when I arrive at my favourite cute little coffee shop in Horsham with its crooked facade and low-slung beams. I decide to discuss Corinne with Dom tonight, and if he thinks I should tell Briony, then I will. He's always my best sounding board. But right now, I'm about to do something he won't be happy about. I'm meeting up with Jamie Headley, Dylan's brother.

I order a cappuccino. Jamie is late, so I take out my phone and do a Google search for my name. I know it's egoistic, searching for oneself, but when you're a writer, there is a masochistic compulsion to read reviews and see where your books are in Amazon's ratings. Fortunately for me, as a children's writer, I don't get many reviews, but the ratings give me an indication as to how many of my books are being sold.

'Oh my God!' I mutter out aloud. I have got five new reviews on *The Gurgles* and four new reviews on *Rooms for a Rhino*. And they are all terrible! *The Gurgles* has three one-star reviews and two two-stars, whereas *Rooms for a Rhino* are all one stars. How is that possible? Has Corinne persuaded her army of supporters to slate my books online? I click through on the names, hoping they'll enlighten me, but all the reviewers seem to be genuine, leaving reviews on other books – mostly four- and five-star reviews, at that. And none of the reviews are for the books we've recently read in book club. Not knowing where these reviewers are located, I can't accuse Corinne of whipping up bad publicity for me because I've got absolutely no evidence.

A knot of panic pulses in my sternum. Howden Brook

Publishing will surely dump me if they read stuff like this. I go back onto Google and see that someone has written something about me on Mumsnet. It's vitriolic. The author of the long missive claims to be an educationalist, and he or she is stating that my fantastical novels are likely to do children more harm than good. In a nutshell, they're telling parents to stay well clear of my books.

It is so bloody unfair.

~

'YOU LOOK ABOUT AS miserable as I feel,' Jamie says, slipping onto the chair opposite me. 'Bad news?' he asks, glancing at the phone that I'm gripping so tightly, my knuckles are white.

I set it onto the table. 'Yes. I've got some dreadful reviews on Amazon.'

'Reviews?' Jamie asks.

'I write and illustrate children's books.'

'Oh yes. Sorry, I forgot. Dylan mentioned you changed careers. Ignore the bad reviews. It's only mean-spirited people who leave them. They know they're not able to write books themselves, so they just take their jealousy out on people who do. Think about it. If you don't like something, what do you do?'

'I'd say nothing.'

'Exactly. I honestly think that reviewers de-personalise books and paintings and other creative works. They forget that a real person has toiled away for weeks and sometimes years to create it. Anyway, enough of my musings; can I get you another coffee?' He stands up.

'No, I'm fine, thanks.'

When he returns, he sits down and the dimple in his cheek winks at me. He looks so similar to Dylan, it is almost uncanny.

'How are your parents?'

'Not so good,' Dylan says. 'Mum has sunk into a depression and rarely gets out of bed. Dad is angry all the time.'

'I'm very sorry.'

He shrugs. 'I'm curious as to why you wanted to see me?'

'I'm not sure if you know, but I recruited Dylan way back. I quit working at the agency a few years ago, but Dylan and I got along well, and I always stopped for a chat whenever I went into the offices. Has Dom offered you or your parents any money?'

Jamie shakes his head.

I bend down and take my cheque book out of my handbag. I've already written the cheque, so I just tear it out and hand it to him.

'One thousand pounds!' he says, staring at it.

'I know it's a derisory amount, but it's to bide your parents over until you can sort things for them. I'm still hoping that SAID will pay out something, but I know they're struggling a bit at the moment. They've lost a few accounts recently.'

'Honestly, Stacey, I wasn't expecting anything. And one thousand pounds is not derisory. So long as it's not hush money and you don't know something that—'

I cut him off. 'Bloody hell, no! I just feel so terrible for your family. I think you know as well as I do that the rumours around Dylan struggling at work are a load of nonsense.'

'I don't know that, Stacey,' Jamie says, sadly. 'I thought I knew my brother, but after that suicide note, perhaps I didn't. Nothing makes sense.'

I'm not sure what to say now, and I wonder for one horrible moment if he's going to hand the cheque back to me. But he doesn't. He folds it up neatly and places it in his wallet. I am relieved, but I'm also concerned. How on earth am I going to explain it to Dom?

9

TAMARA

'Welcome,' Dom says, as he opens the front door.

I hand him a bottle of red wine and a large bouquet of flowers. 'I wasn't sure what colours Stacey likes, so I've gone neutral.'

'Very kind of you and quite unnecessary.' Dom stands aside to let me in.

I walk into the airy hallway, which is dominated by a huge vertical window at the far end, directly opposite the front door. A large chandelier constructed from glass baubles in shades of ambers and greens hangs in front of the window. Personally, I think it's gaudy. Dom takes my coat and puts it on a hook in a cupboard.

'Come in, come in!' He beckons me forwards. My heels clip-clop on the wooden floor. They have done very nicely for themselves, have the Nicholsons, based on the grandeur of this house. It looks old on the outside, with its low-slung roof and traditional brick walls, but on the inside it is all modern and sleek lines. The kitchen is white. At least, I think it's predominantly white, but it's difficult to tell with all the clutter. There is stuff everywhere; kids' drawings on the walls and on the fridge, books and papers scattered between cups and serving bowls. I would have a permanent eye migraine living amongst all this paraphernalia. I wonder how they can fail to see the mess. It's quite a contrast to Dom's office, which is now neat and tidy.

There is a large glass table in the corner with eight white dining chairs. The table is laid for three, but the far side is piled high with papers.

Stacey's not here. I had expected her to be toiling over the stove.

'What can I get you to drink?' Dom asks.

'Just a glass of water please,' I say.

'No wine?' he raises an eyebrow.

'I'm driving.' But that isn't the real reason. I want to keep all my wits about me.

He pours me a glass of sparkling water from a bottle he extracts from the massive American-style fridge, and then there is the sound of running feet and Stacey appears holding two empty mugs, one with a teddy bear on the front and the other bedecked with a horse.

'Hi Tamara, welcome! Sorry I wasn't here to greet you, I had to put the kids to bed.' She holds up the mugs. 'They took longer than normal to drink up their hot chocolates and do their teeth!'

'No problem,' I say. 'You've got a beautiful home.'

She laughs. 'Goodness, you're looking very smart. You'll have to excuse me.' She looks down at her baggy jeans and long-sleeved T-shirt. Her attire is quite a contrast to my pale grey jumper dress that hugs my curves. 'Supper will be ready in ten minutes or so. Dom, why don't you take Tamara next door to the living room?'

'Can't I help you?' I ask.

'It's kind of you, but there's nothing much more to do.'

'Would you like to have a look around?' Dom asks.

'Yes, that would be great. From what I've seen so far, your

home is gorgeous.' I follow him out of the kitchen, glimpsing a large utility room off to the side, a basket of clothes piled high.

'Did you have to do much work to your house, or did it come like this?'

'Our fortune was someone else's misfortune. The owners had just refurbished the house when their business went bust. They had to sell quickly, and we managed to pick it up for a bargain.'

Some people get all the luck.

He shows me the large living room with two sofas and several armchairs dotted around a fireplace, and then he opens a door to what looks like a conservatory. It must be light-filled during the day time, with its glass walls.

'This is Stacey's office and studio. She works at that table.' He points at a large pine table. There is a smaller table easel on the table and a large free-standing one to the side. Against the back wall, the only one that isn't constructed from glass, there is a tall haberdashery chest of drawers made from pale oak, with glass fronts. At the base are two large drawers.

'What a lovely piece of furniture.' I point to the chest.

'Yes. Stacey has always hankered after one of those. I found it at auction and gave it to her for her birthday.

Lucky Stacey, although personally I'd prefer diamonds.

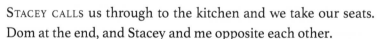

STACEY CALLS us through to the kitchen and we take our seats. Dom at the end, and Stacey and me opposite each other.

'This is delicious,' I say, taking a mouthful of watery, taste-less soup. If this is what Dom has to put up with every night, I feel sorry for him.

'It's lovely to meet you.' Stacey smiles at me, her face all open and unsuspecting. 'Dom told me that you had a successful meeting in Liverpool.'

'Yes. We should hear on Monday or Tuesday if we've won the contract.'

'Fingers crossed you'll have a double reason to celebrate next week. The annual Design Awards dinner next Thursday is the highlight of the year,' Stacey says, smiling. 'It would be great if SAID win an award.'

'Have you won before?' I ask Dom.

'No, but this year is the third time we've been shortlisted.'

'Fingers crossed, then,' I say. 'What's the dress code, Stacey?'

'It's black tie, but I'll just be wearing an old cocktail dress. Most women don't wear long.'

'Thanks for the tip. Dom tells me you're a writer and an illustrator. I'm in awe!'

'You shouldn't be. I just happened to be in the right place at the right time.'

Lucky, lucky, lucky.

'That's not true. You're exceptionally talented,' Dom says, reaching out to squeeze Stacey's hand. 'My wife has just been signed by Howden Brook Publishing, and the book has been optioned for film. She was in London only two nights ago, meeting her agent again.'

'Wow, congratulations!' I say. 'Do you have to spend a lot of time in London?'

'No.'

'Just as well,' Dom interrupts, 'as she has a tendency to miss the last train home!' He blows Stacey a kiss and gives her a little nudge.

'It's only happened twice.' She pauses, then says, 'three times, maybe!'

They both laugh.

'Must be expensive trips?' I suggest.

'No. Fortunately I have friends who live in London. I just stay over.'

'Well, I think it's amazing that you have achieved so much

with your books.' My smile feels tight and I hope it doesn't show.

'Assuming Corinne doesn't screw it all up,' Stacey mutters.

'Corrine?'

'She's a mum at school who is claiming I nicked her idea.'

'Goodness, people can be so jealous of other people's successes. What does your agent say?'

'I mentioned it to Briony when I saw her the day before yesterday, but she dismissed it. I don't think she realises how determined Corinne is.'

'I'm sure your agent must deal with this sort of thing all the time. Hopefully there's nothing to worry about. What I'd like to know is, how do you come up with your ideas? I can't begin to imagine having such creativity.'

'They just pop into my head when I'm in the bath or out for a walk, or sometimes in the supermarket.'

'Stacey's problem isn't coming up with ideas; it's choosing which ones to run with, isn't it darling? She just shoves all the little bits of paper on which she's written or drawn her ideas into the bottom drawer of her cupboard.'

Stacey gives a little laugh. 'Most of them are rubbish!'

'Sadly I don't have any children in my life. Even my sister, who has been married for five years, hasn't produced any sprogs yet, otherwise I'd buy your books.' I let my eyes glaze over as I stare across the room. 'I think it must be wonderful to have a big family.'

'Two is quite enough for me!' Stacey says, laying her spoon down gently into her empty bowl.

'Oh. Don't you want more?' I tilt my head to one side and raise my eyebrows.

'No thank you very much!' She reaches over and squeezes Dom's hand. 'Mister here has had his tubes snipped.'

Dom squirms. *Too much information, Stacey*, I think. I need to get this conversation back on track.

'Anyway, congratulations for all your success with your books! Can you show me any of your drawings? I'd love to see them.'

Stacey removes the empty soup bowls and returns to the table with her laptop. She types in her password, clicks through various pages and then brings up one of her books. She turns the laptop so it's facing me. *Damn.* The angle was all wrong for me to see which keys her fingers typed on the keyboard.

'Have a look whilst I get the next course ready. If you scroll through to the next document, you can see the outline for *Pinkapop's Adventures.*

I um and ah and make all the right noises, but I couldn't care less about the book. She's talented, I suppose, but I haven't got what I need.

A couple of minutes later, Stacey appears with a side of salmon. I put the laptop at the end of the table.

'This is so embarrassing,' I say, my hand over my mouth. 'But I'm allergic to salmon. I'm really sorry. I could have sworn I told you, Dom, but perhaps I didn't. Goodness, and you've gone to all of this trouble.'

'Oh no! I'm really sorry,' Stacey looks mortified. 'I haven't even got anything else to give you. I could whip you up a quick omelette. Would that be all right?'

'Absolutely not. I'll just have some of those boiled potatoes and a large plate of salad. I need to watch my weight anyway.' I pat my stomach, which is washboard flat, unlike Stacey's little bulge. Although I suppose I should give her some slack, considering she's had two children. Life is unfair.

'Dom has had so much on his plate recently, it probably just slipped right out of your memory, didn't it love?' Stacey massages Dom's neck.

'Apologies to both of you,' Dom says. He takes a large sip of beer.

'I feel bad because my mum is Coeliac and gets really sick.

What happens to you when you get the allergic reaction, if you don't mind me asking?' Stacey says.

'I come out in hives.' I pause for a moment and then scratch my stomach. 'This is a bit awkward, but do you think any of the dishes or utensils you've used might have touched the fish? It's just I can feel a bit of a rash coming up.'

'Oh no! That's dreadful. Do you have an epi-pen or something?'

I laugh. 'Honestly, it's nothing much to worry about. It's just a rash and I carry a tube of antihistamine cream around with me. Would it be possible for me to use your bathroom so I can nip it in the bud?'

'Of course. And whilst you're doing that, I insist on making you an omelette. The bathroom is up the stairs, the second room on the left.'

I pick up my handbag and scuttle out of the kitchen.

HURRYING UP THE STAIRS, there are six doors coming off the landing. I open the first one. This must be Dom and Stacey's bedroom. There is a super king-sized bed covered with a large white, un-ironed duvet cover and haphazardly scattered pastel-coloured cushions. Stacey is a total slob; clothes are draped over a chair and in a pile at the corner of the room, even though the full length of the wall is lined with cupboards. I can see an en suite bathroom and catch a glimpse of double sinks. And then I notice her handbag, dumped on the floor at the end of the bed. It is a shabby boho brown leather bag. Tiptoeing across the room, I put my hand inside it and find both her wallet and the car keys for a Volvo. I pop the car keys into my bag, zipping them into the inside pocket. I flick through her wallet. She's only got £15 in cash. For a moment, I consider taking it, but then I have a better idea. I take one hundred pounds out of my wallet and put it in hers. It's just as well I keep plenty of cash on me. Smiling, I tiptoe out of the bedroom, gently closing the door behind me.

Back in the corridor, the door to the next room is slightly ajar. I push it gently. A night light suffuses the room with a pale yellow glow. It's obviously a boy's room, with a bed looking like Thomas the Tank Engine. I can't see the child's face as he lies huddled under a dark blue duvet.

'Looking forward to getting to know you, Arthur,' I whisper.

The next room is the family bathroom. I go in there, flush the toilet and run the taps. It's a mess, like everywhere else. The bath is lined with soap suds, and children's toothbrushes lie on the edge of the sink. I need to be quick, but I want to check out Ivy's room before I go. It's the second door on the left, which creaks ever so slightly when I open it. My heart jumps as the child mumbles and turns over in bed, semi-opening her eyes. She whimpers. I hold my breath, but then she turns over again and is silent.

'Hello, Ivy. I'm sure you and me will get along just fine,' I murmur under my breath as I edge out of the room.

Back downstairs, I make inane small talk and eat Stacey's bland omelette, followed by a chocolate mousse that must be shop-bought. I can't imagine her cooking skills extend to anything quite as rich and delicious.

I help Stacey carry the dirty dishes from the table to the countertop above the dishwasher.

'Have you written your acceptance speech, Dom?' I ask, my back turned towards him.

'For what?'

'The Awards dinner, in case SAID win.' I place two water glasses next to the stack of dirty plates.

'There's no hurry for that,' he says.

'It's a good point, Dom,' Stacey says, putting a Nespresso capsule into the machine.

'I always find speeches are best written after drinking a glass or two of wine,' I say, adding a little laugh.

'You haven't drunk anything,' Dom points out.

'No, but you have, so perhaps now is the ideal time to put pen to paper.'

'It's a good idea, Dom,' Stacey says. 'I'll make the coffee and you two can get your heads together.'

'Can we use your laptop?' I ask, picking it up before Stacey has the chance to say no. I sit down next to Dom, the laptop in front of me.

'Yeah, sure,' Stacey says, wiping her hands on a tea towel. She leans over me and types in the password. *IvyArthur.* I'm ready this time.

Mission accomplished.

10

STACEY

Monday morning and the alarm goes off at 6.30 a.m. The last thing I feel like doing is getting out of bed. I have awoken with a pounding headache.

Dom leans over and gives me a kiss.

'I slept terribly,' I say.

'Do you want to stay in bed and I'll drop the kids off at school this morning?'

'That would be wonderful. Thank you, darling. It'll let me get on with the illustrations. I'm feeling sick with worry, I'm so behind.'

'I'm sure you'll be fine, love,' Dom says as he peels back the duvet and stretches his legs out of bed. 'It's a big week for work this week.'

'Just as well you've got Tamara to help you out,' I say, taking a sip of water from the glass next to my bed. 'She's great. I'm glad you've got someone like her who can take on some of your load.'

'Yes. If we get the Stanwyck contract, I'll probably have to give her a raise. Not bad for the first few weeks of work.'

'Fingers crossed,' I say, hauling myself out of bed.

'I mean it, love. Stay in bed. I'll get the kids up.'

'Oh Dom! What did I do to deserve such a wonderful husband?'

He grimaces and disappears into the bathroom. I lie back down and close my eyes.

I can't sleep through all the noise of Ivy and Arthur getting dressed, running up and down the stairs, clattering in the kitchen and Dom shouting at them to hurry up. And then our bedroom door opens and Dom puts his head around.

'Are you awake?'

'Yup,' I say, sitting up in bed.

'The post has just come. What is this?' Dom holds up a bank statement.

'I can't see from here.'

'You wrote out a cheque for one thousand pounds. What for?'

Dom isn't mean when it comes to spending money, but I always discuss with him before buying large-value items, and despite SAID's success, money is an issue. We have a large mortgage to pay off, we pay for private schooling for the kids and we run two expensive cars.

'Please don't be angry with me, but I wrote out a cheque to Jamie Headley. I wanted him to have money for his parents.'

Dom's lips tighten and his eyes narrow.

'It's just you haven't gotten around to giving them anything, and it seems so wrong that their son died and now they are being penalised financially as well.'

'It's not appropriate, Stacey. It looks like blood money, as if we've done something wrong or were culpable for his death.'

'No it doesn't. I talked it over with Jamie and he's accepting it as a gift. We have to do something.'

'You should have discussed it with me first.'

'Bye, Mummy!' Arthur rushes in, pushing past his father, and throws himself onto the bed.

'Bye bye, darling. Have a lovely day at school.'

Ivy comes in too. 'Are you all right, Mummy?'

'I'm fine sweetheart, just a little tired. Be good for Daddy and I'll see you after school.'

Dom leaves without saying goodbye to me.

I SPEND an hour tidying up the house and then I settle down to work. Despite the day getting off to a bad start, I make good headway; so good that I lose track of the time. When I glance at the clock, it is 3.10 p.m. and I need to be at school for 3.15 p.m. I'm going to be late.

I rush upstairs, grab my handbag, pull my anorak off the coat rack, lock the house and race into the garage. Because the car is kept in our locked garage, I rarely bother to lock the car doors and, as normal, they are open. Shoving my bag onto the passenger's seat, I press the start button of the car.

Nothing happens.

I try again.

Still nothing.

I tip the contents of my handbag onto the passenger seat, and all the muck of crumbs and wrappers and old receipts tumble out. My car keys are not there. That would explain why the bloody car won't start. Perhaps I put the car keys in another handbag?

'Shit!' I mutter and race back into the house. I search the pockets of all my coats, my other handbags, the bowls in the kitchen, my bedside table. But my car keys are nowhere to be found.

I have no choice but to run. We don't live far away from school, and I should probably walk or run it more often, but the car is so much easier, especially at this dark and miserable time of the year.

I shove my wallet and house keys in my pockets, lock up the house and set off at full pelt towards school. Out of breath, I stop for a moment and send Mina a text, asking if she could pick up Ivy and Arthur for me. And then I try calling school, but I get the answer machine. I could call a taxi, but it will be faster to run. So I carry on, the stitches in my side jabbing me, my breath ragged. I am so damned unfit.

As I round the street to school, I pass a couple of mums in their cars, driving away, staring at me open-mouthed. Yes, I'm late. Again. Yes, I look dreadful. But shit happens.

I race up the path and the school yard is empty. Now what?

I ring the bell to the main entrance, and am relieved that young Miss Jones, Ivy's form mistress, comes to the door.

'I'm sorry I'm late,' I gasp. 'Time ran away with me.'

She opens her mouth as if she's going to say something, but then thinks better of it.

'Ivy, Arthur, your mum is here,' she says. The children slink out of the office. Arthur's face is red and there is snot on his nose.

'Oh darling,' I say, bending down to hug him.

'I thought you'd forgotten us,' he mumbles.

'I would never forget you,' I say. 'I'm sorry I'm late.'

'Please, don't be late again,' Miss Jones says.

I nod contritely and, taking each child by the hand, walk out of the school.

'Mummy, can we have a dog for Christmas?' Ivy asks.

I sigh. Ivy is shrewd, asking for things she knows she can't have when I am in the wrong.

'No, darling, you can't.'

'But why?' she whines.

'I want a dog too,' Arthur says. 'I'm going to ask Father Christmas.'

'That's enough, both of you,' I snap. 'You know Mummy doesn't like dogs. Stop asking.'

'Don't worry, Ivy. Father Christmas will bring us a dog. We've both been good this year,' Arthur says in his innocent, high-pitched voice.

I don't know what to say. We've been through this argument too many times. I cannot have a dog. I will not have a dog, and my children will just have to realise that Father Christmas doesn't always make dreams come true.

After a few hundred yards, Arthur bursts into tears and sits down on the pavement. 'I'm tired, Mummy,' he sobs. I end up carrying him all the way home.

11

TAMARA

We still haven't heard if we've won the Stanwyck contract, which is frustrating. I need to nail something big, and this is the one I want. It would give us something extra to celebrate at the Design Awards dinner on Thursday night. SAID is already up for winning fastest-growing South Eastern agency, but I haven't been here long enough to take any credit.

I have prepared a dossier of ideas for cost savings and am running through them with Dom. We are sitting in his office, which is a small glass box adjacent to the meeting room. Most of the time, he keeps the blinds open so he can look out at his staff and they can see him, busily typing away or brainstorming concepts with Jeff. But today, because we're discussing cuts, I suggested he closed the blinds. He obliged.

I think Dom was a bit taken aback when I tidied his office. It's not like I removed anything; I just made it easier to find things and implemented a proper filing system. I explained that, in my last company, they had a tidy desk policy, so everything was cleared away at the end of the day. He looked so horrified, I back tracked and said that it wouldn't work at SAID. His team is too creative.

I am just about to tell him which members of staff I think we should let go, when I glance at the clock. I can't believe I have let time slip away like this.

'Dom, don't you need to be at your accountant's for 2 p.m.?'

'Goodness, yes! I must get a move on. Just need to nip to the loo. What time was the taxi due?'

'Five minutes ago.'

As soon as he is out of the office, I bend down to his briefcase and put the relevant files inside it, his diary, his notebook and his Mont Blanc pen. I put his phone in his jacket pocket, and his set of five keys I hide under a large pile of papers.

When he rushes back in, I hand him his briefcase and jacket.

'I took the liberty of putting all your things in your briefcase. Your phone is in your jacket pocket.'

'Thanks, Tamara. I don't know what I'd do without you!'

'We'll carry on with the cost-saving discussions later, when you're back,' I say.

'Of course!'

He grins at me and rushes away.

With my back to the open plan office, I move the pile of papers and palm his keys, hiding them underneath my stack of files. I saunter back to my desk, drop the keys into my handbag and clear my desk of all papers. Just because everyone else's workstations are a mess, doesn't mean mine needs to be. I hope that as I become increasingly indispensable, Dom will chuck Jeff out of his office and install me. There's only so long I can bear being in an open plan office.

'I'm nipping into town,' I say casually to Ellie, the office dogsbody and giraffe-like girl who is responsible for the phones. She's on my redundancy list. 'Call me on my mobile if there are any issues.'

She nods at me. It's pretty damned obvious she doesn't like me.

~

I CATCH the bus into the centre of Crawley and make my way straight to a high-street locksmith. There is a queue in front of me and I debate calling the whole thing off.

'How quickly can you copy these?' I ask, shoving the bunch of keys onto the counter.

'Thirty minutes, forty tops.'

He looks at me curiously. I wonder whether he's going to ask if they belong to me, but he doesn't. He just taps the prices into the till. I pay him in cash.

I spend the next thirty minutes drinking coffee and trying, but failing, to read the newspapers. I'm too pumped up to eat anything. And then I'm back at the locksmith, tapping my foot as he finishes off putting the keys through the copying machine. When he's done, I grab both sets and make a dash for the bus stop.

'Crap!' I say out aloud as my bus pulls away just as I get there. Money is tight, especially since I put £100 – which I really can't afford to give away – into Stacey's wallet, but I decide to hail a taxi anyway. I need to get back to the office before Dom.

When I'm in the back of the cab, I put the copied set into the side pocket of my handbag, along with Stacey's car key, which is still zipped into my bag. I make a mental note to put them in a drawer for safe keeping when I'm home tonight.

I saunter into the office.

'There was a call for you from Stanwyck,' Ellie says as I pass her desk.

I glare at her. 'Why didn't you call me on my mobile?'

She stares back at me. I definitely need to get this cocky girl fired. 'They said it wasn't urgent, but if you could call back at your convenience.'

I stride away and make a beeline for Dom's office. To my horror, he is sitting at his desk.

I try to back out of his office, but it is too late. He looks up and sees me.

'I'm glad to see you took a lunch break for a change,' he says, 'although an hour and a half later than most people.'

'Sorry I'm late.'

'I'm joking, Tamara. You work too hard. I've got to leave shortly. Stacey needs me home to look after the kids. She's going out tonight.'

He can't leave. I've got his keys in my bag. How the hell am I meant to distract him?

'Don't you have a babysitter?' I know it's a stupid question and none of my business, but I need to buy myself some time.

Dom shakes his head. 'Yes, but we don't like to use her too often. She's booked in for the Awards dinner tomorrow night.'

'No grandparents?'

He throws me a strange look. 'Mine are too elderly, and Stacey's live over an hour away. So no, it's just me. Stacey's best friend, Mina, helps out a lot. I'll do some work when the kids are tucked up in bed.'

If I wasn't feeling so nervous, I would relish the fact that it's as if he needs to prove himself to me. I perch on the edge of the glass table, my bag still over my shoulder.

'I love kids. I'd happily babysit if you ever need me to.'

He looks at me with surprise. 'That's very kind of you, but I think you do quite enough to babysit the team here! I wouldn't dream of imposing on you.'

'Seriously Dom. It would be a joy, not an imposition.'

'Thanks, Tamara. I'll bear that in mind. Can we take a rain check on the costings? I've got a couple of things I want to finish up before I leave.'

'Yes, sure,' I say. But how am I going to get his keys back onto his desk? He obviously hasn't needed to take anything out of his filing cabinet in my absence. I have no choice but to leave his office.

I sit down at my desk, but I can't concentrate. After five minutes of achieving nothing, I put a call through to Stanwyck, all the while watching Dom, who is still hunched over his keyboard.

'Tamara, thank you for calling me back.' Mark Stanwyck has one of those plummy, upper-class British accents, drawling out his vowels. I wonder what the Scousers make of him.

'I've got good news.'

I dig my fingernails into the palm of my hand. I hate it when people try to dramatise their words and fail to get to the point.

'Yes,' I prompt politely.

'We're awarding you the business. We were impressed by your strategic thinking. We're obviously a bit concerned that you are based on the other side of the country, and we did moot having the bulk of the comms implementation done by a local firm. But we've decided to go with SAID. We would like you to prepare the strategy—'

I zone out. Dom has got up and is putting his jacket on. I need to get the keys to him before he realises they're missing. Mark is still talking, but I'm not listening to a word he's saying.

'Mark,' I butt in, 'would you mind having a quick word with Dom? He's just about to go out, but I'm sure he would like to talk to you directly.'

I don't give Mark the chance to answer, and jab the hold button. Then, clutching the keys in my hand and hoping they aren't visible, I dash over to Dom's office.

'Dom. I've got Mark Stanwyck on the phone. He'd like to talk to you, but for some reason I can't get the call to transfer to your office. Would you mind talking to him at my desk?'

Dom looks surprised, but strides to my desk. I can't stay in his office. I'm in full view of everyone, so I turn on my heel and go back to my desk, where Dom has picked up the phone. I collect a lever arch file and gesture to Dom, pointing to myself and then to his office. I walk back into his office, aware that his eyes are on my back. I place the lever arch file on his desk and slide his keys underneath it. Then I open the file, take out a page and lay that on his desk. Meanwhile, I slip some more papers over the top of the keys. Just as I'm turning around to leave his office, Dom is standing in the doorway.

He pumps the air with his fist. 'Yes! Tamara, we did it!'

'That's fantastic news. I'm so glad! Maybe Mark Stanwyck will let us have a sail on one of his yachts!' I grin. 'I was just leaving you a paper with some projections on it, but they're irrelevant now.'

I turn to his desk and pick up the papers I just put down.

Dom's smile reaches from ear to ear. 'Really, Tamara, you are doing such a good job.'

I look coyly towards the floor. 'I'm just doing what I'm paid to do.'

'Talking about that, let's have a chat in the morning.'

He puts his hand on my arm and gives it a little squeeze.

Bingo.

I watch him walk out of the office, his shoulders held back, tall, reasonably good looking and without a care in the world. Opening the app on my phone, I put a tick next to the word 'keys'. If I could award myself a gold star, I would.

12

STACEY

'You are so handsome!' I grin at Dom, who is adjusting his bow tie in our bathroom mirror. He wears a suit so rarely, it's easy to forget how gorgeous my husband is when he dresses up.

'And you aren't so bad yourself!' he says, leaning down to give me a kiss.

'Stay away! You'll ruin my makeup,' I jest.

We are getting ready for the annual Design Awards dinner, and SAID has been shortlisted for an award for the third year in a row. I really hope Dom wins it this year. He and the team deserve the honour. Despite the downturn after Dylan's death, now they have won the Stanwyck contract, the business seems to have picked up.

He was in such a good mood when he came home yesterday evening, I didn't want to ruin things by telling him how I've lost the car keys and was late to pick up the kids again. Instead, I surreptitiously nabbed his copy of my car keys and used those today.

I slip on my silky black dress. It has three-quarter-length

sleeves and a sweetheart neckline. It's not the height of fashion but it suits me, and is my go-to feel-good party dress.

THE DINNER IS HELD in a large seafront hotel in Brighton. The location befits the occasion; unfortunately, the room itself could be a basement conference room anywhere in the world. There are lots of circular tables, all laid up for ten people with silver cutlery and sparkling glasses on white tablecloths. The centrepieces are sculptural flower arrangements made from Birds of Paradise. They look good, but I'm not sure anyone has given much thought as to how they will obstruct the views across the tables. Each agency's table is marked with its name.

It's the same crowd every year, and as we walk in, Dom greets his colleagues and his competitors alike. Seven years out of this world means I don't know many faces, but a few are familiar. I accept a glass of champagne and we make our way towards our table. Jeff is already there with his husband. The rest of our party includes Dom's two longest-standing clients and their partners, Jeff's number two – a young man called Phil – and Tamara. Only Tamara is missing. We greet each other and then sit down. Unlike last year, we have place names. I'm seated on one side of Dom and Tamara on the other. I wonder who planned this. I would have thought it was more appropriate for Dom's clients to sit either side of him. The noise levels are high, and then just as the compere rings a bell, Tamara slips into the empty seat.

She is breathtakingly stunning, and I doubt there's a man in the room who doesn't notice her – or a woman who doesn't want to look like her. With hair swept up into a chignon, she is wearing a ruby red halter-neck dress in satin – more fit for a white-tie ball than an Awards dinner, I think – that sweeps down to the floor. Although she is over-dressed, she doesn't seem to care. She greets everyone with fluttering eyelashes and a demure expression.

She leans behind Dom and reaches out towards me. 'Thank you so much, Stacey, for a delicious dinner. It was such a pleasure to meet you.'

'It was a pleasure to meet you too,' I say, noticing that Dom is throwing Tamara not-so-very-subtle glances.

She then places a manicured hand – scarlet-painted fingernails to match her dress – on Dom's arm and whispers something in his ear. He grins widely and nods. Other than that first time when Dom brought Briony home, I have never been jealous and am utterly positive that Dom has never cheated on me. We are a strong team. But in this moment, I have a little flicker of concern. They really are very friendly, and she is exquisitely beautiful. And then the starters arrive, little parcels of smoked salmon wrapped around salmon paté for all of us, and a plate of green salad for Tamara. As we all tuck in, Tamara turns to the client sitting on her left and engages him in an earnest conversation. It's only then that I realise I have been holding my breath.

As is usual during these dinners, people get up between courses and move amongst the tables to greet ex-colleagues.

'Stacey!' a voice exclaims. I turn around and face Gill. She and I worked in the same firm straight out of college and I haven't seen her in well over five years.

'Wow, how great to see you!' I stand up and give her a hug.

'You need to come and meet my new husband. We got married last month!'

'Congratulations!' I stand up, put my hand on Dom's shoulder. 'I'll just be a moment,' I say, and then follow Gill to the other side of the room. After a few introductions and promises to stay in touch, I return to our table. Tamara is sitting in my place talking to Dom, her face close to his, her eyes fixed on his.

'Did you want to swap places?' I ask Tamara. I can't help the chilliness in my tone of voice.

'Sorry, Stacey. No. I just needed to tell Dom and Jeff something.' She gets up, lifting the train of her dress, and moves over to her vacated chair.

I take a large swig of red wine and make inane small talk with Jeff. A wave of sadness comes over me as I realise that it should be Dylan sitting at this table with us, as it has been the previous seven years. The main course is beef with dauphinoise potatoes. The meat is a bit tough and I quickly finish my glass of wine. I know I'm tired and have been very stressed of late, but the wine is going to my head much faster than normal.

'When's the awards happening?' I ask Jeff as I try to stifle a yawn.

He points at the stage just as the compere taps on the microphone and announces that the time has come to recognise the best players in the industry. The lights dim and a couple of people who I feel I should recognise, but don't, leap onto the stage. Their outlines are becoming a bit blurry. I take a swig of water and then feel a swell of elation. How lucky I am to be here with my gorgeous husband! How well we've done! If there was a band playing right now, I would be up on that stage, boogying away. I glance around at everyone and a warmth cascades through me. What lovely, beautiful people they all are. And I'm one of them!

And then they announce the award for the fastest growing agency in the South East.

'You're going to get it!' I say to Dom.

The others around our table stare at me. Dom says, 'Shush!'

Did I speak too loudly?

And then the compere announces, 'Dom Nicholson of SAID' and I just can't help myself. I fling my arms around Dom, throwing myself onto his lap. I am so proud of my husband! But in the process, I knock a glass of red wine and it spills all over him, and me. It is hilarious. I collapse with laughter, so much so, I wonder if I'm going to wet my knickers. The spotlight is on us and I point my fingers at Dom. Look! Look at this superstar! He's my husband.

But, to my dismay, Dom pushes me away. 'Look what the hell you've done!' he whispers in the strangest tone of voice. 'Oh God!'

Tamara shoves some white napkins towards us and starts to dab Dom down. That should be my job. Dom shoves his chair back and stands up, red wine dripping all down his white shirt and black evening suit. Whoops!

He runs up to the stage and leans in to talk to the microphone. 'Sorry about that. My wife got a little over-enthusiastic!'

'To bloody right I did!' I yell. 'Go, Dom, go!'

Silence falls. Jeff grabs my hand and leans into my ear. 'Stacey, you've drunk too much. You need to be quiet.'

'Haven't,' I slur. It's getting increasingly difficult to articulate my words.

And then Dom is back at the table. He glares at me.

'What?' I say.

'You're pissed, and that was really embarrassing.' He looks away from me.

'Aw, come on Dom. It was jussa bit of fun.'

Tamara gets up and moves over towards me. I don't want the scarlet woman near my husband. The stupid cow knocks my bag off the back of my chair and it falls to the ground. I bend down to try to collect all the stuff and shove it back in the bag, but I am so dizzy I almost fall off my chair. I'm only saved by Jeff grabbing me.

Tamara and Dom are both crouched on the ground picking up my wallet, my phone, my lipstick. I can't really focus anymore. I hear a gasp. I'm not sure if it's Dom or the stupid cow.

'What is it?' I ask. But I can't make out what Dom's saying.

He grabs me under my arm and says, 'We're leaving now.'

'But why?' I wobble precariously.

He doesn't answer, just grips me harder. It almost hurts. And then Tamara is taking my other arm and they are steering me out of the conference hall.

'Would you like me to take her home?' Tamara asks. The room is spinning.

'No, it's kind of you. If you could stay here and smooth things over, that would be great.'

'Of course I will.'

When we're in the taxi, I want to lay my head down and sleep. I let my eyes close to stop the dizziness.

'Stacey?'

'Yeah,' I mumble.

'What the hell are these?'

He holds something up, but I can't focus my eyes properly.

'Stacey?' His voice is hard and cutting. I'm not sure I've ever heard Dom talking like this. 'Why is there an open packet of condoms in your handbag?'

13

TAMARA

After helping Dom get Stacey into the taxi, I return to our table. I've missed the serving of dessert, but that's fine. I don't tend to eat sweet things anyway. My waistline is more important than the transitory enjoyment of unhealthy sugar.

'Could I have a cup of coffee, please?' I ask one of the waiters.

'That was awkward,' I say, sitting myself next to Jeff and pushing Stacey's wine glasses out of the way. 'Does Stacey have a bit of a problem?'

'No!' Jeff snaps. 'I've never seen her like that. It was very odd. It wasn't as if she'd even drunk that much.'

'Dom was telling me that she's under a huge amount of pressure with regard to the new book she's writing. Perhaps she had a few before she came out.'

'Perhaps.' Jeff clearly doesn't wish to bad-mouth his employers. I then excuse myself and have conversations with our clients, explaining who I am and the difference I hope to make to SAID and their accounts. After Stacey's shameful behaviour, I need to restore confidence. And when I think my work is done, I slip away, collecting my coat and hailing a taxi. It's an expense I can't afford, but public transport links between the two towns are appalling. The last bus is at 7.30 p.m., and the train requires at least two stops. At least the journey will give me a little time to wind down and take stock.

I consider sending Dom a text enquiring after Stacey, but decide that would be overkill. Anyway, I know exactly how Stacey is.

My apartment is on the second floor of a small block of six apartments. I'm lucky. It's quiet and relatively spacious for the centre of town. My neighbours are friendly, if a little too nosey, elderly folk. They seem quite happy to have me in their midst. I'm quiet and have no visitors. I've taken the apartment on a six months lease. If all goes to plan, I won't need it for much longer.

I hang my coat up on the stand, kick my high heels off and walk to the small kitchen. There is an unopened bottle of Dom Perignon in the fridge door, ready and waiting for my congratulatory drink. I take it out, pop off the cork and carry the bottle and a glass into the second bedroom, the room I use as my office. I place them on the desk and then pad into my bedroom and remove the evening dress. I will have to return it to the dress hire company tomorrow. I try not to think about the other people who have worn it before me. But it smelled clean and looked divine. I put it inside its plastic bag, slip on a pair of comfy pale grey cotton pyjamas and go back into the study.

I wasn't meant to add or change any locks in the rented apartment, but I ignored that one. I've installed a lock in the door. I can't risk prying eyes.

Sitting down on my swivel chair, I pour myself a large glass of champagne, put my bare feet up on the table and lean back.

I raise the glass in the air and say my toast out loud: 'To me!'

I let my eyes wonder across the noticeboard. There are photographs, printed-off book reviews, and my intricate lists.

The centre photograph is one of Stacey Nicholson, taken when she was walking out of the entrance of Waitrose, unsuspecting, looking as if she hasn't got a care in the world.

I raise my glass again.

'Bitch, you deserve everything that's coming to you!'

THE NEXT MORNING, I am in to work early. It's been a busy day, and Dom and I have been sitting in his office working through the strategies for Stanwyck for the past two hours. Dom looks exhausted; large grey rings under his eyes and lines extending from his lips that I could have sworn weren't there this time yesterday.

He leans back in his chair and stretches his arms above his head. 'I need a break.'

'Me too,' I say, trying hard to stifle a yawn. 'Where's the award you won? We need to display it by the entrance to the office and get a jpeg so we can update our email signatures.'

'I've left it at home.'

I glance away and bite my lip. 'Is Stacey all right? She was a bit worse for wear last night.'

'It was totally out of character behaviour. I've no idea what came over her. I can't remember a single occasion when Stacey got drunk – not even at our wedding. She doesn't like being out of control.'

'I'm sure it'll all be forgotten by next week. So long as she is all right. It sounds like she has a lot on her plate at the moment.'

'Yes, she does.' Dom's face closes down. I can tell he doesn't want to continue this conversation.

'Can I get you a sandwich? I was going to pop out.'

'Thanks, Tamara. Yes, anything will do so long as it hasn't

got cheese in it.' He puts his hand into his trouser pocket and produces his wallet.

'It's fine.' I bat him away. 'I'll let you know how much it is when I come back. Would you like a coffee too?'

'Yes. A double espresso. Thanks.'

When I return, Dom has pulled the blinds in his office and his door is closed. I knock gently.

'Come in.'

He is frowning deeply and pressing his knuckles into his eyes. This is a man who needs cheering up. I must conjure up something to make him feel better, fast.

I put the sandwiches on his desk and take the lid off the steaming espresso.

'Can I sit here?' I ask. I have never eaten lunch in Dom's office before.

'Sure,' he says, in a tone that suggests he couldn't care less one way or another.

'I've got some good news for you,' I say.

'Oh yes?'

'I've been analysing the strategies that work for our clients and those that don't work so well. One of the things you seem to have steered away from is celebrity endorsements.'

'That's because the PR agencies tend to handle it.'

'I know for a fact that there is a new celebrity endorsement company that is looking for funding. They're following the same model as a business set up in the States, and they analyse celebrities to ensure that they have a perfect match with the brand's values. For instance, they research their personalities, the feelings consumers have towards that celebrity – such as their likeability, attractiveness, trustworthiness and such. Then they do a risk assessment to make sure that the celebrity doesn't fraternise with people who take drugs or have any dodgy dark secrets. Finally, they look at how closely the brand's values and the celebrity's values match with the ideal audience.'

Dom is sitting upright now. 'Where would we come into this?'

'If you could raise some money, we could be the company's largest shareholder and have first dibs on the best celebrities worldwide. It could launch us from the fastest-growing agency in the South East to the best in the UK. Think what a competitive advantage we'd have?'

'I've always steered away from funding,' Dom says through a large bite of sandwich. 'We've grown SAID organically.'

I put my barely-eaten sandwich on the desk and pull my chair around so I'm sitting right next to Dom. 'Can I go onto Google?'

We are sitting so close together I can feel his body heat and his breath on the side of my neck as I lean over to grab his mouse and keyboard. I type in rapidly and bring up the details of the company I have in mind.

As I turn to look at him, my eyes wide, my tongue poking just a little bit between my lips, I notice his pupils enlarging. His hand touches mine, and the spark is there. I know he felt it, but then he shifts away from me; subtly, but still away. I move my chair back to the other side of the desk. Dom is a good boy and I'm moving too quickly for him. As he studies his screen, I lean forwards on his desk, giving him a good view of my cleavage.

'I'm a member of a private angels group, and they send me information on all the most exciting companies looking for investment,' I say.

He glances up at me, his eyes flickering to my chest and then quickly fixing on my eyes.

'You're an angel investor?' He sounds surprised.

'My husband was. I do it in a modest way.'

'I was going to ask why you needed to work here!' His face relaxes for the first time all morning.

'I love working here and of course, I need the salary, now I'm single.' I pause and run my index finger along my bottom lip. 'Although perhaps not for much longer. I've got a hot date tomorrow tonight!'

And then the phone rings.

Dom picks it up, and all hints of a smile fade instantly.

'Yes, of course, Miss Jones. No, I hadn't realised my wife was late to collect the children again a few days ago. How long are you able to stay with them? I can be with you in approximately fifteen minutes, subject to traffic. Yes. I am very grateful. Thank you.'

Dom slams the phone on the table. The grey pallor, the deep lines and the teeth on edge are all there as he flings some papers into his briefcase and grabs his jacket.

'Is everything all right?' I ask, then add, 'Well obviously it isn't. Can I do anything to help?'

'My wife has forgotten that it's early collection from school today, and Arthur and Ivy have been left behind. I don't know what the f...' But he stops himself.

'We've still got a few things to cover off on the Stanwyck proposal and I'd love to show you more about this new business opportunity.'

He is nearly at the door. 'Can it wait, Tamara? Until Monday?'

I shake my head. 'Not really. We're back in Liverpool on Tuesday. We need to finish it off today or over the weekend. Jeff has to work out some logo concepts on Monday.'

He sighs and runs his hands through his hair.

'I've got an idea,' I say. 'If it's convenient with you, I'll bring everything to your house in a couple of hours, once you've had time to sort things out at home.'

'Thanks, Tamara. I honestly don't know what I'd do without you!'

And then he's gone.

I lean back in my chair and give myself a mental pat on the back. Stacey is falling apart and I haven't even started on her yet.

14

STACEY

My alarm clock wakes me. Groggily, I lean over and switch it off, and then, to my horror, I realise what the time is: 2 p.m. How can I have slept all day? I look down at myself and realise I'm fully dressed, albeit looking a scruff. I sit up in bed and rub my eyes, trying to recall what has happened. My mobile phone is lying on the floor next to the bed. I pick it up and, to my horror, see six missed calls. Four from the children's school and two from Dom.

Shit! What has happened?

'Oh my God!' I repeat aloud as I pull on a jumper, find my handbag and rush downstairs, tripping on the final two steps. I jab the phone and call school, but it goes straight to voicemail. What the hell has happened? I run to the garage, clamber into the car and press the electric doors. 'Hurry! Hurry!' I mutter. As I'm waiting, I press the play back on my phone.

'Mrs Nicholson, this is Miss Jones speaking. As per the notices both your children received, today is a half day. You are not here to collect them. I wish to get away for the weekend and once again I am having to wait for you.' I jab the phone to end the message.

I drive like a lunatic. I know it's not sensible, but nothing seems rational at the moment. As I skid around a corner, my stomach lurches and I recall little fragments of last night and this morning. I want to put my face in my hands in shame, but I need to get my babies first. Parking at a crazy angle on the single yellow line, I switch on the hazard lights, lock the car door and race up the school path as fast as I possibly can. Once again, Miss Jones is sitting on a chair just outside the office.

'I'm so sorry,' I pant. 'I just don't know what's happening at the moment. Please, please forgive me.'

'Ivy, Arthur, your mum is here,' she says wearily.

And we have a repeat of last time. Arthur throws his arms around my legs. Ivy gives me the cold shoulder.

'Mrs Nicholson, the head would like to have a word with you next week. Perhaps you could make an appointment to see her.'

'Is everything all right with the children?' I gasp.

'Your children are fine,' she murmurs.

I blink hard to stop the tears. An over-reaction perhaps, but the humiliation is overwhelming. For this young teacher, probably ten years my junior, to imply that I am a bad mother is just too much. If I stay a moment longer, I will either burst into tears or shout at her. Wishing to do neither, I grasp both my children's hands and walk them firmly out of the school yard, down the path and into the car.

'I am really sorry, darlings. Mummy wasn't feeling well after something she ate last night, and I fell asleep when I shouldn't have done. It's unforgiveable.'

I've always had an abhorrence of mothers talking about themselves in the third person, and here I am doing exactly that.

'Rosie said that we're going swimming with her after school on Monday. Is that right?' Ivy asks.

I thought I had managed to dodge Mina's suggestion.

'Please, Mummy! Please!' Arthur begs.

'We'll see,' I say.

'That means no.' Ivy sulks. She leans her cheek against the car window and blows hot breath onto it, drawing random patterns with her finger. She knows that annoys me. I cannot cope with the children playing up this afternoon, not with the raging headache that is now thumping in the middle of my forehead.

'Actually, it means yes. Yes, you can go swimming,' I say, and immediately feel a clenching in my gut.

It isn't until I hear the front door slam, just ten minutes after we get home, that I fully recall Dom's fury from last night and again this morning. If he looked angry then, he looks as if he's about to explode now.

'In the kitchen, now!' he says, pointing to the kitchen. He shuts the door behind us and leans against it. 'Why the hell didn't you collect the children from school? And why didn't you answer your phone?'

'I did collect them.'

'Yes. Five minutes ago. And you didn't even bother to let me know. I was called out of an important meeting to go and collect my children. And where were you? Fucking your lover? Is that more important than your own children?'

I am so shocked at Dom's words, I just gawp at him.

'W...what are you talking about?' I stutter.

'So you've conveniently forgotten the half-empty packet of condoms that fell out of your bag, have you?'

I shut my eyes and shake my head. It is all coming back to me now. 'They are not mine. I've never seen them before. I can't remember the last time I even saw a condom.'

Dom and I have never used condoms. I was on the pill and then, after Arthur was born, he had a vasectomy.

'You are losing it, Stacey!' He jabs his finger at me. 'And I understand that it's not the first time that you've forgotten or been late to collect the children.'

'I know, and I'm sorry. But please, keep your voice down. The children will hear!' I start pacing around the room. 'I admit I've been under pressure. I admit I probably had too much to drink, but I have never cheated on you and I never will. You've got to believe me!' I step back towards him and grab his arm, looking at him beseechingly. He pulls his arm away from me. Why would I ever cheat on Dom? We have the perfect relationship; well, at least, I think it's perfect. Of course we argue from time to time. Which couple doesn't? But we always make up before going to sleep. Always.

'Last night was the ultimate humiliation and it should have been a night of celebration,' he spits, running his fingers through his hair.

I hang my head. There's so much about last night that I can't remember, not least drinking a lot. Nothing makes sense. And then I wonder: Am I really losing it? Perhaps I am. After all, it wouldn't be the first time.

Dom sits down, his elbows on his knees, his chin in his hands.

'I need to know if you're having an affair. You've had the opportunity. Three visits to London staying overnight; here alone all day.'

'I am not having an affair!' I am sobbing now. 'How can I make you believe me?' I move to grab his hands, but once again he pushes me away.

'You can't, Stacey, because I don't believe you. At best you are having a break down, at worst you are lying to me. Or perhaps both. Trust is all we have, and I think it's gone. You need to see a doctor.'

'How can our trust be gone? I've never lied to you. Never! Look at me Dom!' I insist. But he doesn't. He will not meet my eyes. And then I totally lose it. I pick up a cold mug of tea, probably from breakfast, as I clearly haven't tidied up the kitchen today, and chuck it at Dom. As the liquid drips down his hair, soaking his shirt, he throws me a look of such disgust, I wonder if we can ever come back from this.

'I'm so sorry!' I collapse on the floor. 'I'm so sorry, darling! I don't know what's come over me. Please forgive me! I love you with all my heart and I would never do anything to hurt you or the children!'

And then the doorbell rings.

Dom ignores it. I ignore it.

I hear the patter of little feet.

The doorbell rings again.

'Hello. You must be Ivy. My name is Tamara and I work with your Daddy. Is he home?'

15

TAMARA

Well, this is awkward. It's obvious that Stacey and Dom have had the most almighty humdinger of a row. Even their little girl, Ivy, looks stumped when we walk into their large kitchen that should be all neat and tidy and white but, as before, looks as if a bomb has been dropped.

'What's happened to you, Daddy?' she asks, staring at Dom, who is dripping wet from what looks distinctly like tea.

Stacey pushes past me, muttering "Sorry," but not before I see her tear-stained face and bright red blotches on her cheeks.

'Mummy?' Ivy asks.

'Not now, Ivy.' Stacey runs up the stairs.

'I've arrived at a very bad time.' I'm stating the blatantly obvious.

Dom throws me a wan smile.

'Shall I go?' I take a step backwards, towards the hall. 'I can leave the files.'

He gathers himself together. 'No, no. Please stay. Ivy can help you make a cup of tea. There was a bit of an accident and I just need to go and get changed. I'll be ten minutes, max.' He bends down in front of Ivy. 'Will you show Tamara where the cups and the tea bags are?'

She nods, her eyes like little saucers. She is the spitting image of Stacey, although with lighter-coloured hair.

When I hear Dom's footsteps disappearing upstairs, I turn to Ivy. 'I think we should mop up the mess first, don't you? Can you show me where Mummy keeps her cleaning materials?'

The child shakes her head as if she is slow to digest my words. I expect the scenario we find ourselves in is not a common occurrence, otherwise her reactions would be different.

She leads me to the utility room, which is almost twice the size of my kitchen, in which there is a bank of cupboards, a washing and drying machine and a long hanging rail. 'In there,' she whispers, pointing to the tall cupboard at the end.

I open the cupboard. It's a jumbled mess of brooms, mops and a vacuum cleaner. I remove the mop and a bucket. 'How old are you Ivy?'

'Seven and a bit,' she whispers.

'Old enough to make a cup of tea, then. Why don't you put the kettle on for us.'

I walk back towards the kitchen. She hesitates, then follows me.

'Mummy says I shouldn't use the kettle.'

'Well, Mummy's not here. So if you don't tell, I won't!' I tap the side of my nose. She looks at me with wide eyes and the flicker of a frown.

Five minutes later, the floor is clean and I have a couple of tea bags brewing in an Emma Bridgewater spotted teapot. Dom appears, his hair wet from a quick shower and wearing a tight T-shirt and jeans. He's in decent shape.

'Ivy, go back to your bedroom or play with Arthur. Mummy will make you tea soon. Tamara and I need to do some work in the living room.'

'But me and Arthur want to watch telly.'

'No buts. Off you go, please.'

I'm glad that Dom is firm with his children. I can't stand bad-mannered kids.

'She's adorable,' I say as Ivy stomps out of the room.

AFTER AN HOUR OR SO, clattering noises come from the kitchen. I can hear the children chatting away but can't make out what they're saying. Dom is concentrating hard on the presentation, but I don't feel he's up to his normal quick thinking and creativity. Eventually he stands up and stretches.

'I need a drink. Can I get you another tea?'

'No, I'm fine thanks.'

He pads out of the living room and it gives me the opportunity to have another good look around. There are photos in photo-frames of differing sizes and shapes everywhere, charting Dom and Stacey's wedding through to pictures of the children at every age and stage. I see a photo of her parents, but not the picture I'm looking for. No surprise, I suppose. I stare at the paintings on the walls. Most of them are signed by Stacey. They're not to my taste: too naive and brightly coloured, but I accept that she is a decent artist. I can hear them now, speaking in loud whispers, and then I almost jump when the door opens.

'Hi, Tamara. Sorry, but I'm not feeling well. I've got a massive migraine. I'm going to put the kids to beds and go to sleep myself. Not sure how long you'll be here for, but I've suggested to Dom you call in a takeaway if you're hungry.'

Stacey looks awful. Her face is blotchy and free from makeup, and her pale-blue long-sleeved T-shirt is splattered with dried up spots of tea.

'I hope you feel better soon,' I say.

She nods and leaves the room. I glance at my watch. It's already 6 p.m. Dom notices me looking at it.

'Do you need to go? Didn't you say you have a date?'

I stifle a grin. 'That's tomorrow night. I don't have any plans tonight. Why don't we finish off the work and then we can both have relaxing weekends?'

He stretches his arms into the air and rolls his neck around.

'Sounds like a plan.' He kicks his boat shoes off and sits on the sofa bare-footed, his right leg crossed over his left. 'Let's work for another hour or so, then I'll put the kids to bed and, if you're up for it, I'll order a takeaway. Chinese or pizza?'

'Definitely Chinese,' I say. My stomach gurgles in anticipation, and we smile at each other.

A LITTLE OVER AN HOUR LATER, the presentation is finished and Dom has ordered our food.

'Would you mind if I leave you for ten or fifteen minutes. I need to tuck the kids up in bed?'

'Of course not.'

He hands me the television remote. 'Watch the news. Make yourself at home. I'll be as quick as I can.'

'Honestly, there's no hurry Dom. Wish Ivy a good night from me.'

His eyes twinkle as he leaves the room. When I hear footsteps and voices upstairs, I know it is my time. Tiptoeing towards Stacey's study door, I pause with my hand on the door handle. It eases open without a creak. I have a quick look around, do what I need to do, and then I'm out of there, sitting comfortably on the sofa, watching the evening news.

FIFTEEN MINUTES LATER, Dom is downstairs and the Chinese takeaway arrives. I would like to decant everything onto proper plates, but Dom seems happy to simply put polystyrene containers out on the kitchen table. I'm a bit disappointed. I had assumed that Stacey was the slob, but perhaps Dom has got lazy having lived with her for so many years.

'I need a beer. Would you like anything? Wine perhaps?'

'I wouldn't say no.'

We eat for a while in silence and then I reckon it's time.

'I'm sorry if things are a bit tough for Stacey at the moment. Is there anything I can do to help?'

'That's kind of you, Tamara. She's just going through a rough patch, what with the work deadlines and various other stresses.'

'I don't know how she does it.' I wave my hands around. 'She manages your beautiful house, is bringing up two delightful young children, and is a full-time author and illustrator. I would definitely fall apart if I had to do all of that.'

A fleeting expression of sadness sweeps across Dom's face.

'She forgot to collect the kids from school twice this week,' he says. 'I'm worried about her.'

I would like to climb onto the table and dance around. Instead, I throw him a concerned look and ask, 'Has anything like this happened before?'

Dom glances at the door, as if it's going to magically open. It doesn't. I know he wants to tell me but is struggling. He sighs and his shoulders droop.

'Stacey had some mental health issues in the past, before we met each other. I've never had reason to think that she would suffer again, but now I'm not sure.'

'It sounds like you could both do with a holiday. What about one of Stanwyck's boats?'

He closes his eyes for a moment. 'My idea of heaven but,

alas, Stacey's idea of hell. She is phobic of water. She'll take a bath but that's it. No swimming, no pools, no sea.'

'I can't imagine not liking the sea. I have a little holiday house on the coast. It's my bolt hole where I go to save my sanity.'

Dom looks surprised. I suppose someone on my salary and in my position wouldn't normally have a second home.

'It's Airbnb'd most of the time.' I look up at the ceiling as if I'm pondering another solution. 'Did I tell you that I used to volunteer with the Samaritans?'

He shakes his head.

'I don't normally talk about it and I leave it off my CV. I can't bear do-gooders who volunteer for charities just to bolster their own credentials. Anyway, I'm a good listener, if ever you need an ear.' I glance away, hoping to appear embarrassed at blurting out too much about myself.

'Thanks, Tamara. I appreciate that. I'm sure Stacey is ok. It's just a temporary thing with too much going on'.

He leans back again and takes a large gulp of beer.

'Thank goodness mental health is so high up on politicians' and doctors' agendas these days,' I murmur.

'You're right. Stacey used to see a psychiatrist. Perhaps it's time for a return visit.'

I place my hand over his forearm, my index finger gently rubbing his bare arm. The golden hairs catch the light. 'I'm sure she'll be fine. She's got you and your beautiful children.'

I remove my hand, lean backwards and stretch. 'I'm going to tidy up now, and then I'll leave you in peace.'

When I'm seated in the car, I go onto my phone and tick off a couple more points on my list. My plans are progressing very nicely indeed.

16

STACEY

The weekend was awful. The worst weekend of our marriage. I don't know who cried more, me or him. After hours and hours, I think I persuaded him that those condoms weren't mine and I am not having an affair. I even got him to talk to Sally, the friend I stay with in London, who confirmed that I had indeed stayed with her. The trouble is, as soon as a little doubt like that is planted in someone's mind, it's like a tick that has buried itself in flesh and is almost impossible to remove without leaving some poison behind.

He suggested I see Dr Brinksome again, the psychiatrist who I saw shortly after Ivy was born because I was terrified I was getting postnatal depression. I wasn't. I persuaded Dom that it hasn't come to that, but in the middle of last night, when he was fast asleep with his back to me, I wondered whether Dom might be right. My mind is so fragile, and perhaps it is disintegrating again.

We have tried very hard to remain civil and normal in front of the kids but they are sensitive, and this morning I don't have to chase them at all. They get dressed quickly and are down in the kitchen eating their breakfast, as good as gold. Dom is finishing off his coffee and is ready to go to work.

I've had to admit to him that I lost my car keys. What I haven't done is tell him that I found £100 in my wallet. I have absolutely no recollection of taking out £100 from the cashpoint. I always take out £50 at a time. I went and had a look on my online banking, and there is no debit of £100. It is baffling. But I don't want to ask Dom if he gave me the money, because then I'd be admitting that I'm forgetting things.

As I'm contemplating the week ahead, the postman pushes the letters through the letterbox and they land on the floor in the front hall with a plop.

'I'll get them.' No one looks up.

There is the normal junk post and two other letters. A bank statement for Dom and a formal letter for me. I tear it open. It's from my publishers. When I read it, I burst into tears. *How can they do this to me? How can that bitch Corinne do this?*

'Stacey, what is it?' Dom comes out into the hallway and takes the letter from me. He reads it, then places his hands on my shoulders, guiding me back towards the kitchen.

'Sit down,' he says. He reads the letter through again, more slowly this time.

'It is not the end of the world. Your publishers are saying that they've received a solicitor's letter claiming there has been an Intellectual Property infringement. They're not providing you with any details, but they are putting *Pinkapop's Adventures* on hold whilst they investigate.'

'But why hasn't this come through Briony? She's my agent. I thought she dealt with stuff like this.'

'I don't know. We'll have to ask her. They're also asking you to submit another idea. Did you read this paragraph?'

'Yes, I did, but it's *Pinkapop's Adventures* that everyone loves so much. I haven't got any other good ideas!'

'Stacey, that's a load of rubbish. You've got a whole drawer full of ideas.' Dom stands up. 'Look darling, this is a temporary setback. Nowhere are they saying that the project is cancelled. You know that Corinne is making it all up. What I suggest you do is dig out some more ideas, draft them up and have a chat with Briony. I bet you that this nothing but a storm in a teacup.'

I look up at him, so grateful for my steady husband. 'You're right. I'm sorry. I'm overreacting to everything at the moment.'

He gives me a kiss on the forehead. 'I need to get a move on. We've got to get the presentation ready for our meeting in Liverpool tomorrow evening.'

I sigh. I'd forgotten that Dom is away again.

'And I still think it would be a good idea for you to see Dr Brinksome again. Think about it.' He pauses. 'I am going to take the children to school for you. Ok?' He peers at me.

I sniff and nod. 'But you'll be late for work?'

'Tamara can handle things. Go and make yourself a cup of tea and relax.'

'Hurry up, kids, I'm taking you to school,' he shouts.

I wipe my eyes and go out into the hall to hug Ivy and Arthur. 'Have a lovely day, darlings,' I whisper into their hair.

'Is Mummy crying?' Arthur asks.

'Mummy isn't feeling very well at the moment, but it's nothing to worry about. I'll race you to the car.'

FEELING A LITTLE CALMER, I make my way to my study. Dom is right. I have numerous ideas written out on the backs of envelopes, little sketches on scrap pieces of paper. It's just that none of them seem nearly as good as *Pinkapop's Adventures*. I bend down and pull open the drawer. I lift out the pile and place them on my desk. I flick through the first two. They bring a smile to my face as I always recall where and when the ideas came to me. But when I pick up the third piece of paper, it is as if my brain has frozen.

I don't recognise the writing.

I don't recognise the lined yellow paper it's written on.

It is not mine.

With a shaking hand I lay it down and read it. The scribbles sketch out the whole story of *Pinkapop's Adventures*. The little creature with a big head, wide eyes, in pale pink with blotches on her body. Pinkapop takes children on dream adventures, going up into the sky in Dream Hoppers. Pinkapop hides in children's favourite toys. It is as if someone has taken all the ideas out of my head and sketched them on a piece of paper, just without the drawings.

I think I'm going to be sick. I rush to the downstairs loo and dry heave into the sink. I need to get a grip, calm down. Is this Corinne's writing? Did she give me the idea after all? Have I completely forgotten?

I sink to the floor and lay my cheek on the cool ceramic tiles. I am going mad. I am forgetting everything. Perhaps I have been having an affair as well? Could I really forget something like that? I let out a sob.

I can't tell Dom. I just can't. He would be absolutely devastated. I don't know how much time passes, but eventually I stagger up and find my phone book.

'This is Stacey Nicholson. Please can I have an appointment with Dr Brinksome. It's urgent.'

'I'm afraid Dr Brinksome doesn't have any availability until Tuesday next week.'

'But that's more than a week away,' I exclaim.

'Would you like me to put you on his waiting list in case he has any cancellations?' the secretary suggests.

'Yes please. Yes.'

17

TAMARA

I love the feeling of bubbles in the base of my stomach; that anticipation that something wonderful is going to happen, not just because – for I don't believe in fate or leaving things to chance – but because I've fulfilled every task in my complex plan and it is all coming together beautifully.

My overnight case is stashed under my desk. Dom's is up against the wall in his office, where I'm sitting now with Jeff and Dom, working through the final pages of the presentation. Jeff has done a good job and I'm pleased with his designs.

I bought a similar suitcase to Dom's. It's smart, black, with four wheels and lots of pockets. Tonight, Dom and I are going back to Liverpool and I can't wait!

It's just gone noon when Dom's phone rings. It's his mobile, and the special ring tone that tells me it's Stacey calling. Why the hell she can't leave him alone in the middle of the day, I've no idea. He puts on that special voice that he uses just for her, quieter, at a lower pitch.

I point to Jeff and me and the door, indicating whether he'd like us to leave. He shakes his head.

'Yes darling. Yes, that's great news. Of course I'll be there. If I leave now it will be fine. Please don't drive. Get a taxi. See you soon.'

My head starts pinging. Why the hell is Dom leaving? He stands up and reaches for his jacket.

'Is everything all right?' I ask.

'Stacey's not feeling so well and she has a doctor's appointment. I need to go with her.'

'I hope she's ok,' Jeff says with a frown. 'Are you still going to the meeting in Liverpool?'

Dom pauses and looks at his watch. 'If I can't make it, would you go instead?' he asks Jeff.

I stand up. 'Dom, needless to say, Stacey's health comes first, but it would be really bad if you weren't there for our first big meeting. We could catch a later train if necessary.'

Dom scratches his head. 'Ok. I'm going home to collect Stace. If the doctor is on time, then I can get her home and meet you—'

I interrupt him. 'Just call me when you're back at home and we'll decide where to meet. If necessary, we can meet at Victoria Station. I'll text you with the times of the latest train out of Euston.'

'Thanks, Tamara. Realistically, I think I need two hours from now, so we'll probably still make the train we're booked on.' He puts his arms in his jacket. 'I don't know how I coped before you came along to organise us all!'

I catch a glimpse of darkness cross Jeff's face. I'm sure Dom didn't mean to be disparaging towards the deceased Dylan, but it was a bit heartless, even if it bolsters my confidence.

'Send Stacey my best wishes,' I say as Dom leaves. 'See you later.'

As he disappears down the corridor with the wave of a hand, I realise that I am being presented with a golden opportunity. It's on my list, but the opportunity has materialised

somewhat sooner than I anticipated. I need to think quickly
and act even faster. I stand up.

'Thank you so much for these amazing designs, Jeff. I've
never worked with anyone as talented as you. I'm going to take
the time to really prepare for the presentation and make sure
I'm word-perfect.'

'Ok.' Jeff stands up too and collects his belongings. Three
minutes or so later, he is on the phone at his desk and doesn't
even look up when I leave the office with the A3 presentation
folder, my suitcase and my handbag.

As I walk past Ellie's desk, I say, 'I'm off now. I'm meeting
Dom. We'll be back from Liverpool tomorrow night, so I'll see
you the day after. Ring me on the mobile if anything crops up.'

'Will do,' Ellie says. She doesn't look at me when she
speaks.

MY ANCIENT SILVER Ford Focus is on its last legs and I doubt it
will make it through the next MOT. I always park it at the back
of the large car park, far away from the communal office block,
double-checking to ensure no one I know is watching me. This
morning, I parked it underneath an old oak tree. It's only now
that I notice a substantial branch is hanging down almost vertically, ready to plunge to the ground and smash through
anything in its path. For a moment, I consider 'dislodging' it
and claiming for damages, but I quickly dismiss the idea. I've
got bigger fish to fry. After placing my case and the folder in the
boot, I get into the driver's seat, put my foot on the accelerator,
pray that the motor won't let me down, and race as fast as I can
towards Horsham.

Stacey and Dom live on the outskirts of Horsham in a little
cul de sac of large homes probably built in the 1950s and
upgraded several times thereafter. They are all different and

have a degree of character. The Nicholson's home looks as if it has been upgraded the most recently, as it has dark grey aluminium windows and a white plastered exterior. The garden, both in the front and to the rear, is mature with plenty of rhododendrons and azaleas and other unrecognisable shrubs, all bare and prickly at this time of year.

I park on the roadside, nearest to their neighbour's house, and sit in my car for five minutes, just to make sure there's no activity. All is quiet, unsurprising at this time of day, although I suppose there are yummy mummies at home, doing whatever they do in the middle of the day. I hop out of the car, carrying my handbag. If anyone sees me, I'll just say I'm working with Stacey on her books.

I stride confidently up the Nicholson's driveway, my feet crunching on the gravel. Just as well I'm wearing flats. After ringing the front door bell twice and then sneaking around the side of the house to the back door, I am confident there is no one home. I wouldn't want to surprise a cleaning lady. I pull on a pair of leather gloves. I decide to enter by the back door, which is tucked around the side of the house, and thanks to the unattractive Leylandii forming a fifteen feet hedge with the neighbours, it's not visible from the road or either of the neighbour's houses. Dom's keys weren't marked, so I'm not sure which of the copied keys is for which door.

The fourth key turns easily. I pause for a moment. I didn't see an alarm system in the house, but there is a box on the outside that I'm fairly confident is fake. But I need to be prepared in case I set off an alarm. I plot my escape route – down the side of the garden, keeping close to the shrubs. Then I take a deep breath and open the door.

Silence.

And then I am startled by the rapid movement of something near my feet.

Bloody hell! A little black cat has just run out of the house.

Shit. Shit. Shit. I can't go hunting a cat.

'Pussy, pussy!' I say in a stupid little high-pitched voice. 'Come here!' But it ignores me and darts off into the bushes. I grind my teeth. Bloody pets. I leave the back door ajar in case it decides to come back in by itself.

I am disappointed in myself. How come I don't know they have a cat? It wasn't present on the previous occasions I was in the house. I hope the damn thing returns before I leave.

But now I need to focus. I slip paper shoe covers over my pumps and walk in through the utility room. I pass a cat litter tray and bowls. Now I'm sure. This cat definitely wasn't here a few days ago.

I tiptoe upstairs, the paper shoe covers crackling with every footstep, and make my way straight to Dom and Stacey's bedroom. I curl my lip with disgust. It's even more messy than the last time I was here. Stacey is a slob. Onwards to their en suite bathroom. There are cupboards beneath both sinks. Dom's side is better organised than Stacey's, but it's in Stacey's cupboard that I find a packet of sleeping pills. A 28-day blister pack of Temazepam, with twenty-three pills remaining. I check the label; they were only recently prescribed. *Oh Stacey, you are a good girl. You're making my life so much easier.* I pop out 18. I have a further rummage in the cupboard and find an old packet of Amitriptyline. Wonderful! A combination of tricylic antidepressants and sleeping pills will certainly work a dream. I pop out several of those. After carefully closing the bathroom cupboard, I tiptoe back into the bedroom.

It's easy to work out which side of the bed Stacey sleeps on. The right-hand side, nearest the window, is messier. She has a cute little photo of Dom and the kids in a miniature leather frame next to her alarm clock, and several pairs of earrings lie discarded on the bedside table. I open the drawer. Inside are some more pills – painkillers, mainly – a pair of ear plugs, some tissues and a heavy gold necklace. I consider palming it, but decide not to. No need to complicate things. Instead, I shove the almost-empty blister pack just under her side of the bed, a centimetre behind the valance so that they won't be seen but will be easily found. *Poor little Stacey, who kicked the empties under her bed before she climbed in.*

I walk downstairs and have a nosey in their kitchen cupboards. Shambolic. Disgusting. But I find what I need: the pot of cocoa. I take one of the little freezer bags I always keep in my handbag and put the pills inside. I then root around the kitchen drawers and find a spoon. Using the back of the spoon, I crush the pills. When I reckon they're a fine-enough powder, I stir some into the cocoa. The white powder shows up a bit against the brown cocoa granules. Frustrating. I stride to the fridge and take out a carton of milk and stir some of the powder into the milk. Not too much, because I'm no child killer.

As I'm putting the milk back into the fridge, I notice a quarter-filled bottle of white wine. Perfect. Dom doesn't drink white, so this must be Stacey's. It's a cheap bottle of Sauvignon Blanc. She has dreadful taste. Carefully, I tip the bulk of the powder into the wine bottle and shake the bottle hard. I hold it up to the light, and although it's hard to tell through the green glass, the wine doesn't look too cloudy. I put the bottle back in the fridge, wipe the spoon down and put it back in the cutlery drawer. Then I shove the freezer bag back into my handbag. I check that everything is as I found it. With my mission complete, it's time to have a good nosey around.

I walk back upstairs. I'll start in Dom and Stacey's bedroom, see if she writes a diary or has anything she shouldn't have in her knickers drawer. I can't help smiling at the thought. She doesn't deserve Dom. A drawer full of greying M&S knickers. Thick woollen tights more suitable for an aging granny. Some cheap-looking clothes. Supermarket-bought makeup. It's not like they can't afford better quality. A laptop is on top of the chest of drawers. I flip the lid up and see that it has been left switched on. Thanks to Stacey's carelessness when I was here for dinner, I know the password: *IvyArthur*. Quickly, I bring up Outlook, compose an email, find the recipient's email address, schedule the email to be sent out at the correct time, shut down the programme and then, just as I close the lid, I hear something.

The slamming of a car door.

Too close.

I scoot towards the window, my back against the wall next to the heavy-weight pale green curtains, just as you see the cops doing in movies. I peek around the side of the fabric.

Shit! Dom and Stacey are home. Already. How's that possible? Dom is walking towards the front door of the house, while Stacey is just getting out of the car. They are talking to each other quite loudly. How the hell am I going to get out without them seeing me?

I race down the stairs, almost tripping headfirst as I do so. I just manage to right myself by gripping the metal stair rail, then skid along the corridor. Just as I slip into the kitchen, I hear the front door open. I need to get to the utility room, but how the hell am I going to do that without them seeing me?

'I can't believe you didn't notice that you had let Molly out!' Dom sounds exasperated. 'Mum would have a hissy fit if she knew.'

'But I didn't let her out, Dom. Molly was curled up in her basket when I left. I promise you!'

'Darling, this is exactly why we went to see the doctor.' Dom's tone of voice is a mix of patronising and concern. If I wasn't so focussed on getting the hell out of here, I might enjoy their conversation. 'Well, then, you must have left a window open. Or the back door. I'll go and check.'

He can't check the back door. I am hiding behind the kitchen door. He'll have to walk right past me, and then he'll see the back door wide open. My heart hammers in my chest. I try to control my breathing, but I can hear myself so loudly. If they catch me, it will be all over. I have only two choices: give myself up or kill them. I glance around, but can't see a knife rack. Too much bloody clutter.

'I'll look, Dom. You need to get away.'

'I'm worried about going to Liverpool and leaving you. I know what Dr Brinksome said, but until we've got you stable on the new medication...' Dom's voice trails away.

Stacey is sobbing.

'Come here, darling,' Dom says. Footsteps approach. Have I got time to make a run for it?

The damned cat comes into the kitchen, takes one look at me and meows. I would like to kick the thing, but all I can do is give it evil eyes. At least it's not hissing at me.

'I know what you think,' Stacey hiccups. 'And sometimes I think you're right. But I don't feel like I did last time. I promise. I've just been stressed and forgotten a few things.'

I hold my breath and decide to go for it. Skidding across the floor, I swear the damned shoe covers sound like the rustling of a newspaper.

I'm not wrong.

'What's that?' Stacey says.

'Probably the cat. Come on. I'll make us a cup of tea and then we'll discuss whether I should go or not. Tamara is quite capable of handling the meeting alone.'

I am in the utility room, where the back door is still ajar and letting in freezing cold air. Only twelve feet or so to go and then I'll be out. But their footsteps sound so loud, as if just a foot away from me. I peer through the crack in the utility room door. They are. Right there. Stacey puts her hand out as if she is going to open the utility room door, which will push it back to where I'm standing. I normally have nerves of steel, but right now I think I'm going to be sick. *Control yourself, Tamara. Control.* I dig my fingernails into my palms and hold my breath.

And then, just when I think it's all over and I'll have no choice but to kill them, a telephone rings.

For one horrific but brief moment, I wonder if it's mine ringing in my bag. But when Stacey's footsteps move away, I let out a little sigh and realise it wasn't mine. Of course it wasn't mine. I'm not that bloody careless. I set it to airplane mode before leaving the car.

Stacey's voice fades away as she walks out of the kitchen, so that now I can't hear what she's saying. And then Dom puts the kettle on.

Dom is my saviour. Again.

I wait until the kettle is at maximum screaming pitch, and then I dart towards the back door and, thank the Lord, I'm out. Pulling the paper covers off my shoes, I gently close the back door. I head to the front of the house, keeping tight to the exterior walls of the house and ducking down as I pass by any windows. Once there, I walk briskly down their drive, not too fast because I don't want to attract attention to myself from any nosey neighbours, but quickly enough so that just a few long seconds later I am collapsed in the driver's seat of my car, trembling but safe.

18

STACEY

D r Brinksome has given me some pills and booked me in to see him again next week. I was worried that Dom might tell him about the packet of condoms or make some snide comment about me having an affair, but he didn't. My husband was lovely. He held my hand and was supportive and gentle.

But then we got home and his mother's bloody cat had escaped. I am sure I locked the doors and closed all the windows. I got in even more of a state because I know the happy pills won't take effect for at least a couple of weeks.

I told Dom to go to Liverpool, to attend the meeting. He's done enough for me today. I will get through the afternoon and the night without him. I have to.

And now I'm standing in the school yard, waiting for the children. I'm wrapped in my thick, ugly, grey goose-down coat with the hood pulled low over my forehead. I'm lost in my own little world, standing away from all the other mums and not even pretending to be on the phone. I suppose my body language says it all, because no one approaches me.

And then the children are rushing out and Arthur hurtles

into my legs, almost knocking me over. Ivy is carrying a big papier-mâché globe – her latest art masterpiece – which is in danger of turning into a sodden mush if we don't get it out of the rain pronto. We race back to the car.

Arthur is gabbling about his day and Ivy is proudly telling me how she got top marks in art for the second time this term. It isn't until we are pulling into the driveway that she says, 'Mummy, aren't I having a piano lesson today?'

'Oh shit! Oh shit!' I slam my foot on the brake and thump my hands on the steering wheel.

'Mummy said a naughty word! Mummy said shit!' Arthur sings.

'Enough!' I shout.

The children fall silent. I turn to look at them. They are staring at me, aghast. I never shout at my children – at least, not unless it is absolutely warranted. What the hell am I doing?

'I'm sorry Arthur, Ivy. I've had a difficult day and I didn't mean to shout at you. Ivy, I totally forgot about your piano lesson. Do you want to still go or shall I call Mrs Ponder and apologise?'

'I can miss it,' Ivy says in a small voice. 'I haven't practiced enough this week anyway.'

I sigh with relief. The last thing I feel like is driving to Coolham for a piano lesson. But why the hell did I forget? Ivy has a piano lesson every Tuesday straight after school, every single bloody week.

After dumping their school bags in the hallway, Ivy sits on the kitchen floor cuddling Molly, Dom's mother's cat, while Arthur sits up at the table and sucks his thumb. I don't have the energy to tell him not to.

'What's for tea?' he garbles around his thumb.

I haven't given any thought to meals. 'Pizza,' I say, pulling open the freezer drawer.

'Again?' Ivy moans. 'All we ever have is pizza or fish fingers.'

'That's not true,' I say, and then I have to shove the heels of my hands into my eye sockets because during the last week it has been true. Why, oh why can't I cope?

'What's the matter, Mummy?' Arthur says, pulling his thumb out of his mouth with a plop.

'Sorry, darlings. I'm not feeling very well. There's nothing to worry about.'

'Amber Jenning's mother has got cancer and she's going to die,' Ivy says in a matter of fact tone.

'Are you going to die, Mummy?' Arthur asks, his bottom lip quivering.

'No, I'm not. Come here!' I open my arms and he flings himself into them.

AFTER TEA we watch *Toy Story 3* for about the thousandth time. I sit between the children on the sofa and think how lucky I am to have such wonderful kids. But then tears well up in my eyes. What if I really can't cope?

Ivy interrupts my maudlin thoughts. 'Mummy, will *Pinkapop's Adventures* be made into a movie, like *Toy Story*?'

'Shush!' Arthur scolds his sister.

My little Ivy could not have asked a more pointed question. 'I don't know,' I say, thinking about the writing on the yellow piece of paper. And then I have to get up off the sofa and disappear into the bathroom because I can't stop the tears. And the more I cry, the more terrified I feel.

There's a knock on the bathroom door. 'Mummy, Arthur's pulling my hair!' Ivy yells.

'I'm coming.'

I wipe my eyes with toilet paper and splash my face with cold water. I wait a couple of minutes until my face is a little less red and force myself to smile in the mirror. I've never tried that before. I feel a smidgeon better.

The children are well behaved at bath-time, and when they're dry and in their pyjamas, I go downstairs and make their nightly hot chocolate. It's the same every evening. I put a heaped spoonful of drinking chocolate into their mugs of milk and heat them up in the microwave. Just as the microwave pings, the phone rings.

'Stacey, it's Briony. I heard about the potential IP infringement and I'm not happy. Not happy at all. What new ideas have you got to pitch to Howden Brook?' Briony's tone of voice is all brisk and curt and totally unsympathetic. I can't handle her right now. I just can't.

'I'm sorry, Briony...now isn't...' I swallow and bite the inside of my cheek. 'Can we have this conversation tomorrow please? I'm in the middle of putting the kids to bed.'

'Well no. Not really. This is urgent and—'

'I'll call you in the morning.' I hang up.

This is the first time I have ever hung up on Briony or been rude to her. Normally I am polite, verging on deferential, but right now I can't cope. Tears spring to my eyes yet again. I grip the edge of the worktop and press down on my palms. I must get a grip.

I take several deep breaths and then pick up the milk carton and put it back into the fridge. There is a third of a bottle of white wine in the fridge door. Normally, I never drink before putting the children to bed. In fact, I don't drink when I'm alone in the house, always fearful that I may need to drive somewhere in a hurry. But tonight that bottle is calling me. I take it out of the fridge and pour myself a large glass of wine. I take a few gulps, put the glass down, then open the microwave door, pick up the mugs of hot chocolate and walk upstairs.

Both Ivy and Arthur are lying on top of their respective

beds. They are such good children, and the thought chokes my throat.

I walk into Ivy's room first. 'Here you go, darling.' I put the mug on her pale pink bedside table. 'Twenty minutes and then brush your teeth and lights out.'

'Okay, Mummy.'

I leave Ivy reading *Goldilocks* and pad down the corridor to Arthur's room, his Thomas the Tank Engine mug in my hand. He is lying on his stomach, playing with a little train.

'Drink up, darling,' I say, handing him the mug. He sits up and takes it from me.

'Ergh! It's cold and it's got a yukky skin on it.'

'That's normal when a hot drink has gone a bit cold. Just ignore it and drink up.'

Arthur takes another couple of sips. 'It's horribubble, I can't.' He pulls a face as he places the mug on his bedside table.

I don't have the energy to insist he finishes it. 'All right. Let's do your teeth.' He follows me to the bathroom and I perch on the edge of the bath whilst he brushes his teeth, a task made possible thanks to his special toothbrush that plays Thomas the Tank Engine's theme tune until brushing time is up.

Before switching out their lights, I give both the children extra tight hugs and lots of kisses.

With no energy or appetite to eat, I collect the wine bottle and glass, walk to the living room and collapse onto the sofa.

19

TAMARA

fter all the stress of the afternoon, we make the train
we were booked on. The journey is spent going over
the presentation. Dom is distracted, but I focus hard.
I am determined that the meeting tomorrow morning will be a
success.

We arrive in the now-familiar Premier Inn in Liverpool's
docks, check in at reception and are handed our key cards.
When I made the booking, I asked for adjacent rooms. If Dom
is surprised by that, he doesn't show it.

'Shall we meet downstairs in fifteen minutes and go out for
a bite to eat?' he suggests. I readily agree.

Tonight, I'm dressing down. I wear a pair of tight-fitting
black trousers, black suede boots that come up over my knees –
and cost a bloody fortune – and a snugly-fitting low V-necked
jumper the colour of a fine-bodied red wine that compliments
my new hair and complexion. There is another secret addition
with which I'm particularly pleased. Stacey wears a perfume by
Penhaligon's called Bluebell. I spotted it in her bedroom when I
was there for dinner. It's expensive, and if I'd had a small bottle
with me, I might have decanted it. But I didn't. Instead, I

purchased one of Penhaligon's little tester kits. The alluring scent of Bluebell is now dabbed on my wrists and behind my ears.

In my opinion, the power of scent is both over-exaggerated and underestimated. All of that talk a few years back about bottling synthesized pheromones is, of course, a load of nonsense used by brands as a marketing device, but using scent to evoke memories is powerful. As we meet in the corridor, I stand close to Dom. I know he senses something about me, but I am confident he won't be able to work out what it is.

'Shall we go to the Italian restaurant next door?' he says.

'Good idea. I would quite like to get an early night so I'm on top form tomorrow.'

We walk in companionable silence to the restaurant. He is a gentleman and pulls out the chair for me to sit down. I appreciate good manners in a man.

'Would you like some wine?'

I shake my head. 'No. I'll just have a sparkling water.'

Dom orders a beer and a pizza. I order a vegetarian risotto.

'How is Stacey?' I ask.

'We saw her doctor and he is putting her on some new medication. Hopefully that will do the trick. I'm worried about her.'

'Of course you are. Has she felt any better during the last couple of days?'

Dom shakes his head.

'If you don't mind me asking, what happened when Stacey was ill previously?'

'She had a nervous breakdown and was hospitalised for a while. It was before I met her.'

'I'm sorry to hear that. My brother experienced the same. He's been in and out of psychiatric units all his life. It's so hard for the rest of the family. On the plus side, it's wonderful that she shared what happened to her. So often people hide mental health problems from their partners, especially if it happened long before they get together. That deceit is such a slippery slope.'

A fleeting look of concern passes over Dom's face. He fidgets and pushes his food around his plate. It's magic how easy it is to plant doubts in someone's head, but I decide it's time to lighten the conversation.

'Have you had a chance to consider the celebrity endorsement company I mentioned last week? I was thinking we could request the information pack from the agent.'

'Sorry, Tamara, I just haven't had any time to give it a moment's thought. If you'd like to get the particulars, by all means do so. It's just I don't want to over-expand, and we don't have the funding to self-finance it.'

I settle my eyes on his and put the tip of my index finger between my lips.

'I suppose it was a bit presumptuous for me to be coming up with expansion plans for your business,' I say.

'Not at all. I like it that you're ambitious for SAID. I've never had anyone on board that has thought about the strategic direction of the agency. What are your personal ambitions?' Dom leans back in his chair.

'I just want to do the best job I possibly can,' I say, gazing into the distance. 'I suppose one day I'd like to be on the board of an entrepreneurial company. I can't imagine ever not working. I could never be a stay-at-home mum. That's why I admire Stacey so much, juggling everything as she does.'

'Would you like to have children one day?'

I want to slam my hand on the table and scream 'Mind your own fucking business' at Dom, but I've dug this hole for myself.

'Honestly, I don't know. I have feelings for someone but...' My eyes move slowly from his lips to his eyes and then back again, but just as he begins to shuffle awkwardly, his mobile phone rings. He glances at it, but hits the end call button. I raise my eyebrows.

'I don't recognise the number,' he says.

The phone rings again immediately. He frowns.

When this happens the third time, I suggest, 'You should probably answer it.'

Dom nods and holds the phone up to his ear. Even though the restaurant is quite noisy, I can hear the voice of a hysterical woman.

The blood drains from Dom's face. His left hand grips the edge of the table. I look at him, my head to one side, querying.

'Which hospital?' Dom asks.

'Are the police still there?'

'Is Stacey going to be all right?'

'Oh God! Oh God, I should never have left her!'

Dom sways slightly as he puts the phone down. I think he might pass out. I quickly stand up and move to his side of the table, crouch down next to him, hold a glass of water to his lips and hold his trembling left hand.

'What's happened?' I ask quietly.

'I'm going to have to go home.'

'Ok,' I say. 'But first you need to tell me exactly what's going on.'

Dom's gaze is vacant, uncomprehending. He stutters a bit before getting his words out. 'That was Mina, Stacey's best friend. She received an email from Stace saying that Stacey couldn't take life anymore and that she'd be taking the children with her and that she was sorry. Mina called an ambulance and rushed over to our house. When she rang the doorbell, she was hopeful all was ok because Stacey answered the door, but then Stacey fell down, unconscious. Mina went to check on the kids. Arthur seemed ok, just a bit more drowsy than normal, but Ivy was drowsy and throwing up. Another ambulance was called, and Mina went with the kids to hospital. They're all there now.

She says the children are absolutely fine, and she'll be taking them home. But Stacey. They don't know. She's being treated and Mina hasn't heard anything.'

'Oh goodness, that is terrible,' I say, squeezing Dom's hand. 'I am so sorry.'

'The worst is, they found an empty pack of sleeping pills and several packs of empty painkillers under our bed. I can't believe she would do something like that. It just doesn't make sense.'

Dom pulls his hand away. 'I've got to go, Tamara. I need to be with my family.'

'Of course you do.' We both stand up.

'I'll take care of the bill and I'll manage the meeting tomorrow,' I say. 'Please don't give the business a moment's thought. But how will you get home? You have missed the last train.'

Dom puts his head in his hands. I wonder if he's going to break down.

'Is everything ok over here?' the Scouser waitress asks.

'We've had some bad news. Please could you bring us the bill quickly and then leave us for a moment,' I snap. She scurries away.

'I am going to find you a taxi to drive you home. It'll take about four hours, at least, but it's the fastest way we can get you back. Come on. Let's go to the hotel and collect your belongings and I'll sort out a car.'

'Tamara, thank you. Thank you so very much.'

'You'll be just fine,' I say, clicking my fingers at the waitress. She hurries back and hands me the bill. I leave cash on the table and then, putting my arm through Dom's, escort him back to the hotel.

I accompany him into his hotel room. He hasn't even unpacked, so I instruct him to sit on the edge of the bed. I call around a couple of taxi companies and find one only too eager to make several hundred pounds on a journey to Sussex.

'He'll be here in ten minutes,' I say to Dom. He looks utterly shell-shocked. I reach out for his hand and pull him up to a standing position. 'I know it's probably inappropriate for an employee to hug her boss, but I think you need a hug.' I throw my arms around Dom and hug him tightly. Eventually he relaxes into me, placing his chin on the top of my head. I like the feel of him. Stacey is too damned lucky.

After twenty seconds or so, he pulls away. 'You're a life-saver, Tamara.'

He leaves then.

I lie on his bed. Dom is a good man and I'm sorry that he is caught up in my plot. But not that sorry. Eventually, I sit up and whip out my mobile phone. I tick off several points on my list. I contemplate my success and think about all my achievements over the past twenty-four hours. I want to get it done, but then I remember. Time is on my side.

20

STACEY

When I wake up, I feel as if an elephant is sitting on my body and my head is going to explode. My eyes flicker open, but the bright light sears through them and I shut my eyelids again immediately. Even so, the light shines through. Where the hell am I? Why do I feel the most sick I have ever felt? And then I remember: I *have* felt like this before, a long time ago.

Panic grips me. My heart is racing and I struggle to gasp for air.

'It's all right, Stacey,' a stranger's voice says to me.

I turn to face her, opening my eyes properly now. My throat feels so sore.

'What's happened?' I ask croakily.

'You're in hospital. You're safe.'

'Why? Was there an accident?'

She looks at me strangely. 'I'm a junior doctor and my name is Marianne Crate. You tried to take your own life, dear.'

I try to sit up, and only then realise that my right arm is attached to a drip. 'No. No, I didn't! I wouldn't do that!'

She throws me a look of pity, which makes me scared.

Think. Think. Think. What time is it? Is it night or day? There are no windows. All I can hear are subdued voices. My throat is so sore, and my nostrils are filled with the stench of antiseptic

'Where are Ivy and Arthur?' I barely recognise my own voice.

'Your children are back at home, being looked after by your friend. Mina, is it?'

'Where's Dom?'

'Who is Dom, my love?'

'My husband! Where is my husband?'

'Shush, shush, Stacey. You must calm down now. I'm sure he will be here very soon.'

'I need to go home!' I try to fling the hospital blanket off my body. I'm not even wearing my own clothes but a hospital tunic. Even my underwear has gone. This is like being trapped in a nightmare.

'Dr Patel is the consultant and he will be in to see you shortly. He's accessing your medical records and then he'll have a nice long chat with you. We'll make you better again.'

'But there's nothing wrong with me!' I exclaim, collapsing back onto the hard bed. And then I wonder. Perhaps there is something wrong with me. I ache all over, and the exhaustion is unlike anything I have ever felt. Energy drains from my body and I close my eyes. The blackness is welcoming.

THE NEXT TIME I AWAKE, a dark-skinned doctor is sitting by my bedside, balancing a clipboard on his crossed knee. He wears a buttoned-down, pale blue open-necked shirt and looks at me with a kindly expression. He has dark penetrating eyes and deep wrinkles around his mouth. There is something reassuring and wise about him, something that makes me want to wake up and shuffle myself to a seated position.

'Mrs Nicholson, I am Dr Patel. Do you know why you are here?'

I shake my head and immediately regret it. It still feels as if I have been hit by a sledgehammer.

'You tried to take your own life with an overdose.' His accent has a soft, sing-song tone to it.

'I didn't. I would never take my own life. What's the time?'

'It's 8 a.m. and breakfast will be arriving shortly.' He glances down at the clipboard. 'What memories do you have immediately before you collapsed at your front door?'

I screw up my eyes. I can't remember anything from yesterday evening. I try to think. Dom and I went to see Dr Brinksome. He gave me a prescription for some new medication, but I hadn't got around to going to the chemist to pick it up...I think. Or did I? Dom brought me home. I collected the children from school. And then...nothing. My memory is a blank, black hole.

'I don't think I took the new medicine that Dr Brinksome prescribed me, but perhaps I did and I had a bad reaction to it?'

Dr Patel shakes his head. 'We found considerable traces of sleeping pills and painkillers in your system. I will, of course, be talking to Dr Brinksome later today to access your records. How does life seem to you right now, Mrs Nicholson?'

'It's Stacey, and life seems bewildering. I don't know why I'm here.'

'Do you ever wish you could go to sleep and not wake up?'

'Yes! I feel like I'm in a bloody nightmare. I just want to go home and get back to normal!' None of this makes sense to me. Why the hell am I here?

'You sent a suicide note to your friend, the lady who found you and alerted the authorities. Why did you feel that your life wasn't worth living?'

'But I didn't!' I am getting hot and agitated. I pull the blanket right off me and stare at my bare feet.

He leans closer to me. 'Stacey, do you have voices in your head?'

'No,' I shake my head vigorously, but then I remember a little of what has been happening. The note written in someone else's writing – Corinne's, perhaps; forgetting the children at school; the lost car key; and that general low-level feeling of panic that has been mounting inside me for the past couple of weeks. Have I heard voices as well? I remember a time when I did, but that was long ago.

'No! Things have been overwhelming recently, but there were no voices.'

He scribbles something down.

'Stacey, the police want to interview you. They are waiting outside, but first I wanted to assess you.'

'The police!' I shriek. 'What are the police here for?'

'Do you remember what happened to Ivy and Arthur?'

It is like a sword is jammed into my chest. I gasp. 'My children? What's happened to my children?'

'Relax, Stacey. They are fine now. They were sick last night, and the police want to find out more about it.'

I am shaking now. I pull the blanket back up over me. 'Where are they?' I whisper.

'They are at home, being cared for by your husband.'

'Thank God!' I say, and promptly burst into tears.

'Stacey, I understand from your husband that you had an episode of mental illness about fifteen years ago. Would you like to tell me about that?'

I sniff. 'No. It was totally different. Something bad happened and I didn't cope well with it. Dr Brinksome can tell you.' There is no way that I am regurgitating long-forgotten and long-dealt-with trauma. I spent years working through it, and what happened in the past must always stay in the past. 'I am not ill,' I say. But even I can hear the lack of conviction in my voice.

Dr Patel scribbles some more notes.

'I am going to allow the police to come and have a word with you, Stacey. Afterwards, I will review your medication and we will transfer you to another ward. Have you got any questions?'

'Yes! I want to go home. When can I go home?'

'It is likely to be a little while yet. We need to be sure that you are totally safe.'

He stands up. I thought Dr Patel looked like a nice man when I first awoke, but now I see him as the enemy. I turn my head away and let the tears drip onto my pillow.

'MRS NICHOLSON, we would like to discuss your children with you.' She stands at the end of my bed. Her colleague, a young man, hovers behind her. 'My name is Detective Sergeant Carla Ward, and my colleague here is Police Constable Chris Jennings.' They look perfectly ordinary, and if it wasn't for the badges they flash at me, I would never know they were police.

'Your children, Ivy and Arthur, were poorly last night. Upon further inspection, it was discovered that they imbibed crushed-up sleeping pills in their hot chocolate. In the note that you left for your friend Mina, you stated your intention of taking your children with you when you depart from this life. Could you please explain?'

I open and then close my mouth, then shake my head vigorously, despite still having a pounding headache.

'No! No, I would never write that, never do that! I love my children. They are my life, my everything! I would never, ever harm them! You've got to believe me!' I know I sound desperate, but I can't help wringing my hands, begging them to believe me. 'I have been set up! I must have been. That wasn't me!'

DS Carla Ward raises her thin, painted-on eyebrows. She

doesn't believe me. 'What time did you give your children their drinks of hot chocolate?'

My mind is still blank. I can remember getting the children into the car on the way back from school, but then nothing. I must have given them tea, overseen their baths, got them into bed. But it's as if my memory has been exorcised.

'Mrs Nicholson?' she asks again.

'I don't remember,' I whisper. 'I normally give them a hot chocolate each after their baths, then they brush their teeth. We read a bedtime story when they are both tucked up in bed.'

'Was anyone with you yesterday afternoon?'

'No. I don't think so.'

'We found this empty packet of sleeping pills under your bed. They have your name on it. Please can you confirm they are indeed yours.'

She holds out a see-through plastic bag with a box of sleeping pills in. They have my name printed on the front.

'Yes, I think they're mine. I've had them a while. I rarely take them.'

'Thank you, Mrs Nicholson. There will be a further enquiry and quite possibly a court hearing. If we decide to bring official charges, then you will have the right to be accompanied by a solicitor.'

'What! What are you saying?'

But they don't answer me. They turn and walk out of the small, single bedroom.

21

TAMARA

The meeting at Stanwyck goes perfectly. They like our design concepts and our proposed strategy. I pass on apologies for Dom and explain that his wife was taken seriously ill. They send their best regards and we joke that the best remedy for Dom's wife's speedy recovery would be a trip on one of their yachts. We agree timescales and budgets, and I take the first train I can get out of Liverpool.

I don't intend to return to the office today. There is too much to think about, too many items to tick off my list. So, after crossing London, I take the train out of London Victoria Station to Horsham, and by the middle of the afternoon I am back in my flat, a cup of mint tea in my hand and my feet up on my desk in the study.

I have been desperate to call him all day, so eager to know how Stacey is. Or preferably, isn't. But the sense of satisfaction I get from withholding my urges is almost orgasmic. I never understand people who eat their favourite foods first. I save them up until last. It's the same with work, and that's quite possibly why I'm so good at it. I get the mundane tasks done first, giving myself the juicy treats only when the tedious ones are ticked off. And so it has been like that all today. The anticipation of that phone call.

It's ten past four in the afternoon when I call Dom. I steel myself for his voicemail, a message all planned out in my head. But no. He answers!

'Dom,' I say breathily, 'how is Stacey?'

'She's in hospital; they're keeping her in for the time being.'

'So she's all right? She will make a good recovery?'

'Yes, I think so. They pumped her stomach and she's fine physically. Mentally, it's another story. They think she tried to harm the kids.' Dom chokes back a sob.

'Oh my goodness. I'm so sorry, Dom. That's awful. Have social services taken your children?'

There is a long pause. 'No. They're here with me now. You don't think social services will take the children, do you?'

'They'll probably do an assessment, but I'm sure they won't take the children from you. Are they at school?'

'No. I kept them home today. They're absolutely fine, enjoying a day of playing at home. I'm hoping we can all go and visit Stacey tomorrow, and then I'll take them back to school. Anyway, how was the meeting?'

'The Stanwyck team send their best regards for Stacey's speedy recovery. The meeting went a dream. They loved all our concepts and we're good to go. Please, don't worry about work, Dom. I'm on top of it.'

We are both silent for a moment, and then I say, 'It's quite a burden you're having to carry, Dom. Would you like me to come over this evening? I could rustle you up a light supper, just to help you out a bit?'

'That's really kind of you, but I couldn't possibly impose on you like that. If you could keep things ticking over at work and stay in regular contact with Jeff, that would be great.'

'That goes without saying, Dom. Please pick up the phone if there's anything at all I can do to help.'

I hang up.

I play with the phone, turning it around and around in my fingers. It's a fine balance. Being there for Dom but not intruding. Letting him know I care without him feeling I'm too pushy. I look up at the photograph of Stacey on my wall.

'Bye bye, Stacey,' I say with a grin.

I TAKE a shower and wash my hair. I always feel dirty after travelling. I'm careful with how I blow dry it, giving it a little bit of bounce. I put on minimal makeup and wear a pair of smart jeans with a white shirt and a belt with an extra-large buckle. Smart but casual.

I aim to get to Dom's for 8.30 p.m. It will be after the kids have gone to bed and, hopefully, he will have eaten already. All easy, just me being my caring, laid-back self. I laugh at the thought.

The weather is dreadful, pouring rain and a howling gale, so I decide to drive. After stopping off at the off-licence and picking up a decent bottle of red wine, I head towards Dom and Stacey's house. The house is shrouded in darkness. That is strange. Nevertheless, I hurry out of the car and run up to the front door, my jacket hood pulled low over my forehead. I ring the doorbell and wait.

After a long couple of minutes, a light comes on and the door opens. Dom stands there, bare-footed, in jeans and a T-shirt, unshaven, his eyes sunken and red.

'I thought you might like a friend and a glass of something decent,' I say, proffering the bottle. He seems taken aback.

'I'm sorry for intruding,' I say, shoving the bottle into his hands and turning away. 'I'll leave you to it.'

'No, Tamara, wait! Please don't go. You just surprised me, that's all. It's been one hell of a twenty-four hours.'

'Are you sure?' I ask, hopping from foot to foot to stave off the cold. 'If you'd rather be alone, I totally understand.'

'Absolutely not. I'd love your company. Come in!' He stands back and opens the door for me.

Bingo.

I follow him into the kitchen, where dirty dishes are stacked in the sink, and the only low light comes from the extractor hood above the oven.

'Have you eaten today?' I ask him.

'I made some tea for the kids, but I haven't been hungry. It's fine.'

'No, it's not. Sit down and I'll whip you up a quick omelette.' I walk over to the fridge. There's not a lot in it, but what is there is a mess. I notice both the bottle of wine and the lactose-free milk have gone. 'How about a cheese omelette with a little bit of salad and a big glass of red wine.'

Dom sinks into a kitchen chair, leans back with his hands behind his head and lets out a deep sigh. 'Thank you, Tamara!' His abs show through his T-shirt. He is surprisingly delectable. But no. I must concentrate on what I need to do.

I find a corkscrew in one of the drawers and open the bottle, pouring him a large glass.

'Drink this,' I say.

After ferreting through the drawers, I find the utensils I need and whip up an omelette for Dom. I glance at him from time to time but he remains silent, lost in his thoughts, sometimes with his eyes closed.

'Here you are,' I say, placing the plate and cutlery in front of him. 'Hey! You're not even drinking your wine. You need to keep body and soul together so you're strong for Ivy and Arthur.'

Dom lets out a long sigh. 'I know you're right, but something else happened this evening. I shouldn't be telling you, but I'll explode if I don't share it.'

I lean towards him and show him the palms of my hands. 'You know I won't breathe a word of your personal affairs to anyone,' I reassure him.

'Thanks, Tamara. So, I was rifling around in Stacey's drawers to find her some clothes to take to the hospital, and I found a bottle of aftershave loosely wrapped in wrapping paper.'

I look at him quizzically. 'And?'

'Stacey was cheating on me.'

'But maybe she bought the aftershave to give to you? When's your birthday? Or perhaps for Christmas?'

'I don't wear aftershave. Never have done.'

'Couldn't it have been for her brother or father?'

'Stacey doesn't have a brother, and I just can't imagine her giving something like that to her elderly father. Besides, she keeps all the presents she gives to everyone for Christmas in what she calls her presents drawer in her study. No, this was hidden there for a reason.'

Again he buries his face in his hands. 'She also had condoms in her bag. I had a vasectomy a few years ago. She's cheating on me.'

Dom looks so dejected it is almost laughable. I swallow my smirk and push his plate towards him. 'You must eat, Dom.'

'You're right.' He sighs and picks up his cutlery. But then he puts them down again before eating a mouthful. 'The worst thing of all is how she wanted to take the kids with her. The email suggested that she was going to poison our children. Even if she was in the depths of despair herself, how could she possibly do that? It just doesn't make any sense.' He swallows a sob. 'Stacey loves Ivy and Arthur.'

I squat down on the floor next to Dom and take his hands in mine. 'When people are at their very lowest and can't see any way out, they hurt the people they love the most. Perhaps now she has hit rock bottom, the only way is up. If she's in the hospital, they will make her better.' I let go of his hands and stand up.

'You're right, but I just don't know if I'll ever be able to trust her again. I've lost my wife, my best friend and my marriage. My children have lost their mother.'

I can't trust my reaction to this sentence, so I sit down on the chair next to Dom and bite my bottom lip. 'You're a good man, Dom. A strong man. You will get through this.'

'Oh Tamara, I'm not sure I can.'

He breaks down then. This strong man sobs in my arms. I let his tears wet my shoulder. I let his cheek lean against my breasts. I let my fingers stroke the back of his neck and his hair. We are so close. So nearly…

And then I break away. Now is not the time. Now he needs my support, not my body or my love.

'The omelette will be cold,' I say.

Dom nods, wipes his eyes and picks up his cutlery.

I make a mental note to check where I put emotional dependency on my Gantt Chart. All in all, it's been a good evening's work.

22

STACEY

A nurse appears and gives me a couple of pills in a little white paper cup. She is oriental and has a cute, heart-shaped face.

'What are these?'

'They'll make you feel better, Stacey.'

'But I don't feel ill! There's nothing wrong with me!' I wring my hands and try to get out of bed.

'Stacey, don't make this difficult. Dr Patel wants you to have these. He is a very good doctor and he'll come and visit you when you're on the ward. If you don't take them, we might have to give you an injection to calm you down, and I'm sure you don't want that, do you?'

She is talking to me as if I am a child. I feel like I'm stuck in an alternate reality. I didn't do all those awful things they accused me of. I would never, ever hurt my darling children. I love them more than life itself. Or do I? If I love them more than life itself, then would I want to take them with me when I leave life? My head is a jumbled whirl.

I tip the pills into my mouth, take a sip of water from a plastic cup and swallow them together.

'Well done, Stacey,' the nurse says. 'A couple of the porters will be along shortly to take you to the ward.'

'What ward?' I ask. But the nurse has already left the room.

I DOZE OFF. When I wake, walls are whizzing past me as if I am on a sledge going down the Cresta Run.

'What?' I try to articulate words, but they sound like strange, unrecognisable vowels. I lift my head slightly and can see that I am in a bed being wheeled through corridors. There is one orderly at the foot of the bed and two at the head. At least the drip has been removed from my arm.

I am trying to dislodge the fur in my brain and coordinate my tongue and lips to ask where we're going, but suddenly we stop. The hospital porter at the foot of the bed uses a swipe card to open a door. And that's when I see the sign. Psychiatric Ward.

'No!' I shout, but even I can tell the word sounds muffled, inadequate. No one takes any notice of me. We go through another set of locked double doors and then we're on a ward. It's all modern, with lino floors and fake wood counters and white walls.

The porter strolls towards a hatch in the wall, where a nurse is writing at a desk.

'Got a Stacey Nicholson for you,' he says.

The nurse looks up. 'Room 7, Rory, please.'

'Room 7 it is then.'

They carry on wheeling me and then turn the bed into a small room full of fitted furniture. There is a bed on a wooden base, attached to the floor. A small desk and chair are also fixed to the ground. An open door leads into a shower room.

'Welcome to your new home,' the porter says. 'Are you up to

getting out of bed by yourself, Stacey?' He talks slowly, as if I'm a dimwit. Perhaps I am?

I sit up and swivel my legs off the trolley bed. I am still wearing the hospital cotton tunic and have bare legs. My pink-painted toenails bring tears to my eyes. They are the only familiar things in this terrifying place. I stand up, but then I sway and feel so dizzy, I have to sit down again.

'Can you give me a hand?' I ask in a whisper.

'Sorry, love, we're not meant to touch you.'

Why? I wonder. *Have I got a contagious disease?* I stand, slowly this time, then hobble towards the fixed-down bed. My legs feel so wobbly, so insecure. The bed is hard and the plastic mattress squeaks as I lie on it.

The orderlies leave without so much as a goodbye. Just a moment later, a nurse comes in with a clipboard and pencil. She is tall and skinny, with a large mole on her left cheek, and blonde hair cut as short as a boy's.

'Hello, Stacey. I'm Wendy and I'll be keeping an eye on you.'

'I don't need anyone keeping an eye on me! I need to go home.'

'The doctor will have explained that you are being sectioned. Do you remember what that means, Stacey?'

'I know what being sectioned means, but there's nothing wrong with me!'

'Dr Patel and Dr Showell have both confirmed that you are suffering from a mental disorder and, to protect yourself and your other family members, you're being detained in this hospital for assessment. Your own doctor, Dr Brinksome has been involved in the decision.'

'How long do I have to stay here?' I look at her, my jaw loose.

'Standard detention by the courts is for 28 days whilst you are assessed and a report is being prepared.'

Wendy perches on the edge of the desk. 'I understand that the police have been involved, Stacey. Is that right?'

I nod.

'It's much better here than if you were detained in prison.'

'Prison?'

I can't take this anymore. The sobs rack through me. Pity. Desperation. Terror. What the hell has happened? I bury myself down under the sheet and blankets, pulling them up over my head so I can lose myself in the darkness of the bed.

After a while, someone taps my shoulder.

'Stacey, it's me again, Wendy. I've got another pill for you to take.'

'I don't want any,' I snuffle.

'You've got no choice, my love. They're to make you feel better.'

I haul myself up the bed and accept the pill and the plastic cup of warm water.

I must sleep, because when I wake up, it's dark outside. The door to my room is open and orange light from the corridor spills in. There are horrible sounds. Those of a woman screeching as if she is being attacked. Footsteps. A man coughing, violent hacks. Loud voices. I have no idea what the time is. My head feels as if it is stuffed full of wool and my body is as wooden as a scarecrow.

TIME IS NOTHING HERE. I don't have a watch or a clock. All I know is that someone comes into my room every fifteen minutes, day and night. I counted the time between visits. One elephant. Two elephants. Three elephants. I got to sixty elephants fifteen times. They don't care if I'm sleeping, and time after time I'm jerked awake, my heart racing, my body slick with a layer of sweat. They bring me food. Disgusting, bland, institutionalised food that I don't eat. I leave it on the tray. I prefer sleep, because then I'm at home or with the kids, or even back at my parents' home, having supper with Mum and Dad.

I don't know if its hours or days later that I hear a familiar voice.

'Stacey?'

I force my eyes open.

Dom.

'Oh Dom!' I struggle to shift myself up in the bed. He looks at me with an expression I have never seen before. Disgust. Horror. Revulsion. For the first time in our marriage, he doesn't greet me with a kiss.

'I've brought you some clothes and stuff from home. A couple of books and some toiletries.'

'Ivy and Arthur. Where are they? Can I see them?'

'No. You're not allowed to see the kids. Not yet.'

Tears well up in my eyes and slip over my bottom lids, rolling down my cheeks. 'How are they?'

'They're fine. They went to school today. They miss you.'

'It's lies that they're telling, Dom. I would never do anything to hurt our babies. You do know that?'

He looks away from me. My own husband cannot meet my eyes.

'Dom! You do believe me, don't you?' I can't help but raise my voice.

The door swings open. 'Everything all right in here? Stacey, are you ok?' She's a new nurse, with ebony skin and a vast bosom.

I nod at her.

'We're fine,' Dom says.

She leaves.

'There is no privacy in here,' I say softly. 'They check up on me every fifteen minutes. There is no lock on the bathroom door and, look around – no belts or ties or anything that I could use to cause damage to myself or others. But they've got it all wrong, Dom. I didn't want to die! I don't want to die! I love you and our life and our family.' The tears are gushing now, and I wait for Dom to pull me into a hug. But he doesn't. He stands there awkwardly, as if I'm some stranger. 'Dom, what's happening?'

He sighs, tries to move the chair to sit down, but realises that it's attached to the ground. He sits anyway.

'You've had a breakdown, Stacey. You tried to kill yourself and the children. How could you do that?'

'I didn't. I would never, ever hurt them. Don't you believe me? Surely you of everybody knows I would never do that?'

'The thing is, Stacey, I don't recognise you anymore. You've been having an affair and—'

'No! No!' I scream. 'No!'

And then two nurses come rushing in and each grabs one of my arms. They inject me.

∼

WHEN I AWAKEN, Dom has gone.

23

TAMARA

They've sectioned Stacey and are detaining her under the Mental Health Act. She'll be in the psych ward for at least 28 days.

Twenty-eight glorious days.

I am in such a good mood, I go shopping. It's Saturday afternoon and nearing Christmas, but even the hordes of shoppers don't detract from the glorious sense of accomplishment and happiness. After parking the car, I amble into Waitrose and pick up a ready-to-cook lasagne, a bag of mixed salad, a baguette pre-filled with garlic butter and another decent bottle of red. In a moment of weakness, I also buy a box of Bendicks chocolates and a couple of jars of jellybeans.

After a long, hot soak in a bubble bath surrounded by flickering candles, I get ready, pampering myself with deliciously-scented lotions and carefully applying my makeup. I put on my dressing gown, then pop the ready-made lasagne into one of my glass dishes and put it in the oven. Then I get dressed. I wear the same jeans as yesterday, but a different top.

At 7 p.m., the oven beeps and I'm ready.

I send Dom a text message. 'I'm coming over with supper.

It's already made, so you can't say no. I won't stay.' I turn my mobile phone off.

I wrap the dish in aluminium foil, then place it on a wooden chopping board and carry it out to my car.

Ten minutes later, I'm parked up outside Dom's house.

CAREFULLY BALANCING the hot dish in one hand, my handbag across my body and the bag with the salad, wine and sweets in the other, I ring Dom's doorbell. This time the door opens instantly. It's as if the door magically opens by itself. Until, that is, I look down. She's smaller than I remember.

'Are you the lady that came here before?' Ivy asks.

'Yes. I'm Tamara.'

'Oh.' She doesn't open the door any further, so I am left standing awkwardly on the doorstep. She's wearing a pink, fluffy dressing gown and slippers that look like little horse faces.

'Is your daddy at home?'

'Yes.'

'Can you let me in?'

'Ok.' She stands to one side and stares at me as I struggle to balance everything. I dash into the kitchen and just make it to the island unit, slipping the glass dish onto the surface. Ivy has followed me in and she stands there, staring at me. 'Where's your daddy?' I ask.

'Putting Arthur to bed. Why are you here?'

I would like to say 'None of your bloody business,' but such a retort won't do much to further my plan, so I sigh. 'I've brought your daddy some supper. I wanted to be kind to him whilst your mummy is away.'

'Mummy is in hospital. She's sick.'

'Yes, I know.' I bend down so I'm level with Ivy. 'She's got a bad sickness in the head and she may never—'

But then I hear loud footsteps coming down the stairs, so I get up, turn my back to Ivy and start unpacking the food.

'Tamara!' Dom comes over and gives me a kiss on the cheek. 'You really didn't have to do this.'

'I know, but I wanted to. How are things?'

'When is Mummy coming home?' Ivy interrupts.

'I don't know, darling. When she's better.'

And then the little black cat slinks around the door into the corridor. It takes one look at me and hisses.

I step backwards. 'Sorry, Dom. I'm terrified of cats and they can always sense it. I was quite badly mauled when I was a kid.'

'Molly wouldn't hurt anyone, would you, you soppy old thing.' Dom bends down and picks her up.

'I didn't realise you had a cat,' I say.

'We don't. She's my mum's. Molly's just visiting for the week. Ivy, can you put her in the utility room, please?'

I remember then that I have something for the children. I take the cartons of jellybeans out of the bag and hand them to Ivy. 'One for you and one for your brother.'

'Arthur's asleep.'

'Perhaps you can give them to him in the morning, then.'

With the cat under her arm, Ivy turns and walks out of the room. Just before she reaches the door, Dom says, 'What do you say to Tamara?'

'Thank you.' She spits out the words as she walks away.

'I'm sorry that she was rude,' Dom says, placing a hand on my arm. 'It's been a tough few days for the kids. They don't understand what's happening.'

I reassure Dom that I am not offended by a seven-year-old. I walk over to the oven and switch it on. 'This needs reheating for fifteen minutes and then should be ready to eat. I'll pop the salad in a bowl and then I'll leave you to it.'

'Leave me?' Dom frowns. 'Oh, you've got a date, right?'

I turn around to face him and laugh. 'I don't have a date! I've given up on internet dating. It's always a disappointment. Hopefully I'll meet Mr Right the conventional way. I was just going to have a date with the television at home, which is why I'm dressed so casually.' I gesture at my designer skinny jeans and black angora V-necked jumper, which is anything but casual.

'In which case, you must stay and keep me company. Have you eaten?'

I shake my head.

'Then please stay.'

WHEN THE LASAGNE is piping hot, I place it on plates and we sit down to eat. I wonder if I'm sitting in Stacey's place, but if so, Dom doesn't say anything.

'Did you get to see Stacey?' I ask.

'Yes. It's very difficult. She's in total denial.'

'I assume that's normal. Did you speak to the doctor?'

'There isn't much to say at this point. They need the full 28 days to assess her. The weird thing is, she seems so lucid. I suppose I had expected her not to be herself. By the way, this lasagne is delicious.'

'Thanks. I love cooking; it's my form of relaxation.'

Just as we're finishing off the remains of the lasagne, Ivy comes back into the room. She pointedly ignores me, walks up to her dad and says, 'When's that lady going home?'

'Ivy, that's very rude. Tamara will stay here as long as she likes. She works with me and we have a lot to discuss.'

'I want my mummy.'

'Of course you do, darling,' I say. 'What does Mummy do with you in the evenings?'

She keeps her eyes on her toes and ignores me. I would slap her, given half the chance.

'Answer Tamara,' Dom instructs his daughter.

'She reads me a story and puts my bedroom light out,' Ivy says in a whisper, still not looking at me.

'Would you allow me to do that?' I ask, wondering if I'm crossing a line.

Ivy shrugs her shoulders.

'What a lovely offer,' Dom says, turning Ivy around to face me. The girl still doesn't look at me. 'Why don't you take Tamara up to your bedroom whilst I wash up.'

I stand up and hold out my hand. Ivy ignores it. She walks in front of me, then runs up the stairs and rushes around the corner into her bedroom. She shrugs off her dressing gown, letting it fall to the floor, then jumps into bed.

I am out of my depth here. I have never read a child a bedtime story.

'What is Mummy reading to you at the moment?'

She looks at me now as if I have a screw loose. 'Mummy's in the hospital. She's not here.'

'Sorry, yes, I know that. I meant what are you reading?'

'*Goldilocks and the Three Bears.*' She chucks a well-worn book towards me. I sit down on the edge of her bed. The all-over pinkness of her room is in danger of giving me a headache.

'That's very old-fashioned,' I murmur. 'Where do I begin?'

'At the beginning.' She rolls her eyes at me.

I don't like this child.

When I've nearly finished reading the book, Dom comes in and sits at the end of Ivy's bed. It is such a cosy scene of domesticity, I have to contain myself to stop my voice from cracking with laughter. I stand up.

'Goodnight, Ivy.'

She doesn't reply.

BACK DOWNSTAIRS, I dry up the dishes that Dom has left draining next to the sink and put everything away. The kitchen is in dire need of a tidy up. I find some cleaning liquid under the sink and scrub all the surfaces. I am startled when Dom pads in.

'Hey you, you're my guest. Put those away!'

He opens another bottle of wine and pours me a large glass. We're both drinking a lot.

'Let's go and sit in the living room and you can tell me more about your ideas for the business.'

But we don't talk about the business. We talk about Stacey. Poor Dom puts on a brave face, but I can tell he is devastated.

'My brother was a manic depressive,' I say, twirling the stem of the glass in my fingers. 'We spent quite a bit of time on the psych wards.'

'You did? How is your brother now?'

I pause as if considering how best to answer that question. I know Dom is looking for hope, but he isn't going to get any from me.

'He died.' I bat away a non-existent tear.

'Oh. I'm so sorry.'

Poor Dom. He is a genuinely nice guy. Stacey has no idea how damned lucky she is. How damned lucky she has been all her cutesy little life.

'Why don't we watch a film, to take our minds off everything?' I suggest.

'Good idea.' Dom searches for the television remote control, which he eventually finds down the back of the sofa. 'What do you like watching?'

'How about an old classic such as *Sleepless in Seattle* or *Casablanca*?'

Dom's face breaks into a smile. Such a joy to see. 'I didn't have you down as an old-fashioned romantic!'

'There's lots about me that you don't know, Dominic Nicholson,' I say, jokingly.

Our eyes lock, and oh, how I want to kiss this man. But he pulls himself out of the gaze, shakes his head and continues scrolling through films. To my amusement, he settles on *When Harry Met Sally*.

'I've never actually seen this film,' he says. Does he not know about the film's most infamous moment?

Dom lowers the lights in the living room and then we both settle down on the sofa, sitting on opposite ends. He puts his feet up on the coffee table. I take off my shoes and curl my legs up under myself, wedging a couple of cushions behind my back. I wait expectantly for the orgasm scene, but Dom's face remains impassive, his eyes locked to the screen. Just before the end of the film, I let my eyes close and quieten my breathing.

'Tamara,' he whispers. But I don't open my eyes. I can feel his breath on my face, and then a blanket is settled around my body, his hands tucking it in along my sides. I can hear him shuffling around the room, so I peek out from under my eyelids.

'Dom,' I whisper.

'Hey. I thought you were asleep?' He comes closer.

'I was. I'm so exhausted, I don't know if I can get myself home.' I try to open my eyelids but blink several times and let them fall again.

'You don't need to go. Why don't you stay the night? We always keep the bed made up in the spare room.'

'I couldn't possibly,' I say, stifling a yawn with my right hand.

'I insist. You've drunk too much to drive. It's really no problem.'

I let out a contented purr. 'You're a darling,' I say. 'If you're sure it's no problem, it will be a joy just to be able to flop into bed. I'll be out of your hair first thing tomorrow morning.'

'There's no hurry. I always take the kids to see my parents on Sundays. Mum cooks us a Sunday roast.'

I stretch my arms above my head, letting my jumper ride up so my flat stomach is revealed.

'I noticed you haven't got much food in the fridge,' I say languidly, letting my head flop back against the sofa. 'Why don't I do a shop for you? I can bring it around tomorrow night.'

'You don't need to do that!' Dom says.

'No, I don't need to, but I'd like to.'

'Honestly, Tamara. You're too good to be true.'

I smile at him and close my eyes.

THE GUEST ROOM has a small double bed and floral curtains in pinks and greens. It's not to my taste, but then Stacey and I only have one thing in common.

'Is there anything I can get you? Would you like to borrow one of Stacey's nightdresses?'

'I'm not really a nightdress kind of girl,' I say. I think I can see a hint of a blush in Dom's cheeks. 'But if you've got a tooth-brush and some toothpaste I could use, that would be much appreciated.'

'Yes, of course.' He scuttles away.

I leave the door ajar and then remove my jumper, and am standing in the bedroom wearing just my black bra and black satin knickers. When I hear his footsteps, I turn so my back is to the door.

He speaks as he steps into the room. 'I've got...'

I turn to face him and immediately feign awkwardness, as if I'd forgotten that I was standing there semi-naked.

'I'm so sorry!' I say, bringing my hands up to my cheeks. 'I'm used to walking around my place with nothing on and I always forget when I'm somewhere else!' I grab my jumper and hold it up in front of me, trying and failing to cover myself up.

Dom doesn't know where to look. His flustering is rather sweet. 'I'll just leave the toothbrush here,' he says, placing them on a small chest of drawers opposite the bed. 'Sleep well, Tamara, and no hurry to get up in the morning. The kids are up bright and early, but please have a lie-in.'

'Goodnight, Dom. And thanks for letting me stay.'

When the house is totally quiet, I tiptoe out of my room. My first port of call is Arthur. He sleeps with his door ajar. The nightlight lets me see where I'm going. Just as well, otherwise I would have tripped on the mess of toys scattered across the floor. I stare at that little chubby, angelic face with dark lashes for a long time, and listen to the gentle whistle that emits from his lips every couple of out-breaths. I switch off his nightlight, then creep out of the room using the light from my phone. I move to Ivy's room. I am more careful here. Ivy is intuitive and I don't like that. She also has a nightlight on. I see the two pots of jellybeans that I gave her, standing on the side of her little dressing table. Gently I pick them up, remove the lids and scatter the jellybeans across the floor.

When I'm back in bed, I scroll through my phone. I'm making fabulous progress and tick off number seven. I sleep a beautiful, dreamless sleep.

24

STACEY

I hate what the drugs do to me. They make the world seem distant, hazy, as if I'm looking through several panes of glass. And they also make me sleepy. That's a good thing, because I don't need to remember the horrors of what has happened and the sheer craziness of being locked up in a psych ward. On the other hand, as soon as I try to think about what has happened, or consider whether perhaps I really did try to take my own life or hurt my children, my brain doesn't have enough capacity to reason it through. I sleep again.

From time to time, I remember my deadline for *Pinkapop's Adventures*. And then Corinne's sneering face breaks through and I cry hot, heavy tears for a career that has been torn to shreds.

I miss Dom. I miss Ivy and Arthur. I realise how often I held my family, and in here there is no one to hold me just when I am craving human touch.

But the worst thing in this place is the lack of privacy. There is none. Every fifteen minutes, someone comes into my room to check I haven't tried to hurt myself. Day and night. They check up on me when I'm in the shower, sitting on the toilet, trying to hide myself away under the sheets.

'How are you feeling, Stacey?'

'Have you taken your pills, Stacey?'

'You need to eat up, Stacey.'

And then there are the other patients. The noise is horrendous. Screams, weird mutterings, cries. Lots of crying. And so, although I hate what the drugs do to me, I am also grateful to them. They dial down everything else.

'It's Sunday today,' Wendy said when she brought me my breakfast tray. It's just as well she tells me the day of the week, because time has merged. I have no idea how long I have been in this place.

And the next time Wendy comes in, she says in an excited voice, 'You have a visitor.' I know it won't be Dom because we always go to see his parents on a Sunday. But me, I'm no longer part of that we, and it's breaking my heart.

'I don't want to see anyone,' I say, my words furring on my lips.

'It'll be good for you,' Wendy blinks rapidly. 'Come on, let's straighten you up.'

They want me to get dressed, to get out of bed, join other people in the day room, but that's the last thing I feel like doing. Besides, I don't have to until tomorrow, when the therapy starts. That's what Wendy has told me.

A couple of minutes later, there is a gentle knock on the door and it swings open. I realise I didn't even ask Wendy who is visiting me, but I assume it is Mina. My lovely friend, Mina.

It's not.

'What are you doing here?' I ask.

'I've come to say hello,' Tamara says, holding out a bunch of flowers that look as if they have been bought on a garage forecourt. Carnations with gypsophila. Cheap and garish.

I don't take them, so she lays them on the desk.

'How are you doing?' she asks. She looks a little flustered as she tries to pull out the chair and then realises it is secured to the ground. But Tamara is one of those people who recovers quickly.

'Dom, Ivy and Arthur are doing fine,' she says, flicking her hair back.

'How do you know?' I wish my head and voice would connect more quickly.

'I stayed at your house last night. Just wanted to keep an eye on everybody.' She looks at her fingernails. They're painted ruby red.

I squeeze my eyes shut. There is something not right about Tamara, but I can't focus on what it is.

'Stacey, I was just wondering if you found your missing car keys?'

I open my eyes and frown at her. 'What?'

'The keys to your Volvo XC90.' She reaches into her bag and dangles them from her index finger.

'What are you doing with my car keys? Did you find them?'

'No, Stacey.' She talks slowly, enunciating every letter as if I am a dim wit. Perhaps I am. 'I took your keys.'

'I don't understand! Why would you want my car keys?'

A slow grin creeps over her face.

'*Pinkapop's Adventures*, scribbled out as a mind map on yellow lined paper. Little creatures with big heads, wide eyes, in pale pink with blotches on body. Pinkapop takes children on dream adventures, going up into the sky in Dream Hoppers. Pinkapop hides in children's favourite toys.'

'What are you talking about?' My voice has raised in pitch by several notes. Despite the drugs, my heart is hammering in my chest and I'm finding it hard to gulp in air. 'How do you know about the note? Did you go rifling through my things?'

Tamara laughs. 'I didn't need to go rifling through your things. I put it there!'

'But why? How do you know about it?'

She laughs. 'You told me all about Corinne, don't you remember? And you showed me the outline on your computer. It didn't take much to work out what your silly little story was all about. But now you're in here...' She waves her arms around and sneers at the room. 'No one is going to believe mad Stacey!'

'What do you want from me?' My head is quivering, the room is spinning. 'What do you want?'

'Can't you work it out, Stacey?'

I wrench the sheets off the bed and swing my legs out. 'What do you want? My husband? My children? My home? Tell me! What do you want?' I'm screaming now. I sound just like all the other patients in the ward.

Tamara just grins at me, a supercilious sneer on her face. 'No Stacey. I don't want any of them, although your husband is rather gorgeous. Much too good for you. The thing is Stacey, I only want one thing. And that is for you to suffer.'

And then I pounce. I can't help it. I grab Tamara's hair and pull it as hard as I can. I pummel her in the chest, in the stomach. I kick. I try to throw her to the ground, but there are lots of hands. Stronger than mine. And loud voices. People telling me to calm down. To behave. Apologising to Tamara. Saying I'm having an episode and it's not uncommon.

'She's a liar!' I scream. 'She's evil!'

But I'm restrained. My arms are pinned back and something is jabbed into my arm. I squeal.

And then there is blackness.

25

TAMARA

When I left Stacey, I felt a pang. I'm not totally heartless. They were talking about moving her to the high-risk unit, upping her drugs. The nurses apologised to me. They fawned over me to make sure I wasn't injured. I wasn't. And then they suggested I wait a few weeks before visiting Stacey again.

That's a laugh. I will never see Stacey again. But I don't feel sorry for her. She deserves this. I've had to wait so long and now it's her time. It's not as if I'm doing anything to her that she hasn't already done to me.

I go to Tesco's to do a shop for Dom. I pile the trolley high with things. None of that fast food rubbish that Stacey keeps in her freezer, but lots of healthy fresh fruit, vegetables and meat.

THERE WAS QUITE A FURORE EARLY this morning when the children woke up. I could hear Ivy screaming at Arthur, blaming him for opening the jellybeans and scattering them across the floor. There were tears and stamping of feet, and Dom was shushing and scolding them for being so noisy. Even when they were downstairs, it was impossible to sleep with the clattering of dishes and the television turned up too loud. I stayed in my room until 9.30 a.m., having taken a quick shower. I don't like wearing yesterday's clothes, but I had no choice.

As I entered the kitchen, Dom was sitting there alone with the newspaper laid out in front of him, staring into space. He started when I cleared my throat.

'Sorry, Tamara, I was miles away. How did you sleep? I'm sorry that the kids made such a racket this morning.'

'I slept beautifully. I'm the heaviest of sleepers so nothing wakes me. It is such a comfortable bed.'

'Can I get you some breakfast, a coffee?'

'It's sweet of you, but I'd better get on my way. There are various things I need to do today. I'll get some groceries for you and pop around later. What time will you be back from seeing your parents?'

'By 5 p.m., usually. But please don't worry. I can do the shop myself.'

'Out of the question. A promise is a promise. I'll see you later, Dom.'

I let myself out of the house.

AND NOW I'M back again. The lights are on in all the rooms and Dom's car is parked by the front door. I place most of the shopping bags on the doorstep and ring the bell.

'Goodness, you've done quite a shop!' Dom says. He greets me with a quick kiss on the cheek.

'I doubt you'll have time to shop this week, so thought I'd stock up today.'

'That's so thoughtful of you. Here, let me give you a hand.'

Between us, we carry all the shopping into the kitchen and unpack it into the fridge and cupboards.

'How much do I owe you?' Dom asks, leaning his backside against the island unit.

'Before we talk about that, there's something I need to tell you.' I pull out a kitchen chair and sit down. 'I went to see Stacey.'

'You did?' Dom looks startled.

'I was literally driving past the entrance to the hospital and my heart bled for her, to think she was all alone on a Sunday when she's normally at the bosom of your lovely family. I took her some flowers and we had a super little chat.'

'Gosh, Tamara. That's...um...' Dom stutters as he frowns.

It is apparent that he is disconcerted by my visit to his wife. I need to put his mind to rest.

'I know it might seem odd that I visited Stacey when I don't know her very well, but I remember how lonely my brother was when he was cooped up in the psychiatric ward. He said that even though you're never alone, it is the loneliest place in the world. And because I was passing, I just thought it would be so cruel not to go and say hello. I really hope you don't mind, Dom?' I look at him beseechingly.

'No. No. Of course I don't mind. It was kind of you.'

'Sit down,' I say, pulling out the chair next to me and patting it. Dom does as he's told.

'Now I don't want you to worry,' I say, leaning forwards towards him, 'but Stacey is not very well today. She was screaming and shouting, and she tried to attack me. I think they are moving her to the high-dependency unit.'

'Oh my God!' Dom leans back and crunches up his face. 'Are you ok?'

'Absolutely fine. I can cope with a few bruises and scratches. I'm more concerned for Stacey. She seems to be deteriorating quite fast.'

Dom jumps up. 'I need to call the hospital.'

'Yes, of course you do. I just wanted to warn you before you speak to the nurses.'

He walks over to the telephone, which is in its docking station on the windowsill. I watch as he dials the hospital. He doesn't say much to whoever he is speaking to, but just nods. When he turns to look at me, he is almost green.

'Yes. Yes. I understand. Thank you. Goodnight.' He hangs up and, with tears in his eyes, walks straight towards me. I jump to my feet, step forwards and throw my arms around him.

'I'm so sorry, Tamara.'

'No, Dom. I am sorry for you and for Stacey. I wasn't hurt.'

I hold him tightly, my upper body pushed up against his. I hope that one of the children will come in, but they don't, so I release him and walk over to the fridge.

'I think we need a plan of action,' I say. 'With so much going on at work, we really need you to be in the office and focused, but at the same time the children need stability.'

'I'm sure Mina will help,' Dom says.

'Mina sounds lovely, but what your kids need is to stay in their own home, surrounded by their toys, and have their daddy tuck them into bed every night. I'd be delighted to help you out. Anything you might need. A bit of cooking, sitting with the kids so you can work, whatever might be of use.'

He rubs his eyes. 'We've got so much going on at work at the moment, but I can't impose upon you.'

'Yes, Dom. You can. And it's not an imposition.'

'Well, if you could do a little bit of cooking. I'm a lousy cook and I think the kids might rebel.'

'It would be a pleasure. Would it make sense if I work from here tomorrow? I could stock up your freezer. If you like, I can pick the children up from school and then from Tuesday onwards, at least you'll have food for a few days and perhaps Mina could look after the children until you get home?'

He squirms. I know he's uncomfortable with my suggestions, but it does make the most practical sense. He is needed in the office more than I am.

'The most important people are the children. They need to keep to their normal routines,' I stress.

'You're right. Thank you, Tamara. Tomorrow I'll get in touch with one of those home agencies to see if I can find someone who can help out. An au pair, perhaps.'

'That sounds like a great idea,' I say, clenching my teeth through my fake smile. 'To be honest, Dom—' I flicker my eyes to the floor. '—it gives me pleasure helping you out. I'm new to the Horsham area so I don't know many people, and my social life isn't exactly buzzing. I'm not even volunteering with the Samaritan's at the moment, as I gave that up when I left London and I haven't got around to signing up again in Sussex.' I throw my hands open in a gesture of supplication.

'In that case, all I can say is thank you. I'd be grateful for your help.'

We are interrupted by Arthur, who comes into the kitchen dragging a large foam dinosaur. His face is blotchy and tears run down his cheeks.

'What's the matter little man?' Dom crouches down and pulls him into a hug.

'I want Mummy,' he says, sniffing.

'Of course you do. But Mummy needs to get better before she comes home. Come on, it's bath time. Let's go and find Ivy.'

I turn around and pick up my jacket and handbag.

'Don't go, Tamara,' Dom says. 'You're more than welcome to stay. I think it's my turn to whip up something for supper. I'm not great in the kitchen, but could probably manage a pasta dish.'

'Are you sure?'

'Absolutely. Let me get these little monsters into bed and I'll be right back down.'

~

TWO AND A HALF hours later we have finished our pasta, but this time I have declined any wine. I'm concerned by how much Dom is drinking and hope he will follow my lead. He doesn't. Then again, he has a lot on his mind.

'I really should be getting home,' I say. 'Would you like me to come into the office tomorrow and get your house keys from you, or what would be best? I've got some work at home, so I can still do things from there or here?'

'No need to come to work. I'll get Stacey's keys for you. In fact, I'll put you on Stacey's car insurance and you can drive her car to collect the children from school, then you don't have to worry about putting booster seats into the back of your car.' He walks to the hall and I see him open the under-stairs cupboard. He returns with a bunch of keys. 'Are you sure you're ok to do this for me?'

'Absolutely.'

'In which case I'll tell the kids' school in the morning that you will be collecting them. They have strict rules as to who is allowed to collect them.'

'I'm glad to hear that. Will Ivy and Arthur be ok with me bringing them home?'

'They're good kids. I'll have a chat with them in the morning.'

And then there is the thumping of feet.

'Dada. Dada.'

'Hey little man! What is it?'

'Done a wee wee in the bed,' Arthur cries.

'Oh dear,' Dom says. 'Let's go and change your sheets.' He takes Arthur's hand and they climb back upstairs together. I follow, even though I haven't been invited. 'Go to the bathroom and take off your pyjama bottoms,' Dom says.

Arthur looks at me and then says too loudly in Dom's ear. 'What's she doing here?'

'Let me strip the bed,' I say.

Dom stands up. 'I'm sorry Tamara. He hasn't wet the bed in over a year. He must be very upset.'

'That's normal.' I bend down and pat Arthur on the head. 'Don't worry about wetting your bed, young man. We'll make sure no one at school knows you're doing this.'

The little boy looks at me, his eyes wide saucers, his bottom lip quivering, and then he bursts into violent sobs. Dom scoops him up.

'Think it's best if I go now,' I whisper.

Dom nods and mouths 'Thank you' to me.

WHEN I'M BACK in the car, I sit for a few minutes. I open the app and then close it again. I have waited so long for this. I had hoped to make further progress tonight, but I must remember to be patient. Attention to detail, and patience. I have those in bucket-loads.

26

STACEY

I am alive, but only just. As soon as I feel like I'm pushing through the smog, they give me more pills and back I sink into the haze, my brain mushy, my senses dulled to such an extent I barely feel, see or hear anything at all. It's as if I'm living inside a fluffy cloud. A rain cloud.

They moved me into another room. It's smaller, and Wendy is no longer my nurse. I think the new nurse is called Imelda, or something like that. I don't like her. She's bossy and has a mean, stretched face.

'What's the day?' I manage to mumble.

'It's Wednesday today and you need to get up. You're turning into a couch potato.' She pulls some of my clothes out of the built-in wardrobe. The top clashes with the trousers. Old clothes Dom must have brought. 'The doctor wants to see you today.' And then she's gone. But she'll be back again in five minutes. And five minutes after that. And five minutes after that. She reminds me of someone – not in the way she looks but in the way she acts – but the name and the image of the person fades from my mind as soon as I feel I'm about to grasp it.

And then, when I'm sitting on the loo, not thinking at all, I remember. Tamara. Imelda reminds me of Tamara. And in that moment, I make a decision. I'm not going to take their drugs anymore. I'm going to get better and get the hell out of here.

I work out how to do it. I take the pills from the nurse, put them in my mouth, stash them down the side of my teeth and swallow the water. As soon as the nurse leaves the room, I scoop them out of my mouth, shove them down the side of the mattress, and when I'm sure that no one will see me going to the loo, I flush them away. But it's not easy. Someone is in my room every five minutes. It's ridiculous.

And so two more days pass, but by Friday I'm beginning to feel a vague sense of normality. The shouts and screams of other patients make me flinch. But I do get dressed. And I do wander down the corridor into the day room, all the time moving slowly, pretending that I am still drugged up. It gives me a chance to check out the lay of the land. There are cameras above the doors and at least one nurse sits at the counter by the entrance to the ward, twenty-four hours a day. With two sets of double doors, accessed only with a swipe card, there is no way I am going to get out of here. I attend the compulsory group therapy lessons and try my best to zone out. It breaks my heart, listening to some of my fellow patients' stories.

In the afternoon, the sun comes out. It's weak and cold, but Imelda tells me I need to get some fresh air. She buttons me up in two jumpers and a thick coat, and leads me through another set of double doors to an outside courtyard. It is fully enclosed, with brick walls about ten feet high. A couple of other patients are there, ambling around and around. I won't find my escape route here, either.

I ask when Dom will visit, when I can see my children. Not yet, they say. Not yet. I tell them I never want to see Tamara ever again, and they agree that she won't be allowed back in. That's some good news, at least. I count down the days I will have to stay here. Another eighteen days until the courts decide my future. I cannot wait another eighteen interminable days.

The monotony of pacing around the courtyard, along with the clarity of thought thanks to no drugs in my system, prompts my memory to return a little. When I first arrived at the hospital, I was on a normal ward. It was only later that I was transferred to the psych ward and then to the high-security psych ward. If I can get back into the hospital, then surely there will be a possibility of escape?

By the end of my twenty minutes 'fresh air,' I feel hopeful, as if I can see a chink of light tugging me forwards through a pitch-black tunnel. As I'm returning to my room, I notice that my neighbour, Billie – a young girl, probably in her early twenties – is being visited by her mother.

I walk straight into her room. 'Hello, how are you doing?'

'Hello, who are you?' The mother looks worn, her hair straggly and grey.

'I'm Stacey and I'm a friend.'

'Nice to meet you, Stacey. I haven't seen you around here before.'

'No, I'm new. Hoping not to stay long.'

She throws me a wan smile. Billie doesn't react.

We make small talk for a short while, and then Imelda comes in.

'Can I have a quick word, Mrs Williams?'

Billie's mother nods and follows her out into the hall. I turn as if to follow them out of the room, but as soon as they disappear, I do a quick U-turn. Unknowingly, Billie's mum has just thrown me a lifeline.

Mrs William's wallet is lying on the desk. I'm surprised they let her bring it in. They put everyone through a metal detector, and anything that might cause harm, such as belts or nail files, are put in lockers. All bags are put away. Nothing is allowed in here that might give the patients a tool for self-harm. I glance at

Billie, but she has her eyes shut and looks as if she's comatose. With my back to the bed and the door, I quickly extract a fifty-pound note and shove it into the elastic waist band of my trousers. I feel terrible about it, and make a silent promise that I'll pay her back as soon as I can.

I race back to my room.

Half an hour later, when I'm lying on my bed, I start groaning. I double over and clutch my midriff.

'What's up?' Imelda asks gruffly.

'Got terrible pain in my stomach,' I say, gasping for air.

'Mmm,' she says, as if she doesn't believe me. She leaves the room, but I don't give up on the act. I lie on the bed and bring my knees up to my chest, rocking backwards and forwards, groaning loudly.

'What's up, love?' Imelda has brought her boss, Rosalyn, with her, and they're both peering at me.

'Terrible pain,' I mutter, willing the tears to come.

'I'll get you some pills to make it better,' Rosalyn says.

'Need doctor,' I cry out as a supposed cramp rips through my body.

I hear footsteps, but don't look up. A few moments later, Imelda puts a hand on me. 'You need to get these pills down you. They'll make you feel better.'

I do my normal trick, praying that Imelda will leave me alone before the pills melt in my mouth. When she leaves, I scoop them out. Over the next hour, I keep up the charade. It's tiring and ridiculous, but I must keep an eye on my ultimate goal.

And then, eventually, Rosalyn returns.

'I think I'm dying,' I pant. 'Please get me the doctor.'

'Ok, love. The doctor is on his way over, but he still might be a while.'

I start crying. Real tears come, ones of desperation. 'Please, no. Please, no. Need a doctor now.'

I hear Rosalyn and Imelda talking to each other in hushed whispers. They take my blood pressure and my temperature, but I move a lot and make it difficult for them to get accurate results. I pray they don't give me an injection to calm me down. I need to be fully conscious so I can keep up this charade.

Rosalyn presses on the lower right side of my belly and I scream. I remember when Dom had an appendicitis, that is where it hurts.

'We're calling for a porter, Stacey, and we'll get you to A&E, where you'll be seen faster. Try to stay calm.'

I feel like laughing. She's telling a psych patient to try to stay calm! But Rosalyn is as good as her word. Five minutes later, two porters arrive pushing a trolley bed. They manage to roll me from my bed onto the trolley.

'Imelda will stay with you until you get to A&E, and she'll hand over your notes to the colleagues over there. These two gentlemen will accompany you at all times.'

I glance at the two porters. They don't look particularly happy with their assigned roles. Resuming my groans and cries, I am wheeled out of the various sets of locked doors in the high-dependency unit, along numerous corridors, into a lift, along more corridors, and eventually we arrive in the back entrance to what I assume is A&E. And what a joy it is. The people here seem vibrant, alive, even if they are in pain. There is a sense of urgency, it's a place where time matters. People are talking normally, quickly, their faces expressive. There are no vacant gazes or manic screams. The porters wheel me into a cubicle and pull the blue, cardboard-like concertina curtains around me. And for the first time, I'm alone. Well, kind of alone, in so far as I can hear everything that is being said all around me. There are no prying eyes and, as far as I can tell, no hidden cameras.

The problem is, I am surrounded by people. I hop off the bed and put a finger in the curtain, peeking through just a centimetre to gauge who is watching me. The two porters are standing guard right in front of my cubicle, their backs to the curtains, watching the comings and goings of the busy department. The curtains fall to the floor on three sides of the cubicle. I bend down and lift the left-hand curtain just a fraction. When I see pairs of feet, I jump backwards. Then I try the same on the other side, and as I'm doing so, I hear a woman say, 'You're all stitched up now, Mr Smith. Take this prescription and get yourself down to the pharmacy. You'll be as right as rain in no time.'

'Thank you, doctor.'

And then I hear the curtain being pulled back and see a pair of trainers and a pair of black crocs walking out of the cubicle.

It has to be now or never.

I lift the bottom of the curtain and shimmy underneath. The curtain to the front of the cubicle is two-thirds open, so I stand behind it, straighten up my jeans and long-sleeved T-shirt and then, without throwing a backwards glance at my two guards, I walk purposefully towards the exit. My heart is thumping so loudly, I wonder if I might have a heart attack. But I keep on walking, swinging my arms purposefully, out through the exit, out through the room packed full of waiting patients and crying children, out to the reception area of the hospital, weaving my way through the crowds. I hear a shout and wonder if they've realised I've gone. I speed up, but I don't run. I must not attract attention. And then I'm outside and it's bloody cold, and I realise I haven't got a coat and I'm only wearing socks, but this is my sole chance and I've got to go.

When I'm in the car park, I run. Despite my feet getting immediately soaked in the puddles, I run the fastest I possibly can. A taxi pulls up at a side entrance and an elderly couple get out.

'Hurry up,' I mutter to myself, wrapping my arms around my torso and standing on the far side of the taxi, hopefully out of view of the main entrance to the hospital. They are painfully slow counting out the pennies. 'Come on,' I mutter

I think I can see one of the porters now at the front entrance, looking from left to right, but it's dark outside and the rain is coming down heavier now. People are putting up umbrellas and headlights blind pedestrians. And still this old woman is fumbling with her purse. She climbs out of the taxi slowly, grimacing with pain. I hold the door for her.

'Thank you, love,' she says as her elderly husband slides his arm through hers.

'Can you take me to Horsham please.'

I hop in before the taxi driver can reply. Just as I am pulling the door closed, I hear a shout.

'Over there!'

I lean forwards to the taxi driver. He has a kindly face and a beard as full as Dylan's. 'I'm in quite a hurry. Please can you go as fast as you can.'

He looks at me strangely, probably because I'm soaked through, but he simply says, 'Of course, love.'

And then we're gone, out through the barrier, and as we're turning right onto the main road, I glance through the rear window. I see my porter throw his arms up.

They know I've gone.

'A bit chilly to be out without a coat, isn't it?' the taxi driver asks.

'We had an emergency. My mum fell and I came here in the ambulance with her.'

'Hope she's going to be ok,' he says.

'Thanks, she's fine. The thing is, I even left my bag at home.'

I see him flinch in the mirror.

'Don't worry. I've got money to pay you! It's just I left my phone and my address book behind. I'm meant to be going to my mum's friend's house to pick up some stuff, but I don't have his address. I know this is cheeky, but could I look it up on your phone? It's been such a nightmare afternoon.'

We're pulling up at a set of traffic lights. He puts in his passcode and hands me the phone.

It doesn't take me long to find the address.

'Please can you take me to Roundover Park, Horsham.' I hand the phone back to him.

Forty minutes later, we pull up outside an unprepossessing apartment block.

'That's forty-nine pounds and twenty pence,' the taxi driver says. I'm shocked it's so expensive. I would have liked to have given him a tip, but I don't have any more money. Instead, I pocket the eighty pence change and stride away from the cab as fast I can, hoping he doesn't notice that I'm only wearing socks.

I let out a loud sigh of relief. I didn't give the taxi driver the correct address on purpose. I'm fairly sure that absconding from a psych ward is a major crime, and in case my face gets plastered over the media as a wanted person, I can't have him knowing where I'm heading.

I jog across the park, both to keep warm and to get there as quickly as possible. My toes feel numb with cold and wetness, and the soles of my feet are painful. Five minutes later, I'm standing in front of an unattractive apartment block. I press the buzzer to number 41a, Upton Road and pray that he answers.

About ten seconds later, a male voice says, 'Hello'.

'Jamie, this is Stacey Nicholson. I'm sorry to disturb you but I need to speak to you urgently. Any chance you could let me in?'

27

TAMARA

I look at my newly-acquired family and beam contentedly. Being a Friday, I suggested to Dom that we give the children their tea a little later and we all eat together. He agrees to most things I say. I think he is overwhelmingly grateful for the normality I'm bringing to their lives.

Twice this week, I have left work early and collected his children from school. I have made tea for them, supper for us and stayed the night. Dom spends hours talking about Stacey. He vacillates between worry and fury and love and incomprehension. I let him talk.

He hasn't mentioned plans for the weekend, and in line with my slowly, slowly strategy, I haven't said anything either. I have a roast chicken in the oven, and the children and I are expecting Dom home any moment.

'Go and put your pyjamas on,' I say to Arthur and Ivy. Neither of them like me telling them what to do, but they've learned not to argue. 'Chop, chop!'

'But we haven't had tea yet,' Ivy says.

'You'll have it with your father this evening.'

'I'm hungry!' Arthur moans.

'And what about our bath?' Ivy says.

'You can live without for one night. Now hurry and get ready.'

I shoo them out of the room.

Barely five minutes later, Dom arrives home. I would like to welcome him with a kiss as if I am a real wife, but instead I stay in the kitchen, pottering with the pans and laying the table.

'The kids are getting ready upstairs,' I say. But before he can answer, the phone rings.

As soon as I see Dom's face, I know something is wrong. He says 'Yes' again and again. 'No, we haven't seen her... Yes, of course I will notify the police if she appears.'

When he ends the call, he lets the phone slide onto the kitchen table and collapses into his chair.

'What's happened?'

'Stacey has escaped.'

'Escaped!' I exclaim. The words *no, no, no,* resound in my head. This is not part of my plan. I don't even have a contingency for it. Who the hell escapes from a high-security psych ward? I need to think, fast. I take a deep breath, turning away from him so he can't see my face.

'What happens if she comes here?' I ask. 'Do you think she intends to harm Arthur and Ivy?'

Dom shakes his head vigorously. 'No, she wouldn't do that. I'm sure she wouldn't.'

I sigh. I lever myself onto the chair and drag it right next to Dom. 'I know you don't want to believe that your wife could do anything so terrible, but they wouldn't have sectioned her if they weren't worried about what she might do. She did try to poison them with crushed-up sleeping pills. And she attacked me.'

Dom moans.

'The most important thing is that we protect the children

and make sure they don't find out that their mum has escaped from a mental institution.'

Dom shivers. I stroke his hand.

'I've got an idea. I might have mentioned to you that I have a little holiday house on the coast. Well, why don't we go there for a few days, just until Stacey is found and given the care she desperately needs? As horrible as it sounds, we don't want Stacey trying to harm Arthur and Ivy again.'

Dom doesn't answer. I can sense his despair.

'I'm so sorry this is happening to you, Dom. What do you think about going to the coast?'

He shakes his head as if awakening from a dream. 'Yes. Yes, that's a lovely idea, Tamara. Are you sure? You've done so much for us already and I don't want to impose.'

'I'm absolutely sure. It's out of season and no one is staying there at the moment. It's near Shoreham. There isn't any sand, but we can still walk along the pebbly beach.'

'Daddy!' Arthur yells, as he comes careering into the kitchen. He has his pyjama top on the wrong way around.

'How's my little man?' Dom asks, picking Arthur up and bouncing him onto his knee.

'I'm too big for this, Dadda,' Arthur giggles.

'Hello, Ivy. How was your day?' Dom reaches out to pull Ivy into his embrace.

'I'm hungry. We haven't had our tea yet,' Ivy moans.

'Well, something smells delicious and I'm sure it will be worth the wait!' Dom kisses Ivy on her forehead. 'If you both sit up at the table like good kids, I've got something exciting to tell you.'

They scoot to their places. 'Is Mummy coming home?' Arthur asks, slapping the palms of his hands on the edge of the table as if playing the drums.

'No,' Dom sighs. I try not to cringe. 'We're going away to the seaside!'

'Yippee!' Arthur cries. 'We're going on holiday!''

'Without Mummy?' Ivy asks.

I concentrate on serving up the vegetables and keep my face expressionless.

'Mummy isn't well, so she can't come with us,' Dom explains.

'*She's* not coming, is she?' Ivy talks in a loud whisper. I can sense her eyes on my back. The girl needs a good slap.

'We're going to be staying in Tamara's house, so yes, she is coming. We'll all have lots of fun.'

'Yippee! Yippee! Yippee!' Arthur sings.

I place the plates of food in front of Arthur and Ivy; extra broccoli for Ivy because she was rude.

'I don't like beans,' Arthur says.

'And I don't like broccoli,' Ivy says.

Dom sighs. 'Just eat up as much as you can. We are very grateful that Tamara is here to help us out.'

'No need to keep on thanking me,' I tell Dom. 'I'm happy to do it.' I eat a couple of mouthfuls and then speak to the children. 'So, kids, when was the last time you went on holiday by the sea?'

'Never,' Ivy says. 'Our Mummy doesn't like the sea.'

'Oh yes. Sorry, I forgot,' I say to Dom. 'Well, you'll love it. It's quite a small house in comparison to this one, but you can see the sea from the windows.'

'Can we go swimming in the sea? We went to the pool with Mina.'

'It's a bit rough and chilly for going in the sea at this time of the year,' Dom laughs.

'Why have you got a house by the sea?' Arthur asks.

'My husband died and he left it to me,' I say. I can see Dom shifting in his seat uneasily.

'Why did he die?' Arthur asks. 'Justin's guinea pig died last week. He went to heaven. Did your husband go to heaven?'

'Enough with the questions,' Dom says.

'When are we going?" Ivy asks, pushing her food around her plate.

'Tonight or tomorrow?' I ask Dom.

'Let's leave tomorrow morning so we have time to pack up a few things. I assume you'll want to go home first?'

'Yes. I'll need to collect the keys. But do you think it's safe to stay here?' I speak the latter part of the sentence in a whisper.

Dom nods, but his face is lined with concern.

I don't stay the night at Dom's, explaining that I have things I need to do at home. In reality, I need thinking time and space.

DAMN, Stacey! How the hell did she manage that? I am pacing around my small study, fury coursing through my veins. I want to hit something, smash my fist through glass, hurt myself. But I know that will only be a temporary reprieve. Experience has taught me that. No, I need to concentrate and use my brain. My brilliant brain. I am cleverer than Stacey.

I can outwit her.

Thank goodness for the holiday cottage. At least I can get Dom and the kids away. But I will need to find Stacey and get her back into hospital or, ideally, a prison cell. I will need to lure her, and right now I have no idea how.

28

STACEY

'I s everything alright, Stacey?' Jamie stands in his doorway looking me up and down, his face a picture of dismay.

'No, it's not. Can I come in and I'll explain.'

'Yeah, sure.' He sounds hesitant, and I don't blame him. I must look a total mess. I take off my sopping wet socks and walk bare-footed as he leads me through into his small living room. His laptop is open on a glass circular table. There is one large sofa covered in navy ticking and a flat screen television on the wall. 'Sorry, this place isn't very fancy,' he says.

'Jamie, I'm going to come straight out with this. I'm on the run from the police and I need somewhere to stay. Somewhere no one will think to look for me. That means I can't go to any friends or family.'

He opens and closes his mouth. 'What have you done?'

'Nothing. Apparently I tried to take my own life and poison my children. But I didn't. Tamara Collins has got something to do with it. She's admitted as much.'

'Who's Tamara?'

'The woman who has taken over Dylan's job, working for Dom.'

'What?' Jamie collapses onto the sofa. 'Has this Tamara got something to do with Dylan's death?'

I shrug my shoulders. 'I don't know. Perhaps not, but I intend to find out. Will you help me?'

'What do you want me to do?

'Right now, I just need somewhere to stay. I've also got no money, but I'll pay you back, I promise.'

'I don't know...' he says, his face scrunched up.

'Please. Just give me one night, maximum two, until I sort myself out. I've promised I will help you out with Dylan's death. The one thousand pounds was just for starters.'

He looks anguished.

'I've got an interview next week with the local paper, and they're carrying out police checks on me. I want to retrain as an investigative journalist. It would totally screw up my future if I'm prosecuted for harbouring a criminal.'

'Jamie, you won't be. I just need to prove that I am of sound mind and that Tamara Collins has set me up. Why she's done what she's done, I've no idea. But I need to find out. It just seems like too much of a coincidence that she's wreaked havoc on my life and has taken over Dylan's job. Please, will you help?'

He sighs. 'Ok,' he says eventually.

'Thank you.' I sit down on a bucket-shaped plastic chair. 'Tomorrow I will go home, get some money and find out what the hell is going on.'

I HAVE A HOT SHOWER. It is blissful. Ten minutes of solitude and warmth and cleanliness. I feel like I need to wash away all the smells and sounds of the psych ward, and rid my body of any remaining drugs. By the time I have finished, I am a new person. Resolute. Ready to fight.

Jamie has left me out a pair of jogging bottoms, a T-shirt and a sweatshirt. They are all enormous on me, but at least they are warm and clean.

'I've ordered us a pizza. I've only got beer. Would you like one?'

'Yes, please.'

'I think you'd better tell me everything from beginning to end.'

And so I do. I tell him all I know about Tamara. What she told me when she came to visit me in hospital. I explain about *Pinkapop's Adventures* and Corinne. I even tell him about the breakdown I had fifteen years ago.

'Why can't you tell the police about your concerns?' he asks.

'Because I have been detained for twenty-eight days under the Mental Health Act. They think I'm mad. If I tell them this story, who do you think the authorities will believe? Perfectly sane, intelligent, well-spoken Tamara, or crazy me?'

Jamie nods his head slowly.

'I'm sorry to put you in this situation,' I say again.

'I'll help you. Let's get to the bottom of it,' Jamie says.

'In the meantime, I'm absolutely knackered. Could I go to sleep on your sofa?'

He grins and brings me a duvet and a pillow, then takes his laptop next door to his bedroom. The moment I lay my head on his sofa, I drift off into the deepest sleep I have experienced in weeks.

I WAKE EARLY, and by the time Jamie is up, I have made us both coffee and have a plan of action.

'Could you lend me a hat?' I ask.

He disappears into his bedroom and returns with a black beanie. I scoop my hair up underneath it and pull it down low.

'You'd better borrow a jacket too,' he says, producing a bomber jacket that swamps me.

'How do I look?' I twizzle around for him.

'Like some weirdo of indeterminate age and sex, wearing clothes several sizes too big.'

'That'll do,' I smile.

'Look, I've got an old mobile phone. It's got about ten quid on it. And here's thirty quid. Take it and pay me back when you can.'

I am so grateful to Jamie, I feel like hugging him. 'Thank you,' I say.

'What's the plan of action?'

'I'm going home. I want to get some clothes and money. I want to see the children.'

'But won't your husband report you?'

'He might,' I say. 'I'll play it by ear.'

'I was going to the gym this morning. Why don't I drop you off?'

TWENTY MINUTES later and I am slinking out of Jamie's battered silver Toyota, the beanie pulled low over my head, wearing several pairs of socks and his too-large trainers, and walking with hunched shoulders towards our house. I decide to do a walk-past first, just to see who's home. I keep my head down, but glance to the side as I stride past our driveway. Dom's car isn't there. The curtains upstairs are pulled closed. That's strange. There is no way that the children will still be asleep at 10 a.m. I wonder if they're not there. It's a Saturday, so it's conceivable he's taken them to his parents for the weekend. Glancing around to check no one is watching, I walk up our drive, but, rather than ring the front door bell, I sneak around to the side of the house.

Dom and I leave a spare key in the small, unused and decaying greenhouse to the left of the garden. I had the ambition to take up gardening, but it has never come to anything. No one goes in the greenhouse. Cobwebs extend across the door. I sweep them aside, inhale the cold damp air and see the three terracotta pots placed upside down on the floor. A large spider scuttles out as I lift up the middle pot and, to my relief, the key is still there, where I left it nearly three years ago. I go out of the greenhouse and, staying close to the hedge, peer up at the house. The lights are all off. Considering how low the clouds are hanging and how grey the day is, I am sure Dom would have the lights on inside the house. I am ninety-nine per cent sure no one is at home.

With a lump in my throat and my heart hammering hard, I pace across the garden to the back door. I knock.

Silence.

Then I slide the key in the door and try to turn it.

The key sticks.

For a horrendous moment, I wonder if Dom has changed the locks.

I take the key out, wipe it down on my leg and try again. This time the lock turns and the door opens.

I slip inside and remove Jamie's trainers. I am surprised that there isn't a pile of un-ironed washing in the utility room. Surely Dom must have run some loads of washing in my absence. I tiptoe into the kitchen and, as I look around, I gasp. I know now what it means when they say your blood runs cold. I shiver. This is not my kitchen.

All my stuff has gone. The clutter, the piles, the photos, the old drawings that the kids have made me, they are all gone. This is like a show home, as it used to look before we arrived and turned it into a beloved family home. I have only been away for ten days and this has happened.

What the hell has Dom done?

It even smells different. There is a lemon freshness to the place, as if one of those air freshener things has been plugged into the wall and allowed to leach out its chemicals.

And then I realise: this isn't Dom. This must be Tamara. Has he let her live here? Or has he got home help? My mind is whirling and my throat is choking up. Has it only taken my husband ten days to expel me from his life?

I throw open some of the drawers. They're neat, cutlery tidily lined up. The hob is sparkling, even the larder has been tidied and cleaned, with tins lined up in rows and cereal boxes placed in descending heights. Bloody hell, I'll never find anything when I come home.

I walk into the children's playroom and I have to blink away tears. Normally this room looks as if a bombshell has hit it. Dom and I agreed that the kids could have one room that is theirs, and so long as it was kept clean, it didn't have to be tidy. But now all the toys are in plastic see-through boxes at the side of the room. My heart is in my mouth when I go into my study, but thank goodness it looks exactly as I left it. Except, it's not. There are piles of stuff that I had around the house, photographs, notes, general clutter. Everything has been dumped haphazardly on my desk.

I go upstairs. I take a deep breath before opening our bedroom door. What if she has moved in here? But no. I exhale so loudly. I want to slump on the bed, bury my head in Dom's pillow, inhale his scent. This room is Dom messy. Whoever has been cleaning up the house hasn't got their hands on our private space. And I am deeply relieved.

The children's rooms have received the deep clean treatment too. Their beds are perfectly made, soft toys balanced on the pillows, everything tidied away in their cupboards. And then I realise that Ivy's favourite toy horse isn't there and Arthur's dinosaur has gone too. Dom must have taken the children away. Finally, I walk to the guest room.

She has been living here. It smells of her. A sickly-sweet jasmine smell. The bed is also perfectly made. I open the wardrobe and there are three suits hanging up and a couple of blouses. I debate cutting them into shreds, but then I wonder. What if these don't belong to Tamara? What if Dom has employed a home help or an au pair, although why an au pair would have such smart clothes, I don't know. So I leave the clothes and shut the door. What if this isn't her scent but someone else's? I lift up the beanie and run my hands through my hair.

I turn and open the chest of drawers. Lying on top of a pile of jumpers is an opened envelope. I ease the letter out of the envelope.

So I was right. Tamara bloody Collins has moved into my house.

The letter is addressed to her. The bitch has been living here, going through my things, taking care of my family.

My hand is shaking as I read the letter.

Dear Ms Collins,

I am writing to advise you that regrettably the care home fees for Mrs Jean Helms will be increasing by 3% as of 1st January.

Who the hell is Mrs Jean Helms, living at Sunnyside Nursing Home in Pulborough? I use Jamie's old phone to take a photograph of the letter and put it back in its envelope in the drawer. I then hurry back to our bedroom and select a few old clothes, items stored at the back of the wardrobe, things Dom will never realise are missing.

I need money, but I can't take any credit cards because they are traceable. My handbag is in the wardrobe. I have thirty-five pounds in cash in my wallet, which I remove. I fumble through Dom's jacket pockets and find another twenty pounds and a few loose coins. It will have to do.

And then I leave, locking up the back door, trying to stop the tears from flowing. But I don't put the backdoor key back in the greenhouse. Instead, I shove it deep into the pocket of Jamie's joggers and set off on foot, on the three-mile walk back to his apartment.

29

TAMARA

I expected the children to be disappointed with my holiday house. It's a far cry from the modern luxury of their home. But I'm wrong. They race around as if it's a five-star hotel. I have to clench my teeth together to stop myself from screaming at them.

Stop! I want to yell. *You'll break something. This isn't a playroom.*

'This is enchanting,' Dom says as he looks around the small living room. I hope he's being honest with me, but I suspect he's just being polite. It's lined with tongue-and-groove panelling, painted in navy and white in a kitsch seaside style. It wasn't my choice and I don't care much about the decor or the house. But, bizarrely, I do care about Dom's reactions. I've probably only been here twice since Alan died. It's an easy little earner for me, bringing in rent from holiday makers in the summer months.

'I'm afraid there are only two bedrooms, so I'll sleep on the sofa,' I say, dumping my overnight bag on the sisal flooring.

'Absolutely not. I will sleep here. I have no intention of booting you from your bed. Children, calm down now! Why don't I take them for a run around on the beach and you can put your feet up. You must be exhausted from looking after us all week.'

I accept graciously.

The solitude is a relief. I need time to think and time to plan.

And most of all, I need to find Stacey and get her sent back to where she belongs.

I lie down on the sofa and scroll through my phone, checking back through my lists and seeing how much I have achieved. I have to accept that I have absolutely no idea where Stacey might have fled to. I simply don't know enough about her life. My next step will have to be achieved through Dom. It's a gamble. A big gamble, but I haven't got much choice.

I MUST HAVE DOZED OFF, because I awake with a start when I hear loud, high-pitched voices. Damn. Dom is going to see me with crease lines down the side of my face. I hope I don't have dried-up dribble on my cheek.

'Hey sleepy-head,' he says, as I stretch and stand up. 'The kids have eaten and I've got us fish and chips.' And then his hand flies to his mouth. 'Are you allergic to cod?'

I laugh, just happy that Dom remembered. 'No, it's only salmon. Cod is fine.'

I hate fish and chips. It's not the taste of it, but rather that the smell contaminates any room it's in. That salty, fishy, vinegary smell. I sure as hell won't be sleeping in the living room tonight.

Dom spends the rest of the afternoon playing with the children. They do a jigsaw puzzle, watch a film on television and do some colouring. I take myself off into the bedroom on the pretext that I need quiet in order to finish off some work.

It isn't until later, when the children are in bed, that I pluck up the courage to put the next major part of my plan into action.

We are drinking wine, sitting on the sofa.

'I've got an admission to make,' I say, leaning back so far that the buttons strain on my blouse. 'I am deeply envious of Stacey.' I hold my breath. This has the potential for going terribly wrong, but I have to take risks now that my plan needs to move off at an unexpected tangent.

'Why?' he asks, crinkling his nose. 'I can't imagine anyone being envious of a woman who has a mental illness—'

'And tried to murder her children,' I finish his sentence breezily.

He sighs.

'But she's married to you,' I say, my voice as husky and low as I can make it.

Dom appears startled.

'I know I shouldn't say that. I'm sorry, Dom.' I put my face in my hands.

I wonder for a moment if I've totally blown it. I know that Dom is upstanding, and that he is very unlikely to have cheated on Stacey. He's a good man. But even good men crack when they're under the strain Dom is under.

I carry on speaking. 'The last thing I want to do is break up your marriage, Dom, but I suspect, with Stacey's affair and everything that has happened, that your marriage may already be broken.'

'We don't know for sure that Stacey had an affair,' Dom says, but he doesn't sound convinced.

'No, we don't. But all the evidence suggests she did. Don't you agree?'

Dom nods.

'You see, the thing is, Dom, I think you might feel the same way as I do. I don't think I've ever lusted after anyone as much as I lust after you.' I close my eyes. 'I know I'm in danger of losing my job and the person who has so unexpectedly become my best friend in the past few weeks, but I just have to say what I'm feeling. I need to be true to myself. And I hope that you'll forgive me for that.'

And the strange thing is, I mean it. I like Dom a lot, and although I didn't when I first met him, I fancy him too.

'Oh Tamara,' Dom murmurs. I open my eyes and lean in towards him. He doesn't move. He just keeps his eyes on mine, and then I feel his lips covering my own and we are kissing, passionately, breathlessly, urgently.

Desperately.

He pulls away and strokes my hair. 'I've never been unfaithful.'

'I know. And I've never made love to a married man. Don't think about it. We can do this once and then forget about it. Pretend it's never happened. Back to normal tomorrow, but for now, oh please, Dom. I need you so badly.'

I run my hands up his back, loosening the shirt from his trousers and running my fingernails along the bare skin of his midriff. He moans and kisses me again. For a man who doesn't wear aftershave, his scent is magnificent. He rips my blouse open and unhooks my bra with surprising adeptness, and then I am straddling him, our hips grinding into each other.

'The children,' he says breathlessly. 'What if they come in?'

'Let's do it in the bathroom,' I say, wriggling off him, undoing and discarding my clothes as I race towards the bathroom. The bathroom has a shower cubicle and a bath, and for a brief moment I pause, remembering the start of this journey and Dylan lying in a tub of blood. But I quickly discard the image as Dom locks the door, switches the shower on, and pulls me inside, ravishing me as the hot water pummels our bodies, melding us into one, quietening our panting. But when I come, violently, unexpectedly and gloriously, I am sure even the sailors on their yachts out at sea hear my screams.

He switches the shower off and we both sink to the floor, covered in soap suds, exhausted, elated.

'I hope we didn't wake up the kids,' he says, nuzzling my neck, his hand already between my legs.

'I'm sorry. I couldn't help myself,' I grin at him.

I lean my head back, my wet hair falling down my back, my lips swollen. His hands are all over me again, his tongue flicking my nipples. This man knows how to make love. I may be sitting on a rather grotty shower tray, but I could be in heaven.

This is so very, very unexpected.

AFTERWARDS, Dom insists that I sleep in the bed and he will take the sofa. I give him sheets, a duvet and pillow, and climb into bed. But my head is buzzing. I feel so alive, so very happy. After thirty minutes or so, I get up and tiptoe through the house to the small kitchen. I need to collect a glass and fill it up with water. I also want to see Dom, check out what he looks like when he's asleep.

With bare feet, I am almost silent as I walk into the kitchen. Using my phone as a torch, I shine it at the open shelf that holds the glasses, and then I hear a noise. It sounds like sobs. I switch the light off and tiptoe back out into the hall towards the living room. As I let my eyes adjust to the darkness, I can make out Dom lying on the sofa. He is crying. My initial reaction is disgust. He is a man. He is crying. But then I soften. Yes, I am dismayed, but as I think this through, I suppose it is understandable. The woman he loved isn't the person he thought he knew. And now he has fallen for someone else and broken his wedding vows. Dom Nicholson is a good man and needs to be comforted.

'Dom,' I say as I walk into the living room. The light from

my phone bounces up and down. He sits up in bed, sniffs and wipes his eyes. I am naked, and that is probably a good thing.

'Budge over,' I say, lifting the duvet up and snuggling in with him. There definitely isn't enough space for both of us.

'I know you're upset and it's totally understandable.' I lean back and pull him down with me, his head lying on my breasts. I stroke his hair and his forehead; I run my fingers over his neat eyebrows and wipe away his tears.

'I've betrayed Stacey.'

'Didn't you say she was having an affair? And...what happened with the children...'

'She denies it all,' he whispers. 'I don't know what to believe.'

'Of course you don't want to think badly of Stacey. She is your wife and the mother of your children, but I really don't think you should be the one that is feeling bad here.' I pause for a moment. 'Besides, we said that this would be a one off, didn't we? Tomorrow is another day.'

I let my fingers travel nonchalantly down his body, twirling the hair on his chest, down his flat stomach, down, down...

'I think tomorrow should start at 7 a.m., don't you?' I murmur as my lips find his.

30

STACEY

'Take my car, I don't need it this morning.'
'Are you sure?' I feel as if I've imposed enough without also borrowing his car.
'I'm sure. I'm not doing anything today.'
'Thank you, Jamie.'
'Take these.' He holds out spectacles with a heavy, black frame without any glass in them. 'I know they're hideous but they're old, and it'll make you look less like you. I've taken out the glass.'

I put them on and pose for Jamie. He laughs. I'm wearing my own clothes, but keeping the over-sized bomber jacket and Jamie's beanie. Perhaps I should dye my hair later.

I'VE ONLY BEEN INCARCERATED for two weeks, but driving Jamie's old car gives me such a sense of freedom, I would like to whoop for joy. But then reality strikes. All I want to do is see Dom and the children. But if I call Dom, will he believe me or will he get me sent back to hospital? For the first time since I have known my husband, I'm not sure how he'll react. He has always been my rock, my staunchest supporter, but his disbelief when he last visited me in hospital has cut through me. And the fact that he has let Tamara into his life so easily, terrifies me. Is she with the children? What is she going to do? The thoughts batter my head. It's obvious that I should speak to Dom and the police, but I am the certified mad woman and my gut is telling me I need to hold fire. If Jamie and I can investigate a bit more and get evidence, then perhaps it's more likely that I will be believed.

I drive out of Horsham onto the A264 up to Five Oaks. I pass the place where we buy our Christmas tree every year and realise I should have bought it by now. Has Dom remembered? Does he know which box I keep the Christmas decorations in? I stifle a sob at the thought that I'm not with Ivy and Arthur, watching their excitement as we attach the decorations, breathing in the aroma of real pine. I feel a sense of panic as I realise I haven't even finished my Christmas shopping. I take the Billingshurst by-pass and then onto the long straight Roman road that eventually ends up in Pulborough.

Sunnyside Nursing Home is in a modern, red-brick block with views over the River Arun and across the plain to the South Downs. It's 9.30 a.m. on a Sunday morning and the car park is almost empty. I hope they will let me in. I remove the bomber jacket and beanie and adjust my blouse and jumper in the hope I will be more respectable. Taking a deep breath, I get out of the car and walk quickly to the entrance. I ring the buzzer.

'Hello, my name is Sarah Collins. I'm here to see Jean Helms.'

The door buzzes and I push it open.

A woman with tightly-curled grey hair and wearing a dark blue uniform is standing next to a reception desk. Her name badge says 'Barbara.' I take a deep breath and remind myself that although she looks like a nurse, she probably isn't one.

'Is it possible to see Jean Helms?' I ask.

'Jeanie?' she sounds surprised.

'Yes.'

'Jeanie doesn't have any visitors except her daughter, who comes once a year. Who are you?'

I can feel myself flushing. I'm a bloody awful liar and need to keep it together. 'I'm her niece. Tamara Collins was meant to let you know that I was coming.'

'Well, it's very nice to meet you. Jeanie isn't up yet. Would you like to wait in the lounge, or would you like to see her in her room?'

'In her room would be lovely. Perhaps we can look through some old photographs. It's been such a long time since I've seen Jeanie. Probably twenty-five years.'

Barbara looks at me a little strangely. I hope I haven't put my foot in it already.

'You do know that our Jeanie isn't how she used to be?'

'Yes, of course,' I bluff. 'I live in Canada now, so it'll just be lovely to see her.'

'If you could just sign our visitor's book, I'll show you where Jeanie's room is.'

It's rather strange signing with a fake name, and my writing looks childish. I follow Barbara along a wide corridor with rooms on either side. She knocks on a door that says 'Jean Helms,' but doesn't wait for an answer.

'Jeanie, love. I've got a visitor for you. Isn't it a lovely surprise?'

Jeanie Helms is sitting in a high-backed chair, gazing out of the window at the expansive view that, despite the grey weather, is still lovely. Her hair is very fine and white, her pink scalp visible through it. She is wearing a long night dress and a dusky pink dressing gown. I wonder if she heard Barbara speak, because she doesn't react.

Barbara turns to me. 'Take the chair and plonk it straight in front of Jeanie. She has good days and not such good days. It's a bit early in the morning to tell which today will be. Any problems and press the buzzer over there.' She points to a red switch on the wall. 'One of us will bring you a cuppa a bit later.'

Before I can thank her, Barbara has gone and the door closes gently behind her.

I do as instructed and pick up the chair and place it in front of Jean. She notices me, then and turns her head slowly, staring at me with unblinking eyes.

'Hello, Jean. My name is Sarah. I've come to talk to you about Tamara.'

'Who are you?' she asks, her pale blue eyes narrowing at me.

'I'm Sarah. I'm a friend of Tamara's.'

'Where's Tam?'

'I don't know right now. Is Tam your daughter?'

'Of course she bloody is.' Jean's body language doesn't match her snappy words. 'What do you want?'

'Just to say hello. Tam has gone away for a bit and she asked me to look in on you. How are you?'

I feel bad subjecting this elderly woman to a barrage of questions and lies.

'Tam said you have some photos and you like talking about the past. Have you got any pictures I can look at?'

She doesn't answer me. Her gaze is totally blank and my heart sinks. And then, just when I'm not sure how to progress with the conversation, she says, 'In the wardrobe.'

I jump up and walk over to the wardrobe. It's a heavy, dark mahogany piece of furniture and the door creaks when I open it. Inside, it is almost empty. Just three coat hangers with clothes hanging from the rail, and a few items neatly folded on the shelves. At the base of the cupboard is a brown box with some books, and at the top is what looks like a photo album.

'Is this it?' I ask, holding up the album.

Again, I get no response, so I pick it up and sit down again. Opening the pages, I see that it is indeed an album, with pictures of a couple with their young daughter. From the clothes they are wearing, I assume the photos were taken in the 1980s.

'Is this Tam?' I ask.

'Where is Tam?' she says.

'I'm not sure, but I will tell her to come and visit you.'

I flick through the album, but the pictures stop when Tam is about sixteen or seventeen. I wonder what happened.

'Do you have any later pictures of yourself with Tam?' I ask.

Again, I wonder if she has heard the question, and then after a long pause, she says, 'Of course not.'

I take a gamble now. 'Tam told me about her falling out with you.'

'Is she still married to that bastard?'

'What bastard?' I say, sitting upright with surprise.

'Whatever his name is.' And then she sinks back into her stupor, her eyes distant and glazed over. She doesn't answer any more of my questions. It's as if I'm not here. Eventually, I place the album back into the wardrobe.

'Can I get you anything, Jeanie?' I ask, but she doesn't respond. 'I'm going to go now.' I stand up, but she doesn't look at me. She doesn't even blink. So I leave the room, none the wiser, except that I know Tamara was married. And perhaps still is.

All is quiet in the corridor. I am relieved that I don't see anyone. Back in the reception area, I quickly write the time that I'm leaving in the visitor's book and scarper.

∼

THE PAIN of not seeing or even speaking to my family is eating me up. I decide to drive back past our home in case they're there, although Sundays are normally spent at Dom's parents. I debate driving over to see them, but my father-in-law's heart is weak enough as it is, and I certainly don't want to be responsible for causing them any further aggravation. Instead, I dial 141 before Dom's number and call him from Jamie's mobile phone.

It goes straight to voicemail. I am about to leave a message, but then I hang up. I didn't ask Jamie if the phone was a pay-as-you-go or on a contract. The last thing I must do is get Jamie into trouble. So, with a heavy heart, I drive back to Horsham.

Our street looks exactly as it did yesterday. Grey, quiet, and there appears to be no one at our home. The curtains are still closed upstairs, and the lights are all off. Choking back tears, I turn the car around and head back to Jamie's.

31

TAMARA

After our second middle-of-the-night liaison – even more exciting than the previous time due to the possibility of being discovered by his children – I return to the master bedroom and sleep a dreamless sleep. I wake up to the chatter of high-pitched voices.

I feel amazing. Sexy, triumphant, on top of the world. The happiest I have felt in years and years. I switch on my mobile phone and tick off the final item on the list headed 'Seduction of Dom'. Yes, what an achievement!

I take a shower and laugh as I remember our antics in the bathroom just a few hours ago. Carefully, I apply my makeup and get dressed, then saunter into the living room.

'Good morning, everyone! Did you sleep well?'

I look at Dom, but he isn't meeting my eyes.

'Look, Tamara. Look at the waves!' Arthur is standing on the rattan armchair, pointing at the sea. I would like to tell him to get his grubby feet off my chair, but of course I don't. 'Look at the white ponies!' he yells.

'White horses, stupid,' Ivy says.

'Be nice to your brother.' Dom speaks without conviction.

They have finished their breakfasts and the dirty dishes are still on the table.

'Did you sleep well, Dom?' I ask.

He looks at me then, but I don't get the hint of a smile and the wink I expect. Just a look of anguish. Bugger. I'm going to have to work harder.

'Yes, thanks.'

'Daddy, can we go to the beach now?' Ivy asks, tugging on Dom's sleeve.

'It's too windy. It will be dangerous today,' he says.

'Please,' Ivy whines.

I switch on the Nespresso machine to make myself a cup of coffee. I pick up the mug and carry it over to the table. 'How about I take you both swimming? There's a great pool in a local leisure centre.'

'Yes!' both Ivy and Arthur exclaim at the same time. 'Can we, Daddy? Please?'

'You look exhausted, Dom,' I say, placing my fingers on his arm. 'Why don't you stay here, read the papers, relax a bit, and I'll look after the kids this morning. We can go out for a spot of lunch, do a quick shop and meet you back here this afternoon?'

He looks at me with an expression of relief. 'Are you sure, Tamara?'

'It'll be fun, won't it, children?'

Arthur jumps up and down. Ivy has already disappeared to, I assume, find her swimming costume.

And then I realise, we came in Dom's car and I'm not sure how I am meant to ferry the children around.

'Is it ok to use your car, Dom?'

'Of course. My insurance covers anyone.'

Arthur races off to his bedroom, and now both the kids are out of the room, I stand close to Dom. 'Don't worry, Dom. Everything will be fine.' I give him a little peck on the cheek and go to find my swimming costume and a stack of towels.

I'M NOT sure I have ever driven a car as fast and as powerful as Dom's Audi. It's hard to stay within the thirty-mile-an-hour speed limit. The kids are strapped into the back, Arthur chatting away excitedly, Ivy quieter as normal.

'Are you a good swimmer?' Ivy surprises me by asking a question. She normally only talks to me when I ask her something first.

'Yes. Why?' I glance in the rear-view mirror, but she's gazing out at the stormy sea.

'Mummy can't swim. She doesn't like the sea.'

'Mina takes us swimming,' Arthur says.

'Why doesn't your mummy like swimming?' I ask.

'Dunno,' Arthur says. He starts humming.

'It's a bit silly being scared of the water, especially if you're a grownup,' I say.

Both the children fall silent. Then Arthur pipes up. 'I don't know how to swim. I wear arm bands.'

'That's ok,' I reassure him. 'I'll teach you.'

At the reception area, I ask to buy tickets for swimming.

'It's lessons first thing this morning. Would you like your kids to join a class?'

'Yes, that's a great idea. It'll save me from having to get wet,' I laugh.

'But I don't want to—'

'Arthur, grow up!' I say. 'Two tickets for the beginners class please.'

'I'm not a beginner,' Ivy says.

I repeat. 'Two tickets for beginners.'

The girl issues me with the tickets and the children follow me to the changing rooms.

'I'm not a beginner,' Ivy repeats, her bottom lip protruding.

'In which case they'll move you up a class.'

'I don't want to go,' Arthur says.

I want to shake him and remind him that five minutes ago he was all excited about it, but instead I bite my tongue and reassure him that it will be fine.

THE SWIMMING POOL IS BUSY. A large portion of the shallow end is cordoned off for the swimming lesson, and a bunch of little kids are already in the water, splashing around and making a racket. The young male teacher is in the water and waves at us. I am bare-footed and we're standing right next to the pool.

'Off you go now,' I tell Arthur and Ivy.

Ivy puts on her own arm bands and, without another word, jumps straight into the pool. Arthur grabs my leg.

'I don't want to go,' he says. Tears start welling up.

Arthur has his back to the edge of the pool. I bend down and attempt to slide his arm bands on, but the plastic sticks to his skin. I get the first band on.

'Ouch!' he says as I try to get the second one onto his left arm. He attempts to pull his arm away. 'I don't want to go.'

'Yes you do, Arthur. Stop being a silly little boy.' I edge closer to him, and as I do so, he takes a step backwards. There is an almighty scream and Arthur falls into the pool.

For a moment I am stunned, not sure whether to laugh or cry. And then I realise this could be my moment. It all happens so quickly.

I jump in.

Fully clothed, I jump into the water to save Dom's youngest child.

I reach him before the teacher does, dragging him up out of the water and tugging him up over the side and onto the edge of the pool.

'Are you all right?' the teacher asks me. He looks terrified, and I wonder if he will get into trouble over this. 'I'm absolutely fine and my son will be too in just a moment.'

I haul myself out of the water and sit down next to Arthur, who is coughing and spluttering and wailing.

'You...you...pushed me!' he sobs.

'No I did not,' I say. 'Don't be ridiculous. You were standing too close to the edge. Now pull yourself together and stop acting like a baby.'

'My throat hurts. And my nose.' His cries turn into gulps.

'Hold your nose and blow hard. It will get rid of any water stuck inside.'

But Arthur is still sobbing and doesn't listen.

'Are you going back into the pool to join the lesson or are you coming with me to get changed.'

'C...c...coming with you,' he splutters.

I stand up, water dripping from my clothes. My hair is sopping wet and no doubt mascara is streaked down my cheeks. All eyes are on me as I take Arthur's hand and grip him firmly as we walk back towards the changing rooms.

'Look at me!' I say to him in a low voice. 'I'm soaking wet all because of you.'

Arthur sobs some more.

I pull his swimming trunks off him and rub him dry roughly. He doesn't stop crying, and when he says, 'I want Mummy,' I have to restrain myself from hitting him. I'm not a monster, but I'm not used to sobbing children.

I squeeze out some of the excess water from my clothes and rub myself down with a towel. Retrieving my bag from the locker, I take Arthur's wrist and tug him towards the entrance, where there is a small shop.

'I'm going to have to buy some clothes. I can't go home like this, can I?' I say snappily. 'It's all your fault. We'll have to take the money out of your pocket money.'

Arthur's cries become almost hysterical.

I DON'T TAKE them out for lunch or to do a shop. Instead we go straight back to my house. Dom can look after his own bloody children.

'What's happened?' he asks, looking up from the newspapers with alarm. Arthur rushes to Dom and throws his arms around his father's neck.

'Arthur fell in and Tamara rescued him. She jumped in with all her clothes on,' Ivy says.

'Did you really?'

'Yes. And I had to buy a new wardrobe. But never mind. At least Arthur is safe. Can I leave the children with you? I need to take yet another shower.'

'Of course. I'm so sorry, Tamara. And thank you. I can't believe you just saved Arthur's life!'

'It's nothing,' I say. When I turn away from them, I have a big grin on my face.

'She pushed me,' Arthur says.

'Don't be so silly, little monster. Tamara saved you. I hope you said a big thank you!'

When I'm in the bathroom and the shower is running, I make a phone call. I am careful to put 141 before the number.

'Hello, news desk.'

'One of my neighbours, a woman called Stacey Nicholson, has escaped from the psychiatric ward and is on the loose. She has been sectioned for attempting to kill her children. I've just seen her skulking around our lane and I'm scared she might endanger my kids.'

'Can I take your name please?'

I hang up.

I peer at myself in the mirror and smile.

STACEY

I return back to Jamie's, feeling dejected. He is in the kitchen making some food.

'How did it go?' he asks.

'Not great. All I've discovered is that Tamara was and perhaps still is married.'

'That's a good start,' Jamie says. He leaves his half-made sandwich on the side and hurries over to his open laptop.

'We can search the archives with that information.'

'What archives?'

'Haven't you done any genealogy research?'

'No.'

'Oh.' He sounds disappointed. 'I'm a bit obsessed with it. I've traced our family tree back to 1556. So, the good news is that I have subscriptions, and all we need to do is input her name. Tamara Helms being her maiden name, we assume, and Tamara Collins being her married name.'

I pull out a chair and sit down next to him.

'And bingo. Here we go.'

'It's that easy?'

'Yup. When you know what you're looking for.'

'Tamara Helms born 16th August 1984 to Jean Helms née Jones and William Helms. Tamara married Zachary Wang Rupert Collins on 4th June 2009.'

'That's quite a name. Is she still married?'

'There's nothing to suggest that she's not.'

'In which case we need to track down her husband, who, with a mouthful of a name like that, might be quite easy to find.'

A little shot of excitement bubbles up in my stomach.

Jamie types away and I wait, becoming increasingly impatient.

'Ok,' he says, stopping typing and leaning back in his chair. 'We've got an issue. Zachary Wang Rupert Collins died on 21st November 2012.'

'Goodness. How old was he?'

'Thirty-two.'

'How sad to die that young. So Tamara is a widow?'

'It appears that way.'

Jamie leans forwards again and starts typing.

'Bloody, bloody hell!' he exclaims. 'Look at this! Zachary Wang Rupert Collins took his own life on 21st November 2012.'

'Oh God!' I say. 'What do you think this means?' The blood is humming inside my head.

'Apparently Dylan took his own life and, despite that email, I'm sure Dylan wasn't depressed. You apparently took your own life, or at least you tried to. And Tamara's husband also took his own life. If Tamara is linked to all three, then we're on to something.'

'But Tamara didn't know Dylan. Surely it was just a coincidence that Dom recruited her to take over Dylan's job? After all, he could have recruited anyone. She wasn't the only candidate he interviewed.'

'True. But I still think it's very fishy.'

'I agree.'

I stand up. I'm hungry now, so I finish making Jamie his sandwich and bring it over to him. Then I raid Jamie's fridge, open a tin of tuna I find in a cupboard and make myself a tuna and cucumber sandwich.

WE ARE BOTH MUNCHING, but Jamie speaks with his mouth full.

'Ok, I'm going to check Tamara out on LinkedIn and Facebook. Here we go. LinkedIn. Her photo looks familiar, but I can't place her.'

'From the funeral, perhaps?' I suggest.

'Maybe.' He scratches his head.

'She has a degree in Natural Sciences from Durham University, she's worked in various marketing and PR roles, never staying for more than a couple of years. Haven't heard of any of these companies. Tomorrow I'll ring around and follow up her references. She hasn't got very many LinkedIn contacts.' He carries on typing. 'Facebook. I can't find her. Do you think she's got an account?'

'How would I know?' I shrug my shoulders.

'Mmm. It's odd. Everyone's on social media these days.'

'Dom isn't. Except for work, and then one of his assistants does it for him. But Dom's a few years older than Tamara, so that's understandable.'

'I still think it's a bit odd. Unless she uses a pseudonym that we don't know about.'

'Dead end, then?'

Jamie grins. 'Far from it. I'm only just getting started.'

'She lives somewhere in Horsham. Can you find her address?'

'I'll have a look.'

I stand up and start walking around the room. After a few

minutes, Jamie says, 'Stop pacing, Stacey. Switch the telly on or something.'

I sit on the sofa and switch on the television just in time to catch the lunchtime news. It's the same old boring stuff – politicians squabbling between themselves in an effort to pump up their egos, increased knife crime... I zone out. That is, until the newsreader says my name.

'Shit!' I sit upright and turn up the volume.

'Stacey Nicholson, an author and illustrator, disappeared on Friday. She may be a danger to herself and others, so the public are advised to keep away from her.' They display the photograph of me that the publishers used, the one where my hair looks all bouncy and I'm wearing a polka dot dress.

'What the...!' I exclaim, jumping up. 'I'm not a danger to anyone!'

'I know it's crap, but as far as the police are concerned, you're unhinged. You tried to kill your kids, you've been sectioned...'

'I know, I know. But...oh God!' I wedge my knuckles into my eye sockets.

'It's only the local news, Stacey.'

'Still. Everyone I know will have heard it. It's a disaster, and it also means that I can't go out anymore.'

'Yes, you can.' He stands up. 'Stay here. Watch a film. I'm going to the shops. I'll be back in an hour.'

JAMIE IS as good as his word. He returns an hour later with a large pair of scissors and hair dye.

'I wanted to get you a wig, but the only ones I could find in Tesco's were witches' wigs, and I didn't think they would work. So you'll need to colour your hair.'

'Blonde,' I say, staring at the packet. 'I've never been a blonde.'

'Here is your opportunity. Off you go. Read the instructions carefully and then we're going to chop it.'

'But I like my long hair!'

Jamie raises his eyebrows at me. I scurry off to the bathroom.

Two hours later and I am no longer me. The pale hair does nothing for my complexion, but Jamie is a surprising dab hand at cutting and I emerge with a cute pixie cut, a look I would never have dreamed I could pull off. With the glasses and the new hairstyle, even I don't recognise myself.

'Now you have a new look, you need a new name. What will it be?'

'Sarah Nichols,' I say. 'I was Sarah when I went to see Jean Helms this morning.'

We are standing in the bathroom, looking at me in the mirror.

'What will the children think? They won't recognise me.'

Jamie places a hand on my shoulder. 'You're still their mum.'

I turn around to face him. 'I need to see them. It's as if I'm being ripped apart on the inside.'

'But you can't risk it, Stacey. Hold on tight until this nightmare is over. Let's do some more investigating into Tamara.'

'The crazy thing is, we don't even know if Tamara is definitely behind all of this,' I say, wringing my hands. 'Everything is circumstantial. I don't even know why she was taunting me with the loss of my car keys. She could have just found my keys, and perhaps she also found the note with the scribbles about *Pinkapop's Adventures*. It doesn't necessarily mean she planted it in my drawer.'

'You're right, we don't know for sure. But one thing I am

absolutely convinced about is that you're not delusional or psychotic; unless, that is, you're a brilliant actress.'

I nod weakly.

'And I still don't think Dylan was suicidal. Watch a film, Stacey, and I'll carry on with the research.'

I sit back down.

'And don't call your husband,' he says as an after-thought.

33

TAMARA

L ast night we debated what to do. We have too much on at work for Dom to take the day off. He was worried about the kids going back to school, especially as Stacey's escape from the psychiatric ward made yesterday's news, thanks to the anonymous phone call that the news desk received from me. The news station clearly did their research. They must have spoken to the hospital and the police. Dom was worried that other kids might tease Arthur and Ivy. I persuaded him that they are too young to understand what is going on.

And so it was decided. Dom would go to work. The kids would go to school. I would stay at Dom and Stacey's house and do some work and some tidying up. Then I will collect the children from school. Driving Stacey's car.

MONDAY MORNING and the children are moaning. They've had to get up much earlier than normal. We drove the forty minutes to their home so they could get changed into their school uniforms, and then on to school. Fortunately Dom has taken complete control of them and I just have to sit back and hold my tongue. We're now in the car, five minutes away from school.

'If you don't mind, I think we should both go into school with the children. I want to have a word with their headteacher about what's going on with Stacey. I can officially introduce you, since you're just a name on the list at the moment,' Dom says. 'I expect rumours are flying and the school will need to be prepared. Do you mind coming in with me?'

'Of course not.'

I really am slipping rather beautifully in as the new wife and mother. As the children run ahead of us up the school path, I notice a few of the other mums staring at me and Dom. I hold my head high as I stride past them, through the playground where all the children are congregating. Dom holds the school door open for me and we walk into together.

The head's secretary is seated in a small anteroom. She is a middle-aged woman with large, wonky teeth and hair in a mid-brown bob that sits flat and close to her head.

'Mrs Whittaker, is it possible to have a quick word with Mr Grimes?'

Her expression is laden with sympathy. 'I'll go and see. Just wait here a moment please.'

It must be less than a minute before a young, good-looking man – mid-thirties, I assume – strides forwards with his hand stretched out.

'I'm very sorry to hear about your wife,' he says. 'Please come into my study.'

The room is small and cluttered. He shuts the door behind us.

Dom turns towards me. 'Can I introduce you to Tamara Collins. She's a family friend and is helping me and the kids out in Stacey's absence.

'How do you do?' He shakes my hand.

'Tamara is collecting the kids after school and looking after them until I get home. Mina will also be helping out.'

'I'm glad you have everything sorted. How are the children?'

'They're doing remarkably well, under the circumstances. They miss their mother.'

'I heard on the news of her...escape.' Mr Grimes shuffles uncomfortably. 'We will of course call the police should she show up here. Our security is very good and all the staff have been notified.'

Dom turns his head away and takes an audible breath. 'Thank you,' he says softly. 'Also, as much as possible, we want to protect the children from any potential unpleasant gossip.'

'Indeed,' Mr Grimes said. 'May I reassure you that we have a zero-bullying policy. Ivy and Arthur will be quite safe here.'

As we are walking out of the school, back into the yard, the children are beginning to line up in their classes. Dom stops, his eyes searching the rows of kids. He sees Ivy, who is jumping up and down, waving. He smiles and waves back. I spot Arthur. He is standing at the back of a row of small children, his face glum. As he turns his head towards Dom and me, I wave at him. He takes one look at me and then he is running, darting between the scores of children straight towards us, grabbing Dom's leg, tears running down his cheeks.

'Daddy, I want Mummy. I don't want her,' he points at me. Subtlety clearly is not this child's strong point.

Dom bends down and puts his arms around Arthur. 'I know, little man. Mummy will be home as soon as she is well enough.'

But we both know that Dom is lying. Mummy won't be home for a very long time. She's absconded from hospital and will either spend a long time in prison or hospital, or possibly both.

'I've got to go to work now. You have a lovely day at school and I'll see you later.' He gives Arthur a tight squeeze. Then a young woman, I assume his form teacher, walks over and holds out her hand. 'Come along, Arthur. We're playing with the dinosaurs today, and you get to choose which one we're going to learn about.'

Arthur releases his grip from his father and takes the young woman's hand.

Children: they're so fickle.

I SPEND the day noseying through Stacey's things, reading her diaries, flicking through her notebooks, trying to get inside her head. I can't deny that she's creative. She draws well and she has lots of ideas for stories and imaginary worlds. She's like a big kid really, but it's hard to respect adults who act like children. I find some photo albums, but none of the things I'm really looking for. It's like she's wiped clean a vital part of her life. What a bitch.

I then take a bubble bath, using her expensive bath oils and rubbing myself down with creams that cost the price of a monthly food shop for a family of four. And then I rifle through her wardrobe. It's disappointing. She doesn't have good taste, and only one designer dress. My clothes are considerably nicer than hers. But at the back of the wardrobe I find a long dress inside a cotton cover. I take it out and lay it on the bed. It's Stacey's wedding dress.

It's made from a heavy white satin, with a deep V-neck cut at the front, nipping in at the waist, and falling away to the floor. The train is long. It's simple, elegant and the type of dress

I would choose. I hesitate for a moment, but then peel back the cotton cover and hold up the dress. It's heavy.

I put it on.

It fits me like a glove. I do a twirl in the long mirror in her dressing room, then I fix my hair up in a messy chignon, a bit like Stacey's was in her wedding photographs.

I wonder what Stacey would think if she saw me wearing this dress at my wedding.

Would Dom mind?

Whipping out my phone, I take a selfie in the mirror. It captures me beautifully. In fact, looking at the picture, I think I look better than Stacey did. I have a bigger bust: my cleavage is perfect. All I need is a diamond necklace and a pair of high-heeled shoes. I try on a pair of Stacey's shoes, but they are too small.

With one last gaze, I try to unzip the dress. But the zip is stuck. This is hilarious! I am stuck in Stacey Nicholson's wedding dress. I can't stop laughing, but then the laughter gives way to sobs and before I know what's happening, I am crying for the first time in years. All of this should be mine. And it's not.

I tug the zip as hard as I can and I hear a rip. I don't care. It undoes and I let the dress fall to the ground. I stand on the fabric as I step out of it, then put it back on the hanger carelessly. It's not like Stacey will ever wear this dress again. I place it back inside the cotton sleeve and shove it to the back of the wardrobe.

I wish I hadn't put it on now. I'm in a foul mood.

34

STACEY

Jamie goes off for his interview, all chipper and excited and smart-looking. I wish him luck, then wonder what the hell I'm going to do with my empty day. I can't even write or draw. I doubt I've got a contract anymore. I wonder if there's a clause in the contract terminating it in the case of mental instability of the author.

At about 10.30 a.m. I can't take it any longer. I need to call Dom. He'll be at work by now and everyone will be gossiping. My poor darling Dom.

I dial his mobile, my heart literally in my mouth. It rings three times and then he answers.

'Dom Nicholson speaking.'

'Dom, it's me.'

'Stace? Oh God, Stacey. Where are you?' I hear him walk across the room and shut the door. I can see him in my mind's eye, all serious and worried and confused. My darling husband.

'Look, I'm fine. You've got to believe me, Dom. I'm not ill. I haven't done any of the things I've been accused of. I have not been having an affair and I certainly haven't harmed the children.'

'Where are you?'

'I'm safe.'

'You're not even going to tell me where you are?'

'That doesn't matter right now. I'm trying to prove my innocence, and I need your help. Is Tamara in the office?'

'What? No. She's not.'

'She's up to no good. She's sneaked into our lives and she's tried to set me up. I think she staged my suicide. It wouldn't surprise me if—'

Dom cuts me off. 'Whooa! Hold on, Stacey. Tamara has been a rock. She's brought in masses of new business here at work and she's helped hold our family together. She's looked after the children and cooked us all meals. Frankly, I don't know what I would have done over the last fortnight without Tamara.'

'Can't you see what she's doing, Dom?' I try to keep my voice calm, but it's nigh on impossible. 'She's infiltrated herself into our lives, into our family. I don't know why, but she has.'

'Stacey, that's ridiculous. Sweetheart, you're having a breakdown and you're wanted by the police. All we want is for you to get the care you need so you can be back with me and the children.'

'But I'm not having a nervous breakdown, Dom! It's ridiculous. I'm perfectly lucid. Listen to me. I am talking to you calmly – well perhaps not calmly, but rationally. It's all a lie. I would never, ever want to hurt our babies. I love them more than life itself.'

Dom is silent, and I am utterly dismayed that he doesn't believe me.

'I want to see you, Dom. And I want to see the children.'

'That's not possible.'

'Please! Please! Can we meet? You and me?'

I wait and will him to say yes. I know I mustn't push Dom when he's about to make an important decision.

'I'll meet you on one condition,' he says. 'You tell me every-thing. The absolute, honest, untarnished truth, however painful it might be for me to hear. Do you promise?'

I want to say, 'I've already told you the truth,' but I know that's not what he wants to hear. Instead I say, 'Yes. I promise. Let's meet in that little coffee shop in Horsham Park. It's the park opposite the theatre. Do you remember? It's where we took the kids last summer?'

'Yes, I know exactly where you mean,' Dom says. 'I'll see you there at 2.30 p.m.'

'And no police,' I say. But Dom has already hung up.

I AM RIDICULOUSLY EXCITED to see Dom. I am sure that when he looks me in the eyes, he will know that I'm telling the truth. If I can't convince my own husband, then I don't stand a chance. Besides, Jamie knows the truth. He believes me. And I barely know Jamie.

I don't have a great choice of clothes, but I select a turquoise jumper and my smart jeans and carefully apply my makeup. As I look at my unfamiliar face in the mirror, I realise I forgot to tell Dom about my transformation. I hope he'll like my new hair style. I suspect he won't.

At 2 p.m. I walk out of Jamie's door feeling excitement and positivity for the first time in weeks. With the beanie hat pulled down low and the bomber jacket that swamps me, I doubt even Mina could recognise me, let alone a member of the public who has only caught a glimpse of my photo in the media. Nevertheless, I keep my head down and my eyes to the ground. As I reach the car park, the nerves start to flutter in my stom-ach. I think of Tamara. Has she brainwashed Dom? Worse still, has she got her clutches on my children? I wish I could call Mina, but I can't expect my lovely friend to cover for me.

I am just a few metres from the front door when two mums from school walk out, laughing. Although I think my disguise is good, I can't risk it, so I decide to hang back and lurk between some parked cars and the hedgerow, waiting for Dom to arrive. I'll let him go in first and then I'll follow. It's cold and I'm shivering. I worry that I look suspicious. I get out Jamie's phone and pretend I'm sending a text. I then pretend I'm on a call. It's almost twenty-five minutes past two. And then, to my utter dismay, a police car turns into the car park. The car stops in front of the entrance to the coffee shop and a uniformed policeman gets out of the passenger side and strides into the building. Thirty seconds later he returns, shaking his head at his colleague. He gets back into the car. They stay where they are, hovering in front of the entrance. I am sure they are here for me. How can Dom have shopped me? Grassed by my husband. My heart feels like it is splintering into a thousand little pieces. And then I see him. Dom, my husband, walks with shoulders hunched, up to the police car. He bends down and speaks to one of the policemen, but I can't wait any longer.

With tears in my eyes, I turn and stride away – as fast as I can without running – along the main road with my head down. I turn into the first side street I come across. Then I hear footsteps that sound like Dom's. I desperately want to turn around to have a look, but I can't. I carry on quickly, steadfastly, until I am several streets away. And then I let the tears flow. I crouch for a moment, trying to steady my breathing and to regain control. But I can't. So, with a wet face and red eyes, I continue the walk back to Jamie's.

I have never felt so betrayed. So utterly devastated.

35

TAMARA

It's just gone two thirty. The children don't need picking up until ten past three, but I decide to leave early. So far, during every pickup, I've managed to avoid talking to any of the other mums. Mina came over to talk to me on the first day. She was asking too many questions.

'I'm just a colleague of Dom's,' I reassured her, but I'm not sure she believed me. I want to make damned sure I don't run into her again, especially when I'm in a bad mood like now. I might say something I later regret.

I ease Stacey's car out of the garage and put the accelerator down, enjoying the thrust of the powerful engine. It's a big Volvo and drives smoothly, and it makes me feel like a yummy mummy. I am very early, so I manoeuvre the car into a space right opposite the school gates. This means I can stay in the car until the children start emerging from the playground.

I switch the radio on, tilt the seat back and close my eyes.

When I open them, I wonder if I'm seeing an apparition. There is a person creeping along the hedgerow wearing a beanie hat and a bomber jacket. It's a small person, so despite the masculine clothes, I assume she's a woman. And now she's peering in through the school gates. I sit up straight.

She's partially hidden by a large oak tree. I need to see her face. I angle my side mirror and then I want to whoop for joy. It's Stacey. She might have dyed her hair a hideous peroxide blonde and swept it up under a hat, she might be wearing a ridiculous pair of glasses, but I know that face. I would know her anywhere, in any disguise.

Bingo, Stacey. You've just taken one risk too far. I reach into my handbag and extract my mobile phone. *You, Stacey Nicholson, are about to be put back in the psych ward!*

Just as I'm about to punch in 999, she does a double-take as if she's noticing the car for the first time. She starts walking towards it, peering as if trying to make out who is inside. Is she really that stupid? And then she sees me in the driving seat. I give her a little wave and a smile. Even from this distance, I can see that she's paled, and then she bolts, running as fast as those stumpy legs will carry her.

Shit. Have I just missed the opportunity? I can't decide. Do I follow her, do I call 999 or should I do both? I punch 999 into my phone.

'What service do you require?'

'Police.'

'How can I help you?'

'I have just seen Stacey Nicholson loitering outside the gates of the school her children attend. I understand that she has escaped the psych ward, is sectioned, and is a potential danger to her children and herself.'

'Could you please give me the address.'

I tell him where I am and the direction Stacey fled in. He asks for my name and address. I tell him the truth. I've got nothing to lose. He thanks me for my assistance and confirms a squad car will attend. They need more than a bloody squad car.

They should send out the police helicopter. There's no point in me following her. I'm certainly not going to degrade myself by giving chase on foot.

Within a minute, I hear the police sirens. That is quick. Good work. I laugh. The stupid cow is still hanging around Horsham. Does she want to get caught?

I AM STILL GRINNING when someone knocks against the passenger window of the car. I jump. Damn, it's Mina, Stacey's friend. I hold up my hand and lower the window on the passenger side.

'Good afternoon, Mina. How are you?'

She appears a little startled by my formality.

'I was wondering if you have heard anything from Stacey? How is everyone?'

'Didn't you just see her?' I tilt my head to one side and smirk. 'She was scoping out the playground. I've literally just called the police. You'd better make sure that you keep a good eye on your kids. She could be dangerous towards them too.'

Mina is tongue-tied. But now is the perfect moment to convert Mina into my friend.

'Actually, I was wondering if the kids and I could come over to your house for tea?' I ask. 'I know it's a bit presumptuous, but Ivy and Arthur are always talking about your children, and it would be better if we didn't go straight home just in case Stacey is loitering there, too.'

'I'm sorry...it's not...we're already committed to activities after school today,' Mina stutters.

'Mmm...I thought that might be the case,' I say, flicking my hair back. 'It appears that the proverb, "A friend in need is a friend indeed" doesn't apply in this instance. Poor Stacey, just when she is desperate for friends, they desert her in droves.'

'That's not true,' Mina says. 'I've tried calling her in the hospital, but I haven't been able to make contact.'

'Mmm – that's what they all say. See you around, Mina.'

I raise the car window and watch as she scurries away.

36

STACEY

I know I should have gone straight back to Jamie's flat, but when I was just a few hundred yards away, I couldn't carry on. I needed to see Ivy and Arthur, even if it was just a glimpse of them in the school playground. I am desperate to check that they are all right. My heart feels as if it has been ripped open, not being able to see my babies. So I turn around and walk back towards their school.

I know it's a risk, as it's only twenty minutes before school finishes. Other mothers will be around. Arthur has playtime, quite often outside, between 2.30 and 3 p.m. Ivy will be harder to spot. But sometimes, if you want something so badly, you don't fully think through the consequences.

I spot my car first. It is parked right outside the school gates. I assume Dom has driven it there. Perhaps he has gone into school to talk to Mr Grimes. But no. Tamara is seated in the driver's seat. She gives me a little wave and holds up her mobile phone.

I run. As fast as I possibly can. It doesn't take a genius to work out that she'll be ringing the police.

I don't know how I do it, but I make it back to Jamie's without being stopped, without being arrested, without falling over.

But now I am collapsed in a heap on Jamie's sofa, still in my outdoor clothes, and I can't stop the tears. Dom has betrayed me. How can he allow that woman to look after my children? Can't he see that she is poisonous? My sobs come as hiccups because I am out of breath and have a hideously painful stitch down my left side. The pain is welcome. It's a distraction from my breaking heart.

Jamie's front door opens and he strides into the living room. 'Stacey?'

I stagger to my feet. 'I'm sorry, it's been a bad afternoon.'

'What's happened?'

I pull off my beanie and his jacket, wipe my eyes and collapse back onto the sofa. I tell him how Dom notified the police, and how Tamara caught me looking for the kids.

'Bloody hell, Stacey. I told you to keep away from them!'

'I know. I'm sorry.'

'Well, I have some good news. I've done more research on Tamara and have some information for you.'

AFTER MAKING us a cup of tea each, Jamie reaches for his notebook.

'I searched the electoral rolls for Jean Helms and discovered that she lived in Chichester from 1982 until 2004. Tamara lived there with her parents until 2002. After that date, I can't find any record for Tamara. Anyway, I then did some searches on the local schools and discovered that she went to Benthamly School in Chichester.' Jamie looks up from his notes and peers at me. 'Are you all right, Stacey?'

'No.' My voice sounds hoarse. 'We lived in Chichester from 1991 until 2006. My parents, my sister and me. I went to school there.'

'To Benthamly School?' Jamie asks.

'No. I went somewhere else. But Craig went to Benthamly.'

'Who's Craig?'

'He died.'

I am shaking. I have tried so hard not to think about Craig. Not to remember those years of hell. The last time I had a mental breakdown. A real one, that time.

'Take a deep breath, Stacey,' Jamie says. 'You'd better tell me about this Craig, and let's work out if he is the link between you and Tamara.'

I close my eyes. 'I was eighteen. It was the Easter holidays, before my A levels. I'd been to a party where there were kids from other schools, and I met Craig. He was funny and good-looking, and I couldn't believe my luck that he was interested in me. We snogged.'

I open my eyes and throw Jamie a watery smile.

'He asked if he could see me again. We agreed to meet up the next day for a walk down at West Wittering. Mum was happy for me to go and I took Bouncer, our crazy, gorgeous mongrel dog. It was high tide and the waves were quite rough. Anyway, we were throwing sticks for Bouncer. Mine didn't go far, but Craig was stronger and a better thrower. He threw a stick that went into the sea. Bouncer ran off after it. The dog was fearless. And then...' My voice breaks.

'It's ok, Stacey,' Jamie says, patting my hand.

I take another deep breath. 'Bouncer got into trouble. I screamed and screamed. Shouted at Craig that he shouldn't have thrown the stick so far and that he needed to go in and rescue Bouncer. And he did. He tugged off his trainers and he ran into the freezing sea. Neither he nor Bouncer came back.' I put my face into my hands as I sob at the memory I have tried desperately hard to forget.

'I'm so sorry, Stacey,' Jamie murmurs.

'It was all my fault. I made Craig go in the sea. How was I to know that he wasn't a strong swimmer?'

'It was a terrible accident.'

'That's what everyone said. But it wasn't. I killed him. Anyway, I flunked my A levels and went on to have a full-blown nervous breakdown.'

'That's awful, Stacey.'

He passes me a piece of kitchen towel and I blow my nose. We are both silent for a while.

'Do you think Tamara is related to Craig somehow?' Jamie asks.

I shrug my shoulders. 'I've never heard her name before. I didn't know any of his friends, so perhaps. But why wait all these years to get revenge?'

'I've no idea.'

'I've also found some more information about Zachary Wang Rupert Collins, Tamara's husband. He died in the same way as Dylan. Sleeping pills were found in his system, and he bled out to death from a cut on the wrist in the bath. I tried to track down his family, but tragically both his parents passed away within three years of their son's death and his brother has emigrated to Australia. If Tamara had something to do with his death, it appears she got away with it.'

'I don't understand what she wants,' I mumble.

'I agree, it seems odd. Perhaps Tamara is related to Craig and is trying to avenge his death. Or possibly she fancies Dom and wants to be in his life. Maybe it was by chance that she got the job and then found out who you were, but that doesn't explain why or if she had something to do with Dylan's supposed suicide.'

'Or we are speculating about all of this, and she is just an opportunist who is taking advantage of my incarceration,' I suggest.

Jamie pulls a face. 'There are too many coincidences here. Are Craig's parents still alive?'

'I don't know. They wouldn't be that old.'

'In which case, let's track them down.'

I'M HUNGRY NOW, after all my exercise. I make us both a simple mushroom risotto with some salad, while Jamie taps away at his laptop, doing more research. As I carry our food to the table, Jamie says, 'Bingo. I've found them. They live in Worthing and they're not even ex-directory. Here's their phone number.'

'What do you want me to do?' I ask, trembling at the memory of Craig's grief-stricken parents doubled over with grief at his memorial service.

'I think you should call them.'

'Oh God,' I mutter. 'Can't you do it?'

'Why would they talk to me, a complete stranger? Do they know you had a breakdown afterwards?'

I shake my head. 'I doubt it. I wasn't exactly their favourite person. They blamed me for their son's death.'

'Time is a great healer. Call them, Stacey.'

We eat our food, and when I place my knife and fork neatly along the centre of the plate, Jamie hands me the phone.

'Call them.'

And so I do. The phone rings and rings, and I hope that they are not there, but then a quivering voice answers.

'Hello.'

'Mr Gill?'

'Yes. Who's speaking.'

'I was wondering if I could talk to you about Craig. You knew me—'

He hangs up on me and I am left staring at the phone.

'Well that didn't work, did it?' I say.

'You'll have to go and visit them.'

'No.' I shake my head vigorously. 'No.'

37

TAMARA

I have no idea if the police apprehended Stacey, and the not knowing is infuriating to say the least. But we can't take the risk.

After Mina has joined a cabal of other mothers, I call Dom.

'Stacey just showed up at the kids' school.' I decide not to tell Dom that I rang the police. I'm still not one hundred per cent sure that he wants her caught.

'Where is she now?' he asks. 'Are the children all right?'

'I don't know where she is. She ran off when she saw me. And yes, the children are fine. They were still in school and don't know anything about it.'

Dom lets out an audible puff of air. 'Stacey contacted me and asked to meet up, but then she didn't show. I'm back at work now.'

'Did you tip off the police?' I ask.

'Yes. Maybe that was a stupid thing to do.'

'It was absolutely the right thing to do,' I say.

'But perhaps she saw the police and did a runner.'

'Perhaps,' I agree. 'The thing is, Dom, if she's still at large, we know she's in Horsham and that means your kids are in danger.'

Dom sighs. 'I just find it so difficult to believe that Stacey would harm Ivy and Arthur. She's the most amazing mother, and she still swears blind that she has never and would never hurt them.'

'Mental illness does all sorts of horrible things to the mind. Dom, we can't risk staying here. I think we should go back to my house in Shoreham. Are you ok if I take the kids there now?'

'Of course, Tamara. I'll organise to get the locks changed at home, and I'll get the alarm reactivated. We haven't bothered with it up until now.'

'That's a good idea. 'I'll take the children home first to collect some of their stuff, then drive down to the coast. See you later.'

'I'll try not to be too late. If the locks are changed tomorrow, we can move back home tomorrow night. See you later.'

As I WALK UP the path to the school, I can't help grinning. Dom said 'we' can move back home tomorrow night. But first I think about tonight. Dom in bed, our cosy, happy, perfect family.

'It's Tamara, isn't it?'

I jump, I'm so lost in my erotic daydream. 'Yes,' I say.

'My name is Corinne. I gather you're Dom's au pair?'

'Do I look like an au pair?' I snap.

'Um, sorry. Nanny then?'

'I'm a colleague of Dom's, a director in his firm, and I'm helping the family out during this difficult time.'

'I'm sorry if I offended,' Corinne says. 'I'm just a bit worried about Stacey. I was wondering if all that aggro around *Pinkapop's Adventures* might have pushed her over the edge.'

'I've no idea what you're talking about,' I say, attempting to move away. Corinne is tenacious and keeps apace with me.

'Would you give Dominic a message for me, please?'

I raise my eyebrows.

'Just send him my best wishes and I hope Stacey makes a quick recovery.'

'I assume you know that she's absconded from the psychiatric hospital,' I say. Corinne nods. 'It's quite possible that she is out to get you, to get revenge for the havoc you wreaked on her life. She's dangerous. You might want to keep all your windows and doors locked, just to be on the safe side.'

I stride away from Corinne, leaving her open-mouthed. Yes, that was mean of me, but needs must.

THE CHILDREN ARE DAWDLING.

'Hurry up,' I snap. It crosses my mind that if the police didn't catch Stacey, she might be lying in wait for us at her home. I am positive I would be able to gain the upper hand in a physical fight, but I would rather not subject the children to that. I may be tough, but I'm not heartless.

I get them in the car, remember to do up their seat belts, and pull away.

'We're going home to collect your things and then we're going back to the seaside.'

'Why?' Ivy asks.

'Because it's not safe at home.'

'Why?' Ivy asks again.

'I want to stay at home,' Arthur says, sticking his thumb in his mouth.

'Well you can't. I assume you know that your mother has escaped?'

I glance at Ivy in the rear-view mirror. Her eyes are wide.

'Can we see Mummy?' she asks.

'No.'

'I want Mumma,' Arthur says. He starts crying.

'Be a big boy,' I say.

But that makes it worse. He is wailing now. I pull the car over onto the side of the road alongside a row of shops, then turn around to face them.

'Look, your mother doesn't want to see you. If she did, she would have handed herself in to the police. Then you could have visited her in the hospital. But now she's run away from all of us. You'll have to try to forget her. I know it's painful. I know exactly what it's like to lose someone you love, but you'll get over it. I promise.'

That clearly was not the right thing to say. Both of the children howl. I restart the car and drive home.

38

STACEY

'I'm coming with you,' Jamie says.

'No. You've done enough already. I don't want to subject you to this,' I insist.

Jamie puts on an anorak. 'It's non-negotiable, Stacey. I'm coming with you. I'm your official driver.'

I can't argue with that, so I follow Jamie out to the car. I keep my head down as we drive out of Horsham and onto the A24 headed southwards. It's another wet and windy day, and I feel as miserable as the weather. I just can't see how I can prove that Tamara is up to no good and I'm innocent. Jamie is hopeful that Craig's parents might know something. I'm not.

The traffic into Worthing is dreadful. Just ten years ago, the journey from Horsham to Worthing took less than thirty minutes. Now we're stuck in relentless traffic jams. I input their address into the sat nav on Jamie's phone and give him directions.

Eventually we pull up outside a small pebble-dash bungalow with a neat garden and a gnome standing on the doorstep. We get out of the car.

'What if they've heard on the news that I'm wanted?' I ask, feeling my gut clench.

'What was your maiden name? You weren't called Stacey Nicholson back then, were you?'

'No, good point. My name was Cassandra Pope. Everyone called me Casey.' The names sound strange on my tongue. If someone addressed me as Cassandra Pope, I doubt I would respond. I have expunged it from my consciousness.

'Casey? You had a different first name and surname? You never told me that!' Jamie exclaims, leaning his hands on the roof of his car.

'I'm sorry. I didn't think it was relevant.'

'When did you change your name?'

'After my breakdown, some well-meaning doctor suggested I have a new start. I don't think he meant that I should have a new name, but I decided I wanted to. So I changed my name from Casey to Stacey via deed poll. It helped me leave the tragedy behind and also meant that if anyone did a search on me, they wouldn't find all the newspaper articles linking me to Craig's death. When Dom and I got married, I took on his surname.'

'In which case I don't think you've got anything to worry about. With your new hairstyle and glasses, you don't look anything like the picture that was circulated about you in the media. Just remember to introduce yourself as Cassandra Pope and you'll be fine. Come along, Casey!'

I throw him a filthy look, but he is striding ahead of me, up the neat stone-paved path to the dark blue front door. He presses the gold front door bell, which plays an electronic version of 'Oh, When The Saints Go Marching In'. Then Jamie steps backwards so I'm the person that Mr Gill sees when he opens the door.

He is haggard; his face is narrow and drawn, and he stands

there stooping, his deep-set blue eyes looking up over his nose like a hawk.

'Yes,' he says, glancing from Jamie back to me.

'Mr Gill, I am Cassandra Pope. I know I'm probably the last person you want to meet, but please, could I just have one minute of your time?'

He grabs the doorframe and starts trembling. 'Haven't you caused us enough grief over the years? And you have the audacity to turn up on our doorstep!'

'Who is it, love?' Mrs Gill appears next to her husband. She hasn't aged as much, or perhaps she was always a lot younger than him. I don't recall. She grasps her husband's arm. 'Are you all right, love?' she asks.

'No. This woman here is Cassandra Pope.'

Mrs Gill opens and closes her mouth without saying anything. Mr Gill makes as if to close the door in my face. But Jamie is too quick for him and puts a hand out.

'The last thing we want to do is cause you any more upset. It's just that someone Craig used to know is trying to destroy Stace–Cassandra's life, and we were wondering whether you might be able to help us work out why?'

'I'm not...I can't...' Mr Gill has tears in his eyes. All I want to do is throw my arms around the old man and tell him how desperately sorry I am. How Craig's death has haunted me the whole of my life. That if I could have exchanged my life for Craig's, I would have done so. I can feel the tears pouring down my face. I try to swallow the sob, but I do a lousy job.

Mr Gill shakes his wife's arm off his and shuffles back into the house. We all watch him go, along the corridor, through the open door and into a kitchen at the back of the house.

'My husband cries every day. He's a broken man. I know it was an accident, Cassandra, but sometimes it's just too much for both of us to bear.'

'I'm so sorry.'

'You don't need to be sorry, Cassandra. It broke you too. I heard that you had a breakdown. We should have reached out to you, but we were hurting so much, we didn't. I think you'd better come in.'

She stands back to let us pass, then leads us into her front room. There is a beige sofa, and matching armchairs and ornaments are placed on every surface: on top of the mantlepiece, on the sideboard, on the windowsill, peeking out from under the net curtains. The television in the corner of the room is old, boxy and large. In between the china animals and crystal angels are photographs of Craig. I haven't seen his picture in years. I remember him as being so good-looking, so charming. But, then, I barely knew him. Now I look at the photographs and see an ordinary boy, a life ended far too young.

'Take a seat,' Mrs Gill says to us. She chooses the beige chair with the upright back. I sink into the sofa and Jamie sits next to me.

'How has your life been, Cassandra?'

'It's been good, Mrs Gill. I am very lucky. I am married to a wonderful man and have two beautiful children.'

'I'm glad to hear it. You're her husband, then?' Mrs Gill turns to Jamie, who blushes scarlet.

'No, no. I'm just a friend helping out.'

'So, what is it you'd like to know, Cassandra?'

It is bizarre hearing her call me that.

'Do you know someone called Tamara Helms. We think she went to school with Craig and may have been in the same class.'

'Oh dear, my memory isn't what it used to be. I can't say that the name rings a bell.'

Jamie fumbles with his mobile phone and brings up a photo of Tamara.

I flinch. 'Where did you find that?' I ask.

'It's on SAID's website. Her photo is alongside Dom's and Jeff's. All the staff photos are there.'

Jamie stands up and walks over to Mrs Gill. He crouches down next to her and shows her the photograph.

'She probably had different coloured hair when she was younger,' Jamie says. I have no doubt that he is going to be a very good investigative journalist.

Mrs Gill puts on her reading glasses and peers at the phone. 'Mmm, there's definitely something familiar about her.' She glances up to the ceiling. 'Let me have another look.'

'Good heavens! I think it's little Tammy. I haven't thought of wee Tammy in years and years.'

'Was Tammy a friend of Craig's?' Jamie asks.

'Indeed she was. They were what you call these days, an item. Boyfriend and girlfriend from the ages of twelve to sixteen or seventeen, as I recall it. My husband didn't approve of wee Tammy. There was never any father on the scene, and Tammy used to dress a bit tartily. She always smelled of cigarette smoke. She had quite a mouth on her. Craig rarely brought her here because he didn't want to get into arguments with his dad, but it didn't fool me. I knew they were up to hanky-panky at too young an age. So she's done all right then, has our Tammy. I have to say, I'm surprised. Just goes to show.' She shakes her head. 'And I haven't thought about her in years.'

'I'm sorry to have to ask this, but do you remember if Tammy was at Craig's funeral?' Jamie asks.

'I wouldn't know, love. There were too many young people there and it's all a haze from that dreadful time. But Tammy wasn't his girlfriend at the time of our Craig's passing. I think Craig tried to dump her and there was a terrible scene. She stood outside our house crying and screaming and chucking stones up at Craig's window. That was at our old house, not this one. My husband was so enraged he threatened to call the police. Quite a hullabaloo, that was. It's funny. I'd totally forgotten about it.'

'I don't suppose you have any photos of Tammy, from back then, do you?' I ask.

'I probably do.' She levers herself up out of the chair.

'Only if it's not too painful for you to look,' I say, wondering if I will be able to keep my emotions in check. Mrs Gill ignores my comment and bends down to pull out a drawer in the pine cabinet next to the television.

'Here you go,' she says, handing me a large claret-coloured photo album. 'If you flick through it, you'll find a photograph of our Craig and Tammy all dressed up before going to some school ball, or prom as you call it these days, to celebrate finishing their GCSEs.'

The photograph Mrs Gill is referring to is towards the end of the album. It's a small 4 x 6 size photograph. Craig is wearing an evening suit, his bow tie crooked. He looks lanky and ill at ease. Tamara on the other hand, is staring straight at the camera, her mouth slightly open in a pout, her cleavage almost falling out of her low-cut, strapless green dress that barely covers the tops of her thighs. Her fingers are stretched along Craig's arm in a possessive manner. The body language suggests that she is holding on to Craig for dear life.

'Is that her?' Mrs Gill asks, as Jamie and I stare at the photograph.

'Yes, Mrs Gill. It is. Thank you.'

'What has the lassie done to you, love?'

'She's trying to ruin my life.'

'Well that's quite dramatic. I'm sure it isn't as bad as that.'

'Would it be all right if we photograph this photo?' Jamie asks.

'Of course, love.'

Jamie takes his phone out and captures the photograph. And then he stops and peers at it.

'Have you seen this necklace?' he asks.

I look closer. It's gold on a gold chain.

'It says "T&C",' Jamie says.

I have another look. 'I suppose it might be T&C. Makes sense – Tamara and Craig. Perhaps he gave it to her.'

Jamie pales, his eyes wide with shock. He whispers in my ear. 'I've seen that necklace before.'

'Can I get you two a cup of tea?' Mrs Gill asks, taking the photo album from me.

'It's very kind of you but we've imposed enough. I don't want to bring back any more difficult memories.'

'No dear, you're not doing that. I love remembering our Craig. It's just my husband who finds it too painful. Well I hope I could help you, and I hope you sort out whatever is going on with Tammy.'

Both Jamie and I stand up.

'Thank you very much for talking to me,' I say to Mrs Gill, and shake her hand. Jamie does the same. 'Please don't get up. We'll see ourselves out.'

WHEN WE'RE BACK in the car, I feel a wave of sadness, but Jamie has his mind on something and is frantically searching through messages on his mobile phone.

'What is it?' I ask.

'I've seen that necklace before.'

'How would you remember a necklace?'

'T&C. I thought it funny. You know, Terms and Conditions. It just needed an apostrophe after the C and an S on the end.'

I raise an eyebrow at him.

'Ok, not funny perhaps. But it caught my eye.'

'What are you looking for?'

'A photo that Dylan sent me. I might be mistaken, but I'm

sure he sent me a photo of a woman he was seeing wearing that necklace. Come on...' he mutters to himself. His fingers are shaking and slipping across the screen of his phone.

As the realization of what he is saying sinks in, we stare at each other. My heart lurches. I bring my hand over my mouth. 'You think Dylan was dating Tamara?'

'I don't know, Stacey. But it's a distinct possibility.' Jamie's voice quivers.

39

TAMARA

'I'll happily collect the kids from school, but is it all right if I take Stacey's car?'

We are in the kitchen, waiting for the locksmith to finish changing the locks on all the external doors.

'Of course. You don't need to ask.'

'In which case I'll get off to work so we're not both absurdly late.'

'That makes sense. Besides it's better if we don't walk in together. I don't want the staff to...well, you know.'

'I'll see you at the office,' I say through gritted teeth.

I fume quietly as I drive fast. It's frustrating that he doesn't want the staff to see us together but, I suppose, understandable. And I'm not happy about collecting the kids from school, despite offering to do so. I'm done with those spoiled-brat children. Perhaps I'll change my mind about collecting them and let Dom do it himself. But this morning I want to concentrate on work. I need to be sure that we are making good progress on the Stanwyck account. I've scheduled a meeting with Jeff to work through his designs, then I'll have a meeting with Dom to put together a brief for the copy. As I walk in, I catch a couple of the younger staff having a good bitch about Dom and Stacey over the photocopier. I put a swift end to that conversation.

The day passes quickly, and soon it's early afternoon and I'm in Dom's office. I wish he would pull the blinds so we could have a quick bonk on his desk, but I suspect that's not Dom's style. Besides, I have to pretend that we're not an item, even though it's quite obvious that we are. We're sitting side by side at the circular table in his office, mooting tag lines to run alongside the new logo that Jeff has designed. It seems that neither of us are on top form today, as we don't make great progress.

An email pings on his computer. He stands up and walks over to his desk, stretching his arms up into the air as he does so. Dom is looking very tired and I'm worried about him. He drops into his chair and uses the mouse to bring his screen to life. As he looks at the email, he goes whiter and whiter. What the hell?

'What's the matter, Dom?' I ask

'I've just...It's just...I need to go out for a moment. Can you excuse me please?' He grabs his mobile phone off his desk and rushes out of the office. Jeff comes up to him and says something, but Dom brushes him off. I get up and watch Dom leave the office.

What the hell is going on?

I control myself and walk slowly through the office, past Ellie, as if on my way to the toilets. I exit and walk out into the communal area. Dom's not there. I wonder if he's taken the lift downstairs. I call the lift and go down to the ground floor, to the large open space that is the reception for the whole building. But he isn't there either.

'Have you seen Dom Nicholson?' I ask the concierge.

'No, not since he came in this morning,' he says. I turn and step back into the lift, returning to the second floor. He could be in the men's toilets, I suppose. I glance around to make sure no one is looking, and open the door. There are only two cubicles and both doors are open. Dom isn't here.

For a moment I'm stumped, and then I see the Fire Exit door that leads to the stairwell no one ever uses. I open the door gently, holding my breath and hoping that it won't creak. It doesn't. I slip inside and then I see Dom. He is pacing on the landing below, on the phone. But then he starts walking down the stairs and I can't hear properly what he's saying, although it sounds distinctly like he's talking to Stacey. Surely not? I can't hang around to find out, so I tiptoe back, ease open the door and hurry back to our office.

'Tamara, can you—'

'Not now, Ellie,' I say, striding towards Dom's office. A couple of people glance up at me. I walk into Dom's office and close the door behind me. Then I sit at his desk and move the mouse. The email that made him turn white is open on the screen. There are two pictures, and they have been sent by Stacey Nicholson.

Fuck.

The first picture is of me and Craig when we were sixteen.

The second picture is the profile picture I used when I joined the online dating site where I met Dylan. Attached to it is a screenshot of a message Dylan sent. 'Hi bro, this is my new bird. She's hot!'

How the fuck did Stacey get hold of those?

I have to think. Fast. Fast. Everything I have worked for is in danger of collapsing. I will not let that happen.

I race to my desk, grab my handbag and coat, and literally run out of the office.

'I'm late for a meeting!' I tell Ellie.

I've got to get out of the office block without Dom seeing me. How can I possibly do that? I jab the button for the lifts. Come on! Come on! I'm hopping from foot to foot, trying to keep steady on my high heels, my eyes on the door to the stair-well. Please stay there, I silently will Dom. Hurry up lift!

And then the lift pings and the doors open slowly. I step inside and jab the button for the ground floor. Just as the doors are closing, I catch a glimpse of Dom's back as he walks towards the office. I pray that he didn't see me. Quite possibly, I am just seconds ahead of him.

'Did you find Mr Nicholson?' the concierge asks.

I remove my heels and run in my stockinged feet, ignoring the question, across the cold marble floor and then out into the car park, where little stones dig into the soles of my feet. The tarmac is freezing cold and damp, but I don't care. I run as fast as I can towards Stacey's car, so grateful that her fancy motor doesn't require me to point a key fob at it, and opens simply by recognising the fob in my handbag. Chucking my belongings onto the passenger seat, I start the car and put my foot down on the accelerator. I have to go. Now.

I know I'm panicking, not seeing straight, not thinking straight, and I try to calm down. Breathe slowly. In and out. But this was not part of my plan.

The car skids around the corner but holds the road. Thank goodness. I have no intention of ending up in a ditch. I just need to be calm, think rationally, work out my next steps.

And as I race the car along the dual carriageway on the A264 between Crawley and Horsham, I work out what I need to do next. I slow down a little, careful to drive within the 70-mile-an-hour speed limit. I let my shoulders relax and exhale loudly.

40

STACEY

As soon as Jamie found Tamara's profile picture on Love2U.com, I emailed the photographs to Dom. First there was the picture of Tamara and Craig, and then I sent the screenshot from Jamie's phone, showing that Dylan was dating Tamara. I accompanied the photographs with a message. 'I'm about to call you. Please answer the phone.'

Jamie is driving. We agreed that I should go to Dom's offices and meet him as soon as possible. Jamie wants to be there too, but this is a conversation I need to have with my husband alone.

I wait three minutes, and then I call Dom.

'It's Stacey,' I say. 'Did you get the photos?' I can hear Dom walking. He sounds breathless.

'Yes, I got them.'

'Are you at the office?'

'Yes.'

'Good. I'm coming to meet you. We need to talk.'

'What is all of this, Stacey? I don't understand these photos you've sent me.'

'I think you do, Dom. Tamara is seeking revenge on me. She's using you and everyone else to ruin my life.'

'But the photos?'

'The first one is of her and Craig. He was the boy who drowned trying to save my dog.'

'Craig was Tamara's boyfriend?'

'Yes.'

'But that happened more than fifteen years ago,' he exclaims. 'Why has she only taken revenge now? It doesn't make any sense, Stacey!'

'I think Tamara is very, very clever and cunning. She has made you need her.' I hear Dom gulp, and for the first time I wonder if Dom has been unfaithful with Tamara. I swallow bile.

'But if Craig was going out with Tamara, what were you doing with Craig?'

'According to his mother, Craig dumped Tamara. She didn't take it well. Hold on, Dom. Turn left here and then first right,' I instruct Jamie.

'Who are you with?' Dom asks.

'Jamie Headley, Dylan's brother.'

'Why on earth are you with Jamie?'

'Because we think Tamara might have killed Dylan.'

'What!' Dom explodes. 'Are you accusing Tamara of being a murderer? And you expect me to believe that, Stacey? It's ridiculous. Remember, it's you who have been sectioned, not her. Whilst she may or may not have had a relationship with Craig, it is insane to insinuate she killed Dylan!'

'Dom, we're just pulling into the car park outside your offices. Will you meet me?'

'Yes, but—'

'There can't be any buts. You've got to promise you won't call the police. I have all the evidence to prove to you that

Tamara is not the person she says she is. Do you promise?' I reiterate.

'I promise.'

'I'll meet you at the back of the offices, where the dumpster bins are. I don't want anyone to see me, least of all Tamara. I'll be there in thirty seconds.'

I gesture to Jamie to turn to the left, around the side of the building towards the deliveries sign.

'Ok. I'm going back to the office to get my jacket and I'll see you there in a moment.' Dom hangs up on me.

'Do we trust him?' Jamie asks. The question is like a dagger in my heart. Jamie is asking whether we trust my husband! But, based on what has gone on before, he has every right to ask that question.

'I think so.'

'Stay in the car. Get down into the passenger footwell and I'll do a drive past to make sure that Dom is alone and no one is watching. If I see a police car, I'll hoot and we'll just do whatever we've got to do.'

Jamie drives slowly past the door for deliveries and a little further on, to where there are five large rubbish bins.

'Ok, I see him. He just came out of the side door. I'll turn the car and wait here.'

'Thanks, Jamie. I lean over and squeeze his arm.

'Shit, Stacey. What have you done to your hair?'

'Thanks for that,' I say sarcastically. 'Look, I know it's a lot to take in, but I am not crazy. Tamara has set me up and I can prove it to you.'

I show him Tamara's profile picture on the dating app. She had blonde hair then, but it's unmistakably the same person. And then I show the messages that Dylan sent to Jamie, expressing his excitement that he was going to be dating such a hot woman. I point to the necklace around Tamara's neck, the gold T&C.

'Have you seen Tamara wearing that necklace?' I ask.

Dom nods. His expression is pained.

'Most of her CV is made up,' I say. 'We've checked with her supposed previous employers. Also, she doesn't have a degree from Durham University.'

'But Tamara is brilliant at her job! She won us a huge tranche of business, and I've never known anyone as organised and astute as she is.'

'That may be the case, but she categorically did not work at the places she said she did. Who knows what she has really done!'

Dom leans his back against the brick wall and squeezes his eyes shut.

'We can't prove it, but Jamie thinks she might have killed Dylan in order to get his job.'

Dom's eyes flick open. 'That's ridiculous, Stacey. She was the best candidate for the job. Are you suggesting that she conned me? I have spent a lot of time with this woman. She is not a murderer!'

'How can you know that for sure? You can't. And if Jamie and I are right, she has conned you and everyone else along the way. Did you know that she was married?'

'Yes, she told me. Her husband is dead.'

'Did she tell you how her husband died?'

'No. It didn't seem appropriate to ask.' He shuffles.

'He committed suicide in exactly the same way Dylan supposedly did. He overdosed on sleeping pills and then cut his wrists. And don't you think it's odd that I supposedly overdosed on sleeping pills?' I grab Dom's hands. 'Yes, I was stressed. Yes, I still am stressed. But I would never try to kill myself. The thought of hurting our children...it's just too much to bear.'

'Oh Stacey,' Dom groans. 'What the hell have I done? If this is really true, I am a total idiot. I've betrayed you and I'm so sorry.'

Dom is shaking. My strong Dom is quivering, and now it is me who is having to be the strong one.

'We need to confront Tamara and find out what really is the truth,' Dom says.

I want to hug him, but he steps away from me and wraps his arms around himself.

'I agree,' I say.

Dom opens the back door to the office block and I walk in.

'Let me go first, Stacey. If everything you've said is correct, I don't know how she's going to react when she sees you.'

Dom takes the stairs two at a time and I run up them after him. With his hand on the door handle on the second floor, he turns to look at me. It's the strangest look, as if he hasn't seen me before, as if he is discovering something for the first time.

'Actually, Dom, I think I should stay here. What if a member of your staff shops me to the police? I'm still a wanted woman.'

'You're right. Stay here and I'll bring her with me.' He squeezes my hand and then disappears.

I PLAY out all the possible scenarios in my head. Tamara denying everything. Tamara trying to push me down the stairs. Tamara calling the police. The one scenario I don't imagine is what happens. Within a couple of minutes, Dom is back.

'She's gone,' he says.

'What do you mean, "she's gone"?'

'She told Ellie she was late for a meeting and rushed out of the office. But Ellie says there's nothing in the diary. I think she might have read your email to me. It was open on my computer. That means she knows we're on to her.'

'Oh God! What are we going to do now?' I cry. 'We need to tell the police everything.' I hold up the mobile phone Jamie loaned me. 'The proof is all here, isn't it?'

Dom puts his hands on my shoulders. 'Stacey, you've been sectioned. If we ring the police, you will be arrested and taken straight back.'

We stare at each other.

'You're right,' I say quietly. 'We mustn't call the police. Not yet. Or maybe you can and I'll stay in hiding?'

Dom's face is pained.

'I'm so happy to see you, Dom,' I say, stroking his cheek. 'I've missed you and the children so much. You will never know how much.'

'The children!' Dom says.

'I need to see them,' I say.

'Tamara is meant to be collecting Ivy and Arthur from school this afternoon.'

'What!' I exclaim. 'No!'

41

TAMARA

There are no cars parked on the road outside the children's school. Not surprising, since it's only 2 p.m. The playground is quiet and the gate creaks as I open it. I am calm now and walk confidently up the path towards the main school entrance. I press the buzzer on the locked door and a female voice says, 'How can I help you?'

'My name is Tamara Collins. I'm the guardian of Ivy and Arthur Nicholson, and on their approved contact list. I totally forgot to tell you this morning that they have a dentist's appointment.' There is a camera angled at me, its light flickering.

The door buzzes open and I walk inside. I wonder if all schools have the same smell – an unpleasant mixture of old, boiled food, antiseptic, body odour and a generic mustiness. I assume I need to go to the headmaster's secretary, so I walk along the corridor, past a long display of children's paintings that evidently are their attempts at self-portraits. Ivy's is at the end, and hers stands out as the most accomplished of the lot. I am pleased for her and bizarrely proud. I knock on the door to the small anteroom Dom took me to when we met the headmaster.

'Come in!'

'It's Ms Collins, isn't it?' Mrs Whittaker, the headmaster's secretary, nods at me.

'Yes, that's right. You'll have to forgive me, but I forgot that I'm meant to notify you in advance if the children need to come out of school early. We have a dentist appointment at 2.30 p.m.'

'You know it isn't normally allowed? Appointments need to be made out of school hours. But as the Nicholson's are having a difficult time at the moment, I'm sure Mr Grimes won't mind.'

I smile at her, even though I would like to smack that smug look off her face. How these little gatekeepers relish their power.

'Please can you wait here and I'll go to Ivy and Arthur's classrooms to collect them.'

'Thank you very much. I'm extremely grateful,' I say. 'Please can you ask them to be quick, otherwise we'll be late for their appointments.'

I can't sit still. My mind is on overdrive, trying to work out what to do. If Stacey convinces Dom that I am responsible for her incarceration, then the game is up. I think back to Dylan's death. Although the coroner's report hasn't been issued yet, the police declared it suicide. I was so careful. Surely they can't pin anything on me?

If I'm left alone in an office, I normally have a quick look at the papers on the desk, but this is a school, and I'm not interested in school reports or the antics of children, so I ignore Mrs Whittaker's desk and walk out of the room. I pace up and down the corridor, listening to the faint rise and fall of a teacher's voice talking to a class. Hurry up, I mutter to myself. What if Dom is on his way here?

~

It MUST BE a good ten minutes later that the school secretary appears with both Ivy and Arthur. They are wearing their school coats, Ivy has her rucksack on her back and Arthur is dragging his school bag along the ground. They both look glum.

'Cheer up, children. It's not so bad at the dentist,' Mrs Whittaker says brightly.

Ivy stares at the woman as if she is crazy.

'Come on, darlings, we'll be late if we don't hurry.' I hold out both of my hands but neither of the children taken them. I throw an embarrassed glance at Mrs Whittaker, but she doesn't seem to have clocked my rejection. As soon as we are outside on the path leading away from the playground, I say, 'You need to hurry. We're going to be really late. Stop dragging your heels, Ivy.'

'Why are we going to the dentist? We only went not long ago with Mummy.'

'He wants to see you again,' I say.

'Our dentist is a lady,' Arthur pipes up, speaking a little too loudly.

'I meant to say "she". I don't know why she wants to see you again. Perhaps you haven't been brushing your teeth properly.'

Arthur is dawdling. I grab his hand and start walking quickly, pulling him along.

'You're hurting me,' he cries.

'I won't hurt you if you hurry up.'

Eventually we reach the car. I snatch their bags from them and open the rear car doors.

'Get in.'

They both climb in the car. I slam the doors closed and jump into the driver's seat, starting the engine and pulling away as I'm putting my seat belt on.

'We haven't got our seat belts on yet,' Ivy says.

'Put them on yourselves.' My eyes are on the road and I

can't be bothered with the children. I glance in the mirror and catch Ivy glaring at me. She's too clever by half, that child. We drive out of Horsham towards Billingshurst.

'Where are we going? The dentist is in Horsham.' Ivy says.

'Stop asking questions!' My fingers grip tightly around the steering wheel.

Arthur starts crying. 'I want my mummy,' he mutters again and again. Ivy reaches over and holds Arthur's hand.

'When will we see Mummy or Daddy?' Ivy asks.

'Stop nagging.'

They are both snivelling now, talking, crying and it's doing my head in. I shout at them, 'Shut up!'

Mistake. That makes it much worse.

I am driving too fast and skid around a corner.

'Fuck!' I yell, yanking the steering wheel just in time. A white van coming from the opposite direction hoots at me and the driver raises his hand in an obscene gesture.

I must calm down. Slow down. If the police catch me for speeding, then it really will all be over. Right now, the children are my greatest asset, and I need to think through what I'm going to do with them.

I'm not a murderer. I'm not a child hater. But if the means justifies the end, then perhaps...

42

STACEY

I rush over to Jamie's car.

'We think Tamara might have gone to get the children! I'm going with Dom to their school.'

'What do you want me to do?' Jamie asks.

'Nothing. Just keep your phone on. I'll call you with news. And thank you, Jamie.'

I haven't got time to say anymore and run over towards Dom, who is pulling his Audi out of its parking space.

It is a miracle we are not stopped by the police. Dom drives like a maniac, hooting at cars that are driving too slowly, even overtaking on the inside on the dual carriageway. I have to tell him to slow down. I'm scared.

We put Dom's phone on loudspeaker through the car and I dial the number for the children's school. It's normally Mrs Whittaker who answers, but her phone goes straight to voicemail.

'This is Dom Nicholson,' Dom says. 'Please can you make sure that no one collects Ivy and Arthur. No one except me. I'll be there soon.'

I end the call. There is nothing else Dom could have said. A mad-woman who isn't my wife, but who I put on the approved contact list, might come and collect my children. Please don't let her take them. No, he said the right thing. Besides, we'll be there in less than ten minutes.

We sit in silence. Dom's knuckles are white around the steering wheel, his jaw clenched; my fingers grip the edge of the seat, my eyes on the road ahead. When we drive into Horsham, Dom slows down and keeps to the speed limit. It seems as if we are driving painfully slowly. I can't stop my foot from tapping up and down.

When we arrive, I rush to open my door.

'No, Stacey. You can't go in. It has to be me.'

I nod reluctantly. I watch Dom as he runs across the road and races up the school path.

He isn't long. Two or three minutes at most. When he returns, his face is white and drawn.

'Where are the children?'

'It's too late, Stace. She's already collected them.'

'What do you mean, "She's collected them"?' I screech.

'She told Mrs Whittaker that they had a dentist's appointment. They've only been gone ten minutes or so.'

'Oh my God! Oh my God!' I wail, rocking backwards and forwards.

'I'm calling the police,' Dom says, dialling 999 on his phone.

'Ok,' I whisper. I am ready to hand myself in. I'm ready to sacrifice my life if I can save my babies. I've always wondered whether a mother really would give her life for her children, but now I know for sure that I would do so in the blink of an eye. Dom speaks with the phone to his ear, so I only hear his side of the conversation.

'Police,' Dom says.

'My children have been abducted.'

'Yes, it's Dominic Nicholson and our children are called Ivy and Arthur.'

'They were taken from school.'

'No. No, it wasn't my wife. She's...' Dom holds the phone away from his ear and looks at me with a pained expression. I can hear the operator on the other end saying, 'Sir, sir!' I shrug my shoulders.

'No. My wife is with me in the car. We are parked outside our children's school.'

'I am aware that she has broken the terms... Yes. No, there is nothing wrong with my wife. The whole thing has been a set up. The woman you need to go after is called Tamara Collins.'

Silence, whilst he listens. Dom is getting frustrated. A nerve is pulsating in his jaw line, and he is clenching and unclenching the fingers of his left hand.

'No, Tamara did have permission to collect the children from school. Yes, I understand. Yes.' The call ends and he chucks the phone onto the floor by his feet.

'What?' I ask.

'I need to hand you in otherwise I will become an accessory to the crime and then our children will lose both their parents. And because Tamara was on the approved contact list, they are not viewing this as an abduction. Shit!'

'You could have told them about our murder theories,' I say.

'Really, Stace? He wouldn't have believed me. We're going to have to go to the police station and show them your photographs. But we haven't got time for that now. We need to find Tamara.'

'Do you think she would harm the children?' I ask, biting my lip so hard I draw blood.

'I don't know. I don't know anything now except I've got so much wrong. I think we should go home. She may just have taken the children there. Otherwise she might have gone to her holiday home. We stayed there.'

'You what?' I gasp.

Dom doesn't answer, but he does look anguished. 'I'm going to call her. Perhaps I can reason with her. After all, as the policeman said, we are jumping to a very dramatic conclusion.'

'If you must,' I mutter.

Dom leans down into his footwell and picks up his phone. He makes the call, but I can hear it goes straight to voicemail. 'Her phone is off.'

'Right, let's go home,' I say.

Dom starts the car and we take the familiar journey home.

As soon as we pull up into the drive, I jump out of the car and rush to the front door.

'Stacey, you won't be able to get in,' Dom says.

'I took the spare key we kept in the greenhouse,' I say, pulling it out of my pocket and inserting it into the lock.

'It won't work.' Dom shifts his weight from side to side and tugs at the hair above his right ear. 'We got the locks changed.'

'You what? Why?'

'We thought you might be a danger to the kids. I'm sorry Stace.'

I am lost for words and take a step backwards. Dom opens the door and we both rush inside.

'Ivy! Arthur!' I yell, racing around the house. Dom runs upstairs. We meet up in the kitchen.

'They're not here,' Dom says, his shoulders sagging.

'The garage,' I mutter, recalling horrific instances of suicides or killings from car fumes. I rush to the door to our internal garage and unlock it.

'My car. It's not here!' I turn to Dom, frowning.

'I put Tamara on your car insurance. I didn't want her driving the kids in her small, old banger. I thought it was for the best.' His voice fades away.

'She could be anywhere,' I say, despondently.

'No. I think she'll have taken the children to her house near

Shoreham. It's her bolt-hole and the obvious place for her to go.'

'You think so?' I ask Dom imploringly. He knows this woman. He has got to be right.

'Let's go.'

We lock up the house and race to Dom's car. We drive onto the A24, again, the fastest car on the road. Dom is concentrating on the bends and I'm trying to keep my breathing under control, trying not to catastrophise. It's almost impossible.

We've just passed the Washington roundabout when Dom says, 'I'm going to call the police again. I'll explain the whole situation. I'll give them the details of your car. At least we know the number plate and they'll use automatic number plate recognition.

'No! Hold on!' I yell. 'I've just remembered something! My car has a tracker on it, doesn't it? Don't you remember, we had all that hoohah a couple of years ago with the insurers and we had to pay for a tracker?'

'Shit, I can't believe you forgot!'

'Well, you could have remembered too. The monthly payments come out of our joint bank account!'

Dom backs down and slows the car. It's like all the fight has been wrung out of him. 'You're right. Can we track it online?'

'I'm not sure. I've never tried.'

'What was the name of the company?' Dom asks.

'I don't know. I can't remember.'

Dom looks as if he's about to break, then he shakes his head.

'We pay on direct debit, so it'll be on my online banking.'

I want to scream at him. This is all Dom's bloody fault. If he hadn't been so taken in by Tamara, we wouldn't be in this horrific situation.

'Take my phone. Go onto NatWest.com and you'll find it.'

He tells me his passwords, which I could have worked out anyway, and soon I'm looking through his direct debits.

'Got it!' I exclaim. 'TrackerToEverywhere. I'll go onto their website.'

43

TAMARA

The journey takes longer than I had anticipated. Eventually we are up over the South Downs and on the A29, past the turning to Arundel with its Norman castle and on the road towards Chichester. I put my foot down on the dual carriageway, but the traffic is heavy and the light is fading fast. It starts raining, and soon it is torrential, with large puddles on the road and the windscreen wipers working at full pelt. But Stacey's car feels solid. It can handle it.

The children are still whimpering in the back. Moaning that they are hungry, need to go to the loo, want their parents. Every so often they force me to scream at them. Their high-pitched moans and cries eat into my brain and stop it from functioning properly.

The traffic on the Chichester bypass is almost at a standstill and it's making me more and more frantic. I can't overtake, can't move forwards. All I can do is wait. On the plus side, if they're coming to get me, they will also be stuck in this heavy traffic.

And then I hear sirens and I think I'm going to throw up. Blue flashing lights are approaching from behind. Cars start pulling over onto the hard shoulder to allow the vehicle to pass. If I had a gun, I would shoot them now. But I don't and can't. The glare of the headlights obscures my view in the rear-view mirror. The car behind me pulls over and now it's my turn. What will happen?

I indicate to the left, as does the blue Vauxhall in front of me. We're all half on the hard shoulder now. Briefly I close my eyes, wondering if this is my final moment of freedom. All that fine planning, all my hopes, dashed once again.

When I open my eyes, the police car has gone past and is edging farther ahead. And now I can see it at the roundabout and turning off the A27 towards Runcton. I let out a loud exhalation.

I must keep positive. I must stay focused.

Eventually we are on the small road leading into West Wittering. I haven't been here for so long, but nothing much has changed. My heart is beating faster. I look in the rear-view mirror. Arthur is sucking his thumb and his eyes are closed. Ivy's face is as white as the moon.

Oh Stacey, I think to myself. *Stacey, you stupid bitch. You made all of this happen. I don't want to do this. I haven't wanted to do any of this, but you've forced my hand. How does that make you feel, Stacey?*

And then I am turning the car into the West Wittering Beach car park. It is almost dark now, and the rain is splattering the windscreen, bouncing off the top of the car. The wheels crunch as we drive in slowly. I exhale as I realise we are the only people here. The sole car in the car park. I pull up on the right-hand side of the car park, as close to the beach as one can get.

'Where are we?'

Ivy's voice makes me jump.

I don't answer, and Ivy doesn't repeat the question.

Stacey, it's your fault your children need to die. How else can I tick off the final points on my list and make you suffer forever? If you had followed my plan, you would have remained incarcerated and your children would have survived. I am so nearly the second Mrs Dominic Nicholson, and Ivy and Arthur would become my children, properly loved and nurtured; taught discipline and academic rigour. But no. You screwed everything up all over again, Stacey. Or should I call you Cassandra now? I wonder if Dominic knows that your real name is Cassandra?

'I need to go to the loo.' Ivy's voice cuts through my thoughts.

'Get out the car, then,' I say.

'But it's dark and raining and I don't know where we are!'

I would have knocked that belligerence out of Ivy, but now I don't have time. I fling open my car door and step outside. I don't care that the rain is torrential, that my hair is plastered to my head in seconds, that it is freezing cold and the waves are roaring. I open Ivy's car door.

'Get out.'

'But—'

'I said, "Get out"!' I yell.

Arthur wakes up. He takes a moment to adjust, and when he sees my face in the car window, he bursts into tears. I walk around to Arthur's door and fling it open too. Without saying a word, I undo the child safety seat belt.

'Get out,' I say.

Ivy is slowly extracting herself from her booster seat.

'Hurry up, both of you!'

Arthur ignores me, so I put my hands in his armpits, grip him around his chest and lift him out of his seat. He tries to hit me with his fists and is kicking out with his feet.

I stare him in the eyes. 'If you don't stop that immediately, Arthur, I will hit you so hard, you won't know what has happened to you.'

His eyes widen with terror. His limbs turn rigid, but he stops kicking. Ivy has walked around to my side of the car. She has the hood up on her school waterproof jacket.

'Where are the loos?' she asks.

'There aren't any. We have to go on the beach.'

Well done, Ivy, I think. She has given us a perfect reason for going down onto the beach. I deposit Arthur on the ground and grasp his wrist tightly in my right hand. I use my shoulder to shut the car door, then grab Ivy's wrist with my left hand.

'You're hurting me,' Ivy says. I ignore her.

These children should be mine. We would have had a boy first, followed by a girl. But no, Stacey took Craig from me. She stole his life. She ripped my heart open and no one, absolutely no one, has been able to heal it.

He was my soulmate. I knew that from such a young age. No one understood me the way Craig did.

I tried to get over him. Of course I did. I still had a life to live. I had high hopes for Zach. We met five years after Craig's death. I'd had a lot of men in the interim, all different shapes and sizes, colours and backgrounds. I needed to cast my net as wide as possible, just in case there could be more than one soulmate out there for me. None of them lived up to the standard Craig had set. Those years in my early twenties were lost in a haze of drugs, drink and deviant sex. Mum disowned me. She found me once, half naked and drugged up on the doorstep. She kicked me out. Can you imagine your own mother kicking you out? At the time I swore I'd get revenge on her too, but it's strange how things come to pass. Mum did me a favour. I had to get my shit together, and I did. I went back to college, studied hard, came off all the substances. I make it sound like it was easy, but it wasn't. Those were months of sheer hell.

And then along came Zach, my knight in shining armour. He was rich, well-connected, ambitious. His eyes reminded me of Craig's, and we had that chemistry I had failed to find with any other man. I swear, he could make me come just by gazing at me. I played the game and was quite the perfect little wifey. We tried to have children. I worked at it as hard as I worked at my job. I got ovulation kits and fertility monitors. I kept detailed charts. But month after bloody month, I failed to get pregnant. The pressure mounted on our relationship and his eagerness for my body waned. He started suggesting that I was at fault; that there was something wrong with me. What fucking audacity. And so Zach had to take his own life. Perhaps it was the tragedy of being unable to father a child, or perhaps he realised that neither he nor any other man could fill Craig's shoes.

All the while, Cassandra Pope was living her happy little life. I looked for her everywhere. It became my life's purpose to find her and get justice for Craig and me. Mainly for Craig. But sometimes even the most carefully laid plans can be trumped by luck. And that happened for me when I began dating Dylan Headley. I research all my potential dates, and when I found where Dylan worked, up popped the photos of SAID's founders, Stacey and Dominic Nicholson. I've been seeking that face for nearly fifteen years. Under normal circumstances I wouldn't date someone as uninspiring as Dylan, but he served a much bigger purpose.

At the thought of Dylan, I realise we haven't been walking fast enough. The children are wailing and tugging to get away from me. I pull them forwards, my face wet with the freezing cold, salty water. And then we are walking on the sand and it gets harder to drag them. The ocean is roaring and, despite the darkness and lack of moon, the breaking waves are white with frothy foam.

'I'm scared!' Arthur screams and tries to sit down. I drag him towards the ocean. Ivy tries to bite my arm, so I kick her shins. I don't want to hurt the children, but I've got absolutely no choice.

'It's your fucking fault, Cassandra Pope!' I scream at the top of my voice. But my words get swept out to sea.

44

STACEY

It takes me a few minutes of fumbling to get onto the tracking website. It seems that, in our panic, both of us have forgotten our passwords for everything. It's like our minds have shut down. I try all our normal passwords, and the relief when the site logs me in is overwhelming.

'She's on the A27, on the Chichester bypass.'

'Chichester? What the hell is she doing there?'

'Oh no,' I exclaim. 'She's turned off onto the A286. Oh God!'

'Where's that?' Dom glances over towards me as he turns onto the A27. But we're at least twenty minutes behind Tamara. More, perhaps, depending on the traffic.

'It's the road to Birdham.'

'What's in Birdham?'

'It's the route down to West Wittering.' My voice cracks as I sob.

Dom hunches farther forwards over the steering wheel.

'The beach?' he asks.

'It's where Craig died. I haven't been back there, ever. How could she do this to us, Dom?' I can't stop the tears now, at the thought of Tamara taking my babies onto that beach. The rain is torrential. It's nearly dark and it's freezing cold.

'Stacey, we don't even know that Tamara has got the children. She could be going there alone. Perhaps she's dropped the kids off somewhere. Perhaps she's there in the hope of luring us to the beach?'

'Does she know there's a tracker on the car?' I ask, sniffing hard.

'I don't know. But it's an expensive car so it's not that unlikely.'

Dom overtakes a slow car and then another. I'm clenching everything now.

'I'm calling the police again,' Dom says. 'Dial 999 on the phone and we'll pretend I'm alone in the car.'

I do as instructed.

'How can I direct your call?'

'Police,' Dom says.

'How can I help you?'

'My children have been abducted. I rang earlier but got fobbed off. This is now an emergency and if anything happens to my children, I will be holding the police accountable. Do you understand?' Dom's voice cracks.

'Please can I take your name and further details.'

'I've already given you lot all the information!' he shouts.

'Sir, you need to calm down.'

I glance at Dom and he is shaking with rage. I hope that he can concentrate sufficiently on driving. The road is wet, headlights are glaring. But he does well. He restrains his temper and slowly goes through all the details again, giving information on our children and Tamara and the location of my car.

'Mr Nicholson, I can confirm that this is now a grade one response. We will be running ANPR and it is likely we will mobilise the police helicopter. Rest assured, we will do everything we can to rescue your children.'

Dom presses the end call key. If he was driving fast before, now he drives like a maniac. All I can do is shut my eyes, pray and hope that my husband doesn't kill us or anyone else.

We screech off the A286 onto the narrow B2179, overtaking all the cars. I don't know how Dom has done it. And then we're pulling up into the bleak, empty car park on West Wittering Beach. There is only one other car there. Mine.

I don't even wait for Dom to stop the engine. I am out of the and Audi racing towards my Volvo. I tug at the doors, but the car is locked and I don't have the spare key. The light is practically non-existent, but by shading my hands over my eyes, I can see into the car. Both Ivy's and Arthur's school bags are on the back seat.

I scream their names, but my voice disappears in the roaring rush of the waves and the howling gale. I am back here. The place of my worst nightmares. And it is even worse than in my nightmares because my babies are out there. I don't know if I can bear this. But I run, as fast as I have ever run in my life, from the car park, onto the sand, towards the edge of the surf. My feet sink into the wet sand. My heartbeat is as loud as the crashing waves, my breath ragged. How can I watch tragedy unfold here again? Surely that is too much for anyone to bear? What did I do to deserve this?

And then I see them. A flash of pale skin against the dark sea. Tamara is standing on the edge of the sand, her feet in the water, her arms around the necks of my two darling children. How is that possible?

'Stop!' I scream, but I'm not sure my voice carries. I run towards them, and then I hear heavy footsteps alongside mine.

Tamara turns. She sees us. We're just a few metres away now. Her eyes narrow. She screams something, but I can't hear what she says. And then she's dragging my babies with her into the water; the waves bashing their legs, their midriffs.

I'm closer now.

'It's all your fucking fault, Stacey or Cassandra or whatever the hell your name is! You stole the love of my life. You killed him and now you've made me do the same. I didn't want to do this but you have to pay. Forever!' Her screams are shrill, intermingled with the terrified cries of my children, choked yells I will never forget.

I am so close now. But then I slip and fall. No! My hand meets the jagged edge of something. A rock, about the size of a large potato. I grab it and, as I stagger to my feet, I hurl it at Tamara's head. It hits her. She stumbles forwards and releases the children. I grab Ivy's arm, which is outstretched towards me.

'Mummy!" she screams. I pull her so hard I wonder if I will pull her little arm out of its socket. And then we both fall backwards onto the freezing wet sand. I tug her up and up until we're a metre away from the edge of the surf. She is crying, shivering violently, soaking wet. I wrap her in my arms. I'm not sure whether the wetness on my face is tears or sea water.

As I look up at the water's edge, I can't see anyone. 'Arthur!' I scream. 'Dom!'

We hang onto each other, Ivy and me. Is my worst nightmare unfolding all over again? *Where is Dom? Where is my baby boy?* I clutch my little girl to my chest, enveloping her head, praying, just praying that our family hasn't been splintered in two. And then I see the pale little arms of my boy reaching up out of the waves, but they're gone in a flash as a wave wrenches Arthur downwards.

'Arthur!' I scream again.

Dom flings himself into the sea fully dressed. All I can do is watch. I hug Ivy so tightly, but we are both shivering and sobbing, our tears and the salty sea water mingling together, frigid on our trembling bodies.

Where is Dom? Where is Arthur? My eyes strain in the darkness, but all I see are the white frothy waves and the spray that catches the faint lights of the shoreline. How is it possible that this is happening all over again? It seems like yesterday that I was caught in the same nightmare, screaming for Craig, screaming for Bouncer.

But this time I am silent. I have to protect my little girl. Besides, I know my screams will be futile, lost in the deafening roar of the ocean. And so I pray. *Please God, bring my boys back.*

We rock backwards and forwards, Ivy and me, as if we are one person. Her face is buried in my chest. I don't need her to see the massive expanse of water rushing forwards and then pulling back. *Please. Please release Arthur and Dom. Please.*

I don't know how long we sit there, quivering, on the beach. It could be seconds, it could be minutes. It seems like eternity. And then I see something. A little farther up the beach. It's hard to make out, but something, someone, is crawling out from the edge of the sea.

'Ivy! Stand up!' I release my grip on my daughter. 'Stay here!' She is wailing now, nonsensical words, but I have to go. I run, the water squelching from my clothes, my feet heavy. And then I am on my knees, crouching over him.

'Dom! Where's Arthur?'

Dom doesn't answer. He rolls to his left and there is my boy, his eyes blinking up at me, and then he's sick, throwing up sea water and bile, and coughing. And I have never felt such relief. Ever.

'Mummy!' Ivy screams throwing herself on us, and we are together, our little family of four. Alive.

And then I see the flashing lights. Lots of them. Blue lights, white lights. And voices. Running footsteps towards us. A dog. The lights bounce along the edge of the waves and along the narrow strip of sand. All noise is dulled by the crashing of the ocean. But then I hear a voice.

'Over here!'

'Mrs Nicholson?' A man in uniform asks, breathlessly.

'Yes.'

'We've called for urgent medical assistance.'

'Mr Nicholson?'

'Yes,' Dom replies, his voice cracking. 'We're fine. We're together.'

My knees give way and, clutching my babies, I sink to the sand once again.

45

STACEY

I t's 6 p.m. on New Year's Eve.
Dom is trying so hard, almost too hard. He blames himself and, to a large degree, I blame him too. He was totally taken in by Tamara. When he admitted he slept with her, I had to walk away from him, the revulsion was so overwhelming. But I'm relieved he was able to be honest with me. After all, he was a victim too.

The week after the episode on the beach was horrendous. I was taken back to the hospital for further mental health assessments. At the same time, the police decided to reinvestigate both Dylan Headley's and Zachary Collins's supposed suicides.

But for our little family, things have improved surprisingly rapidly.

'Mummy, Bonnie is chewing my slipper,' Arthur says, tugging my hand. I follow him back into the living room. 'No, Bonnie,' I say, giving our new Cocker Spaniel puppy a little tap on the nose. She releases the slipper.

'Are you a naughty girl, Bonnie?' Ivy asks, crouching down on the floor next to the puppy and throwing her arms around the dog's neck. She buries her face in Bonnie's fur.

Bonnie was a last-minute Christmas present for the children. My dislike of dogs was never because I was scared of them; just the fear that a dog might cause a perilous event, as Bouncer did all those years ago. But Dom wasn't going to let my fears affect our children, and when he suggested getting a dog, I had to agree. Those beautiful puppy eyes tug on my heartstrings and I know that getting Bonnie will be one of the best things we have done.

'Knock knock!' Mina opens the back door. 'Hello lovely! Any chance you could take a couple of these dishes.' Mina hands me a plate with a sumptuous-looking cake and a tray covered with tin foil. 'Paul's bringing in the booze.'

'Happy New Year!' I say.

Mina's children, Ben and Rosie, dart into the kitchen, giggling and chattering, and disappear into the playroom with Arthur, Ivy and Bonnie.

TAMARA HAS NEVER BEEN FOUND. They tell us that her body could still wash up on a beach somewhere, or perhaps, in the darkness and the rough weather, she managed to save herself. I hope we will find out one day, as I need closure. In the meantime, there is an international arrest warrant out for her. She is wanted for murder and kidnap.

It's Dom I'm most worried about. His confidence has been brutally knocked. He feels as if he has betrayed us all. Jeff has been managing things at work, but all the publicity has undoubtedly affected their business. Dom is still sleeping in the spare room. I can hardly bear the thought of going in there, knowing that Tamara slept in our spare bed. Dom promised me that they didn't sleep together in our bed, and I have chosen to believe him. I hope that things will improve between us because I love Dom from the bottom of my heart, but I guess only time will tell. Perhaps a few glasses of champagne tonight will tip the balance.

For me, things are back on the up. Corinne turned up on our doorstep, her cheeks red with embarrassment. She admitted that, on reflection, she wasn't sure whether I had or hadn't stolen her idea. She has been going through a rough patch and alcohol became her best friend. Mina told me she's making good progress in Alcoholics Anonymous and that she has received a generous settlement from her ex-husband, so money is no longer a problem. It turns out she never sent that solicitor's letter and had no intention of suing me for the intellectual property contravention of *Pinkapop's Adventures*. We think that Tamara must have placed those scribbles in my drawer and sent the fake solicitor's letter. Corinne swears she had nothing to do with it, and again, I'm choosing to believe her.

During the second week in January, we're having a meeting with the head of commissioning for CBeebies. They are seriously considering taking on *Pinkapop's Adventures*, and there has been banter that it is tipped to become the *Teletubbies* of the twenty-first century.

We'll see.

A LETTER FROM MIRANDA

Dear Reader,

Thank you very much for reading *Deserve To Die*. I hope you enjoyed reading it – I certainly enjoyed writing it.

I must apologise to all residents of Horsham and West Sussex for bumping off so many people in this locality! It's a glorious place to call home and my books do not reflect the peaceful reality of this part of England.

In *Deserve To Die*, I slipped in a book within a book. Pinkapop is a little character that was brought to life in a children's leisure attraction and a series of kids' stories that I created over fifteen years ago. If you'd like to see what she looks like, head over to my website (details below)

Special thanks to Becca McCauley and Adriana Galimberti-Rennie for answering my mental health and police procedural questions. Along with Harmen my husband, Becca and Adriana are my early readers and I'm so grateful for your support. All mistakes are mine alone. Thank you to Brian Lynch and Garret Ryan of Inkubator Books who work their magic on my novels, bringing them to life. It is such a pleasure working with you.

And finally – but most importantly – thank you to you and all my readers for your support. I never dreamed that writing books could connect me to people all over the globe. It's such a joy!

If you could spend a moment writing an honest review on Amazon, no matter how short, I would be extremely grateful. They really do help other people discover my books.

With warmest wishes,

Miranda

www.mirandarijks.com

ALSO BY MIRANDA RIJKS

(Book 3 in the Dr Pippa Durrant Mystery Series)

Published by Inkubator Books
www.inkubatorbooks.com